THE GRUMP, THE BRIDE, THE BABY

CALICO COVE
BOOK 3

HAILEY SHORE

PROLOGUE

The Masquerade Ball
June
Vanessa

What's that saying about the bed and making it? The one that basically means – it doesn't matter how awful this thing is you're doing, how much you hate it, or wish you could make it stop – it was your choice, so you have to suck it up.

This is my bed so I have to make it?

Something like that.

There was a whole masquerade engagement party happening in this house right now. In rooms decorated in pink and gold (my signature colors) with servers passing around canapes (keto and paleo) to celebrate my engagement to Simon.

My father was telling everyone who'd listen how proud he was of me. That he loved Simon like a son. I'm sure my brother Jackson loved that. Jackson loved Simon like a foot fungus.

Meanwhile, I was hiding in this dark study, drinking expensive champagne that tasted like dirt, because hours earlier my fiancé had been fucking a girl I knew from boarding school.

I *hated* this bed.

I'd caught them coming out of one of the guest rooms. Disheveled, touching, laughing at their little dirty secret.

Thankfully, they hadn't seen me, so I'd been spared any lying explanations.

Still. Today? He couldn't keep it in his pants, *today*?

This engagement, this whole marriage between me and Simon—was really a business arrangement between my family and his. I knew it. Simon's family got our Dumont connections and we got Simon's family's money.

I tried for a really long time to convince myself I could love Simon. And if I couldn't love him I could be...content with him. I could put together a fairy tale to tell the world, and if the world believed the fairy tale, so could I. And everything would be okay.

Tonight, I looked the part of a fairy princess in my Reformation Barbiecore Veria silk dress. My legs were ten miles long. My hair was a golden sheet so straight and shiny you could see your reflection in it. I was thin enough to please even my mother, who was never pleased.

Still, Simon cheated on me.

He'd probably screw one of my bridesmaids on my wedding day, too.

"This fairy tale sucks," I muttered.

I traded out the empty champagne glass and filled a glass with Dad's good bourbon, and settled back into the leather couch that was all but swallowing me whole.

Which wouldn't be the worst thing that happened to me tonight.

It wasn't always like this. When we first met, Simon had been charming. Sweet. Sexy in his backwards hat, gym body way. He'd wooed me. Flowers, flirting, little gifts. He'd made me feel special for the first time in my life.

I was in love. Or I thought I was. Was there a difference? Maybe that was the bourbon talking, but right now it seemed like love was something you had to convince yourself you actually felt.

Except I knew the difference. Deep down. I'd had the real thing once and I'd given it up.

For Simon. For my family. Because my father had asked me to.

Years ago, the first time I'd caught Simon cheating, it was with a waitress from the yacht club. I'd called him out and he'd said it was a slip up and would never happen again.

The second time, I'd broken up with him. I wasn't such a push over. I'd left him. Made a scene at brunch. I hadn't returned his calls for like...four days.

Except he'd begged and pleaded and I had the backbone of a jellyfish.

I am only guessing they don't have backbones, I don't actually know.

That was when he started to make me feel like the cheating was my fault. If only I'd liked sex more, or was better at it – he wouldn't have had to cheat.

Which, I guess was fair. I didn't *love* sex, the way everyone else on the planet seemed to love it. Simon made it clear I was bad at it. So, could I blame him?

The third time he'd cheated, he'd thought I didn't know. Because I hadn't even bothered to call him out for it. That summer, I'd left Simon in Boston and come up to Calico Cove.

That was the summer I'd met Roy.

The summer that had changed everything, and weirdly, had changed nothing at all.

Because eventually Dad had found me in Calico Cove and said he'd needed my help. That only I could save the family. *Me.*

Sure, yes, I had to get back together with Simon, but that was nothing compared to the shining light of my father's sudden love for me.

How was I supposed to resist that? My daddy needed me.

So I'd fallen for it. I was still falling for it.

The door to the den clicked open and a slice of light was cut out of the darkness I was drowning in. Mom, probably. The announcement was to be made soon and Simon and I had this whole choreographed dance to perform. How I was supposed to do that without throwing up, I didn't know. I only knew I had to make it happen.

This was my bed and I was lying in it.

That's it! That's how the saying went.

"Hey, Messy Nessy."

I gasped at the sound of his voice. At that ridiculous nickname.

"Roy," I whispered.

Was this a dream? It had to be a dream. I'd passed out from the bourbon. Or I'd hit my head or was having some kind of breakdown. Because after what I'd done to him two years ago there was no way he'd ever talk to me again. Even if I ran into him on the street, he would ignore me like he never knew me.

He had every right to.

The door closed and darkness swept around us. I heard him step further into the study. My father's inner sanctum. Roy always was brave. He didn't care this was my father's private space.

I felt him watching me in the darkness, broken only by strips of moonlight shining through the curtains. The urge to turn and look at him was so intense, but equally intense was the urge to throw myself out the window to get away from him.

This guy I'd liked so much. This guy I'd hurt so bad.

Be brave, Vanessa. For once in your stupid life.

I turned my head and found him in the shadows. He was in a tux that fit him like it was custom. Filling it out with muscles built from hard work. Seeing him made me want to smile. Made me want to throw myself at him. Made me want to cry.

"Hi," I said, like a dummy.

"Hi," he said back.

"I'm...surprised you're here."

"That makes two of us."

"If you're here to yell-"

"I don't want to yell, Ness."

He pulled at his tie as if it was choking him.

"You need help with that tie?"

"The fucker," he said, and then just tugged on one end until it lost its knot. He undid the button at the neck and suddenly he looked like a man in an expensive watch commercial.

"You look good," I told him. Understatement.

"I look like an ass in this penguin suit," he said.

Roy would feel that way about a tuxedo. Uncomfortable. Out of place. But he still looked better than any man out there.

"Why did you come?" I asked him, my voice barely a whisper while I waited for an answer I wasn't sure I wanted. Or an answer I desperately needed:

Because I love you, I've always loved you. That summer meant everything to me and I can't watch you lie in this stupid bed even though you made it.

He was frowning. He was always frowning. He had resting frown face. Except when I got him to laugh. Which I'd gotten pretty good at that summer.

Those had been my favorite times. The best times of my whole life, really.

Why hadn't I been strong enough to hold onto him? To us?

"You know how when you have a toothache and you can't stop poking at it with your tongue?" he asked.

I think I am the toothache in this situation.

"I do," I said quietly.

"You gonna marry him?"

"That's a ridiculous question, Roy."

There were hundreds of people in this house all here to celebrate my upcoming nuptials. Who would ask me, the bride to be, a question like that?

Roy Barnes. That's who. He'd come to see it for himself. To poke that toothache one last time. And maybe, because it was a thing he did, to save me. One last time. Save me from this marriage. From myself.

From this stupid bed.

"I don't think it is," he said.

Should I tell him the truth? That I didn't want to marry Simon. I never wanted to marry Simon. That I'd picked my family over him for *reasons*. Would it matter?

He'd save me again, and then what? He'd be stuck with me. A spoiled princess with daddy and *sex* issues. No. It wasn't fair.

Roy Barnes deserved better than Messy Nessy.

"I don't...I can't...Yes," I finally said. I shook my head, trying to find some bravery. Like a captain going down with a ship. "Yes, I'm going to marry him."

He nodded and shoved his hands in his pockets, ruining the lines of the suit.

"You love him then?" he said.

"It's not... it's not about love."

"Geezus, please don't tell me it's about money." His harsh laugh was a knife that sliced at me and I kept my mouth shut. "You're as bad as your father. Whatever, Ness. Good luck."

I wanted to tell him not to go. Tell him I could never love Simon because my heart would always be Roy's. But what would be the point?

He took my silence for an answer and turned for the door.

"Wait," I said, getting up from the couch and following him. I sounded desperate. I was desperate. For just one more second, one more...touch. "Your tie."

He stopped but didn't turn around. I could feel him wanting to storm out. Or to turn and tell me off. I deserved all of it. It was stupid to ask him for anything else.

"Let me fix it."

I held my breath until he turned and bent down so I could reach his neck.

Our faces were close, our breaths mingled. I could feel the warmth of his neck. His skin.

I could always smell the sea on Roy. A scent he could never shake. I could see the stubble on his cheeks and chin, even though he'd probably shaved just hours ago. He kept his caramel brown eyes locked on some fixed place over my head.

Look at me, please. One more time. Just look at me.

Like he heard me, his eyes met mine and instantly I couldn't breathe. A pang of longing hit my chest so hard, I had to look away.

"You're good at this," he said.

"We...we go to a lot of black-tie events."

I tied Simon's tie every time but he never ducked down to make it easier for me. He always made me stretch up on my tiptoes. It was a little thing that felt so big right now.

"Makes sense."

"There," I said when I was done and couldn't stretch it out any longer. I patted his impossibly broad chest, remembering how thick his muscles were beneath his chest hair.

"Ness," he said, and brushed a finger against my cheek.

He was going to say something. Something like I didn't have to go through with this terrible marriage if I didn't want to. How I could make my own decisions for my life.

He was so obviously wrong.

None of this was in my control. Because I gave all that up the summer I met and left Roy.

Thankfully, he didn't say any of that. He just dropped his hand and walked out the door, shutting it quietly behind him.

I don't know how long I stared at that closed door, but it seemed like some deep metaphor for my life.

Until it opened again, and my mother poked her head inside.

"There you are!" she exclaimed. "I've been looking everywhere for you. Come, come. They're about to make the introductions."

I plastered a fake smile on my face because that's what I was expected to do, and followed my mother out into the small foyer outside the ballroom.

Where my bastard, cheating fiancé was waiting for me with a huge smile on his face too.

Run.

Where?

Roy.

"Ladies and gentleman," the DJ announced after getting everyone's attention. "It is my pleasure to introduce the couple of the hour. The soon to be Mr. and Mrs. Turnberry. Simon Turnberry and Vanessa Dumont."

I slipped on my mask.

That was my cue.

1

The Wedding Day
September
Vanessa

I looked down at the glob of lobster mac & cheese that had fallen on the bodice of my wedding dress and tried not to cry.

I did not succeed.

I mean, in the grand scheme of everything that happened today, this smear of cream, butter and cheese, leaving a grease stain on my twenty-thousand-dollar, hand-beaded Swarovski crystal Vera Wang dress, shouldn't have even registered. Except here I was. Crying.

"Are you...I'm sorry, but are you okay?" A woman asked me.

She was leaving with a few items in her hand that she'd just bought at the register of the store, but it was hard to walk by a devastated, crying, non-bride without checking in. She seemed nice. She wore unflattering capri pants and her concern was maybe a little judgy, but it was nice that she asked.

No one except for Jackson had asked me if I was okay in years.

I tried to push my veil off my face, but there was just so much of it, so I yanked it off, sending a small waterfall of bobby pins onto the floor.

"I'm great. Thank you for asking," I said, sniffing. "Could you..." I pointed at the drinks fridge against the wall. I couldn't get to it, surrounded as I was by the ten foot long, Irish-lace train attached to my dress that I'd had to wedge into the small booth with me.

"A drink?" she asked.

"Yes. That would be so nice of you. Like just really nice."

Nice Lady opened the drink fridge and reached for a diet Coke.

"No!" I barked.

Then she reached for the regular full sugar Coke on the top shelf and waited for me to nod.

"Yes. That would be so nice," I said.

She even popped the top on it and set it down in front of me. I guzzled down that can of Coke in three seconds.

"Honey, are you sure you're okay?"

"I was just so hungry," I said with a laugh and a little burp. With renewed vigor, I dove back into what was actually my second helping of lobster mac & cheese. I'd finished the first one so fast, I'd made Verity, who was working at The Lobster Pot today, give me another. "Mom wanted me to be a size four for the wedding."

"Well, the dress looks beautiful."

"Thanks. It's ruined. I mean it's all ruined. The dress. The day. The wedding. Everything's ruined. I ruined it."

Me. Messy Nessy. Maybe everyone should have seen that coming.

"I'm so sorry to hear that," Nice Lady said, although it was obvious now she was looking for an escape.

"Have you had this lobster mac & cheese?" I asked, pointing my plastic fork at what was left in the bowl.

"I have."

"It's the best thing I've ever eaten."

I hadn't eaten in years. Not like I'd wanted to. Not like my body needed me to. No, I ate what other people told me to eat.

My mother. My agent. Photographers. Other models.

When all that time I was so hungry.

Now, I was eating forbidden noodles covered in cheese sauce with big chunks of lobster, and it was changing my life.

One of the crystals fell off the bodice of my dress and rolled off the table, onto the floor. Nice Lady casually picked it up and set it back down on the edge of my booth. She gingerly patted my shoulder as she walked past me and out the door.

The wedding was definitely off now.

I grimaced thinking about the house full of guests, all probably still in a state of shock having watched the bride take off at a full sprint out the front door.

I had one job today. Marry Simon, save my family, make my father happy and in the end ...I couldn't do it. I didn't love Simon. I didn't even like him. Actually... I think I hated him.

I know I hated myself with him.

Jackson, to his wonderful credit, had kissed my cheek and told me his Jeep was right out front. Like he'd known all along I might bolt at the last moment. He'd always given me more credit than I gave myself.

I left The Dumont Estate to the sound of the string quartet coming to a violent stop, while my father shouted my name and the guests gasped and swiveled in their chairs.

I'd jumped in the Jeep, lowered the sun visor, and the car keys had fallen into the creamy white folds of my dress. I took off as fast as the old Jeep would go even as people came out of the front door behind me.

I didn't bother checking the rear-view mirror to see if Simon was one of those people.

The key to a life on the run was to be inconspicuous. Which wasn't the easiest thing to do in a silk wedding dress with a ten foot train. Everyone in Calico Cove would recognize Jackson's Jeep. So I'd left the Jeep at the diner and was suddenly starving. Faint and dizzy and famished.

Pappas' was too obvious a choice. Lola Pappas was Jackson's girlfriend.

No, the better option for food oblivion was The Lobster Pot on the other side of town. I had no problem navigating the walk in my three-inch heels. Having once had to walk down a catwalk draped in twenty pounds of designer couture on five-inch stilettos, these three-inch Jimmy Choo's felt like sneakers.

I'd made the right choice coming here.

Lobster mac & cheese....'nuff said.

Verity left the kitchen to bring me some extra napkins and pointed to the grease stain on my dress.

"I can maybe get some hot water to try..." She didn't finish her sentence.

"It's not like I'm going to be wearing it again," I told her.

"Vanessa, it's Vanessa right?"

I nodded. People in this town didn't know me like they

knew Jackson. I hadn't spent most of my summers here like he had. Summers weren't play time for me. They were a time for improvement and catching up.

I always needed to improve on something.

"Tell me who to call, honey," Verity said gently.

I shook my head. There was no one. I could head over to Jackson's new condo, but my father was sure to show up there. I had no idea what Simon might do. I doubted he actually cared, but he would be embarrassed and that was never a good look on him.

I needed to plan. I needed a place I could lay low. Now that the immediate need for comfort food had been filled, it was time to think.

Only I wasn't the best thinker.

It's why I needed the special tutors, the summer school programs, all that catching up.

I was only good for being pretty and for making other things look pretty.

In my life, I'd never done anything so disobedient as running away from my own wedding. I had no idea what to do next.

My stomach cramped.

"Oh my God. What was I thinking?" I groaned, putting my hand over my stomach.

"Oh honey, do you want to go back to the wedding?" Verity asked me. "I'm sure you can. Lots of brides get last minute jitters. Well, not me, but that's because I was marrying Josh..."

"No, I don't want to go back to the wedding. I meant what was I thinking ordering two servings of mac & cheese. My stomach hates me."

"Oh. Okay. Well, let me get you some water."

I could call an Uber...

No phone.

I could use Verity's phone to call a taxi...

No money to pay the taxi.

No money to pay Verity for the lobster mac & cheese either.

Here I was, stuffed with pasta and Coke with no money, a stained wedding dress and designer shoes.

Verity came back with a plastic cup of water.

"What size shoe do you wear?" I asked her. She looked at me like I was crazy, which was fair. I was considering selling her my shoes for enough money to get out of Calico Cove. Then I glanced over at the community bulletin board on the wall. It was covered with flyers and advertisements for babysitting and pet-sitting services.

Then I saw the yellowed paper with large bold letters that read:

WANTED:WIFE

Now that was a job I was perfect for. I was just about to commit myself for life to a man I didn't love. How hard could it be to do that with someone else?

I already came with the dress.

Hysterical laughter bubbled out of my chest.

Shoving my train out of the way, I got up from the booth and walked over to the board. I pulled out the pin holding up the notice.

"Oh, don't pay attention to that. That's just Roy's idea of a joke," Verity said, cleaning up the dishes behind me. "I think."

"Roy," I repeated softly. "Roy Barnes?"

"His cousin died a year ago and left him with a baby, she's oh, gosh, sixteen, maybe seventeen months now? Anyway he freaked out and put that sign up last summer.

Thought he needed a wife to manage. But they're doing just fine."

"A baby?"

Roy hadn't said anything about a baby the night of the masquerade ball.

Roy Barnes wanted a wife. So much he was willing to advertise for one.

If he put this notice up on a bulletin board in town, he hadn't done it as a joke.

Roy wasn't known for his sense of humor.

I bit my bottom lip and ran my thumb over the phone number on the paper. It was Roy's old number. It had been seared into my memory.

Was this smart?

Maybe not. But my father was about to tear apart this town looking for me.

I needed a place to stay. I didn't have a phone, a car or any money to get out of town. Every penny of my personal funds had gone toward the Calico Cove Investment Bureau - Jackson's company - which currently was invested heavily in Pappas' Diner.

I knew Dad would cut off my access to the family account the first chance he got. Same with the credit cards. He'd probably already done it.

No family money, no personal money. Jackson of course would try and help me out, but we were both cash poor after pulling together the funds needed for Lola to buy and restore the diner.

Not to mention the upscale bar - *The Starboard Tavern* - Jackson was building in the lot behind Pappas'.

It's not even like I could stay with Jackson now that he and Lola were officially living together. Like who wanted to be a third wheel on the bicycle of new love?

Then there was the little matter of Simon.

My father would still want me to marry him. He'd see my escape as nothing more than a setback to his plans. Simon had his reasons for agreeing to an arranged marriage with a woman he cared so little for, he would screw another woman on the same day of his engagement party.

There really was nothing stopping my father from using all his financial strings, guilt strings and flat out mean strings to bring me back home.

I was a runaway bride in need of saving.

I couldn't. *Could I?*

No way Roy would say yes to this.

I had no talents, no skills. To date, my greatest accomplishment had been a year modeling in Europe, walking in really high shoes. However, after designers and photographers determined my face wasn't interesting enough, the jobs dried up.

After that, I'd been nothing more than Simon's arm piece for parties.

Sure, I had been helping Jackson with the CCIB. But all I really did was tell him which businesses I thought would make the best return on his money. Which, let me tell you, was not a highly scientific process on my part. I mostly went with my gut. It was kind of like the work I'd been doing with Lola, helping her with the remodel of Pappas'.

It wasn't skill, it was just guessing with some good taste thrown in.

Roy was a private fisherman, with a house to run and now a baby. Those were serious things. He probably needed serious help.

Oh, and he *hated* me for what I did to him.

The idea was preposterous. Even I knew that.

He saved you once. He showed up at the engagement party. Maybe...

Whelp, the absolute worst thing he could say was...no.

∼

ROY

"I SAID NO NORA, and I meant it. I won't crack. Not this time."

I picked up my screwdriver from my tool box and glared at her. She curled her little hands over the top of the play pen and screamed bloody murder.

She was crying for no damn reason, which sometimes she just liked to do to get under my skin. She was fed, changed, well rested and her teeth were all in now, but every once in a while she got stubborn about something and let me know it.

Today it was because she wanted out of her pen. That wasn't happening. I had the little play pen set up on deck, filled with all of her favorite toys, including the Elmo doll that didn't shut up, while I did some repair work to the rear winch.

Apparently, that wasn't good enough for Nora. Nope.

Life had been a whole lot easier when the bugger couldn't walk. I could carry her in a backpack contraption while I captained the boat. Or she'd sleep in her pen in the cabin below deck.

Now she wanted to be mobile all the time, and that just wasn't safe on a fishing boat.

Those lunatics who put their kids on leashes, maybe it wasn't such a bad idea.

"I gotta fix this," I told her. I'd replaced the bearings in the winch and shit just needed to be tightened, so I only needed about five more minutes. Except Nora didn't understand time. Or patience. These days she only understood freedom.

As fast as I could, I tightened the screws and ran the lines through the self-guiding system, when suddenly Nora stopped crying.

I turned, positive she'd climbed out of the pen, just like in my nightmares, and was either playing with knives or was about to fall into the water.

No, she was fixated on someone walking down the line of slips towards my boat, *The Surly Bird*.

Clearly, I was officially cracked in the head. It was the only explanation for what looked like Vanessa Dumont, in a full bridal gown, navigating the docks as she made her way toward us.

"Are you seeing that?" I asked Nora.

Vanessa was careful where to step in her fancy shoes. When she finally reached me, she stopped and held out the advertisement I'd posted on the board in The Lobster Pot last summer.

"I want to apply," she said. "For the, you know...Wife. Job-thingy."

This had to be my poker crew having a laugh. For which there would be fists in faces.

"Look," she laughed a little hysterically. "I'm even dressed for the part!"

She held up the glittery, lace dress in her arms, revealing the garter just above her knee. The hem was covered in mud and her hair was coming down from whatever style she'd had it in.

Messy Nessy. Once upon a time, I'd given her that name

for a reason.

"What are you doing here, Ness?"

"I told you," she shook the paper in her hand. "I want to be your wife."

It wasn't hard to guess what happened. I knew the wedding was today. Of course, I knew. Everyone in town knew. It's why I'd avoided everyone by spending the day out on the water alone with Nora. Not even fishing, I just took the boat out and was...away.

The wedding should have been over by now. The Best Man should be giving his speech. People should be eating fancy food and drinking champagne. Instead, she was in her dress standing in front of my boat.

In almost the exact same place where she lied to my face, tore out my heart and stomped it into seven million pieces. The irony was upsetting.

She must have had a panic attack at the last minute and bolted.

Not. My. Fucking. Problem.

"Go home, Ness." She'd made her choice a long time ago and it wasn't me.

"I can't do that. I can't go back." She tried to shake some of the hair out of her face. "I *won't* go back."

Well, we both knew that wasn't true.

"You're embarrassing yourself," I told her.

Just like I'd embarrassed myself when I showed up at her stupid engagement party in that monkey suit. Just to hear the words out of her mouth that she was going to marry that asshole.

"Of course I am! You think I don't know that? This must be hilarious for you. I mean, you must be cracking up on the inside."

I wasn't. I didn't know what I was doing on the inside,

but it was not cracking up.

"But here's the thing, Roy," she continued. "I know you. You live to save helpless little creatures. You always want to be everyone's hero."

"That's ridiculous."

Nora shrieked.

"Hi baby girl," Vanessa crooned to Nora. "I see you. Did he save you too?"

"You don't know what the fuck you're talking about," I snapped.

"I know you probably shouldn't say *fuck* around a baby who is just starting to absorb language skills."

Fuck. I'd been working on it, hadn't I? Making sure not every word out of my mouth was a curse.

Vanessa spread out her arms. "In the history of the universe, no one needs saving more than me, Roy. I have no money, no fiancé, my father...I don't know what he'll do, but it's never a good thing when he's desperate. You put the notice on that bulletin board. You need help with that little girl. Here I am. Ready to help."

I stepped up onto the rail of the boat and hopped down onto the dock with enough force that the boards rattled under her feet. That dress she was wearing probably cost more than I made in a season.

"I don't like liars."

"I didn't...," she stopped herself, most likely knowing it was only going to make matters worse. We'd been over this ground a few times. "I'm sorry, Roy. I'm so sorry about all of it."

I didn't like to think of myself as vindictive or vengeful. But Vanessa Dumont was the one fucking person on planet Earth I couldn't forgive.

Because she did something I didn't think anyone was capable of.

She made me happy.

Then she took it all away.

"Well," I said. "My hero days are over. Go back to Daddy. Go back to Simon. Those are *your* people. Remember?"

She looked crestfallen, but it didn't stir me. Not even a little bit.

Which should be some comfort.

Vanessa Dumont no longer had any hold over me.

I glared her down and finally she nodded.

"Okay, okay" she whispered, but it sounded like she was talking to herself. "It's fine. I'll be fine."

She turned and started her trek back up the dock.

I tore my eyes away from her slumped back only to find Nora watching me. Her eyes narrowed.

We did need help. We needed help last summer when I posted that sign, but things were much, much worse now that Nora was mobile.

"Not her," I told the kid. "Anyone else. Just not her."

Except no one else had answered that stupid ad.

2

Vanessa

I stopped at the end of the docks. There was a bench there situated next to a garbage can. A person could sit and watch the boats go out and come back in. Have a cup of coffee, then toss the cup away when they were done.

Maybe I could take this bench, I thought. Take the bench and sit here for the rest of my days. Like a twisted Calico Cove version of Dicken's Miss Havisham.

Who's that old lady sitting on the bench at the end of the docks in that yellow dress that's practically dissolving around her?

Oh her? She's the runaway bride who didn't have a plan and no one wanted to save.

Couldn't she save herself?

No. She didn't know how.

I would become a Calico Cove legend. Like the story

about the pirates who saved the cats in their pirate hats. Or Larry the Lobster at Pappas' Diner.

I would be the *Runaway Bride of Calico Cove.*

It sort of had a nice ring to it, actually. Maybe I could charge people to take pictures with me.

I thought about going back to the diner to pick up Jackson's Jeep. I could drive as far as the gas he had in the tank would take me, then call him to see if he could send me some money. What little cash he had. It would have to be enough.

I looked down at the now stained and ruined dress. I needed to get out of these clothes. If I headed back to the diner, Lola might have some spare t-shirts and shorts in her office. It wasn't much, but at least it was a start.

There was the screech of tires around a corner and I froze as the black Escalade came to a sudden stop. The driver's side door popped open and my father, still wearing his tuxedo, came rushing toward me. His face redder than I'd ever seen it.

Dangerously red.

"Do you know what you've done?" he shouted. "Do you have any idea the havoc you've caused? You...you...stupid girl!"

"Daddy, I..."

"Don't talk! Don't say a goddamn word. You're going to get in that car. I'm taking you back to Simon. You'll apologize. You'll beg if you have to, and tomorrow I'll have a judge marry you."

I shook my head, my hands in fists, clinging to my courage.

"I won't go back," I said, my voice shaking, but firm. Sort of firm. Mostly shaking. "I'm not going to marry Simon."

He took a deep breath and I could see him trying to push

the rage off his face. To perform for me the act of a loving father, and it made me so sad. So sad and so angry that I'd fallen for it before. That he thought I'd fall for it again.

"I need you, honey. Remember?" he said, his voice softening. "You're the only person who can save this family. Don't we mean anything to you?"

"I won't marry him, Daddy," I whispered.

The loving father act quickly vanished. He grabbed my arm so hard it hurt, his red face inches from mine. I could feel his rage like heat rolling off of him. "Your mother is telling anyone who will listen about your mental health issues. Simon looks like the long-suffering fiancé who loves you in spite of your unfortunate condition. Everyone is playing their parts. Except for you. So, you've had your tantrum, now it's time for you to remember who you are!"

I tried to pull away from him, but his fingers dug into my skin. "You're hurting me," I told him.

"I don't care! Get in the fucking car!"

"No!" I shouted in his face. "No! I won't get in the car! No! I won't marry Simon! You can't make me!"

His open palm blazed across my face, snapping my head back so hard my neck hurt. My cheek burned, my eyes filled with tears. There was a buzzing in my head.

Did he just hit me? *My Dad?*

I'd pushed my father a step too far. Defied him in a way he hadn't expected from me. From Jackson, it happened all the time. But not from me. I'd always tried to be so good.

This is what being good gets you in my family.

He had his arm around my waist and was practically carrying me towards the car.

"No!" I whispered. Was that blood? That copper taste in my mouth?

"Get in the car!"

"Let her go."

He was like a lobsterman superhero in his faded jeans and flannel shirt over a white T. The wind ruffling his dark hair. His eyes narrowed to slits. Not even the baby in the purple stroller sucking on the leg of a stuffed bunny could diminish how scary Roy Barnes was.

He never scared me though.

Relief made me dizzy. I knew he would rescue me.

"This isn't your concern. It's family business," my father said.

Roy pushed the stroller to the side and then used his foot to put on the wheel lock, so it didn't roll away. "Where I come from, family doesn't smack the shit out of their daughters."

"Oh for heaven's sake," my father shouted. "I was just trying to slap some sense into her. She's got mental health issues."

"Nah," Roy said, his arms crossed over his wide chest. "She's got daddy issues. Known that for years. Remove your hand or I'll do it for you."

"Touch me and I'll have you arrested."

"You could try, but when Bobby, he's the town sheriff by the way, shows up and takes one look at Ness's face, he's going to know who to arrest. Now you let her go, and I'll let you get back in your car and drive off. You don't let her go, then I have permission to beat the fucking shit out of you. You ever get hit, Mr. Dumont? Ever had your cheek broken? Your nose re-arranged? I'm guessing no. I'm here to tell you, it's not going to feel good. Let. Her. Go."

Whether it was shock or fear, Dad's hand loosened around my waist. I'd been pulling away so hard, I fell to the ground. At least I was free. I crab-walked backwards. Away from my father and towards Roy.

The little girl, who had been silent in her purple stroller, giggled hysterically.

Who could blame her? I had to look ridiculous.

"So help me, Vanessa, if you don't get in this car right now you are forever disowned," my father barked at me, even as he stepped backwards away from Roy. "The only thing you're taking with you is the dress on your back. Do you understand me?"

I got to my feet and looked at my hands which were scraped raw. My cheek throbbed.

So, this was it. Twenty-five years of trying to make this man happy, proud, pleased with me, when the reality was, I was never going to be enough.

"I'm not getting in that car. I'm not marrying Simon. If that costs me my family...so be it."

I said it like a vow.

"You're a bigger disappointment to me than your brother," he hissed.

"Yeah, well you're sort of a big disappointment to me too, *Dad!*"

The car door slammed. The engine which had been running this whole time revved as he sped off, screeching around the corner until he was gone. Out of my life.

Maybe not forever. I doubted I was that lucky.

But certainly, for now.

I turned back to Roy and offered him a weak smile. "Thank you, Roy. You didn't have to-"

He snarled. "He fucking hit you, Ness!"

"Don't say the f-word in front of the baby. I'm fine."

"You're not fine," he snapped. "Your cheek is swollen. Come with me."

"Where?"

"To get ice."

"Okay." I didn't have any fight left in me anyway. I would basically go in whatever direction the wind was blowing. The adrenaline was gone and I felt like a limp rag. I wanted to pull the blankets over my head and sleep for a million years.

But I didn't even have blankets.

I walked alongside him as he navigated the stroller over the wooden dock.

"This doesn't mean I'm saving you," he said.

"Nope."

"We're absolutely not getting married."

"Of course not."

"That would be ridiculous."

"It would," I said.

"You're getting an ice bag and a trip to the bus stop if you want."

"Sure," I said. I didn't have any money for a bus ticket, but now that there was no point hiding from my father, I could head back to the diner and wait for Jackson and Lola.

Roy stopped walking, and instinctively I stopped too.

"Has he done that before? Hit you like that?"

I shook my head and the words I never said aloud tumbled out. "Pinches. My dad liked to pinch me, to let me know when I was failing him. He saved the hitting for Jackson."

All my therapist had ever wanted to talk about was my abusive father and I wouldn't let her. Like if I could pretend he wasn't who I *knew* him to be, he might someday be the man I *wanted* him to be.

Except it was never going to happen. He was the kind of man who hit his children. That's who he was.

"You cryin'?"

Roy hated tears. I could only imagine his life with a baby in it.

I lifted my head and sniffed. "No, I'm not crying. Where are we going?"

"My house. But just for-"

"The ice bag. I know, Roy. Trust me, I get it."

I was Messy Nessy. No one wanted me.

We didn't talk the rest of the way until we reached the parking lot. Roy drove a rusted out pickup truck that was stacked with lobster pots in need of repair.

"Nora has to go in the baby seat, so you need to get in the back of the truck."

The truck only had the one bench seat up front and the baby seat looked secure. Still.

"Don't car seats always have to be in a back seat?"

"Working on buying a new car, okay?" he growled.

Okay. Touchy subject. While he situated Nora in her car seat and handed her a stuffed toy to play with, I climbed into the back of the truck with the lobster pots. It was covered in mud and smelled like dead fish. This wedding dress was never going to recover, but I was free.

Roy

I PULLED up to the house and sighed. There was nothing to be done about it. She was going to see the place as is.

"It's not that bad," I said to Nora, who had her stuffed rabbit pushed up under her nose. She lived to rub soft furry things under her nose, while sucking her thumb. I was told thumb-sucking was bad for her teeth, but I was saving a mint on pacifiers.

I sucked my thumb as a kid. I turned out all right.

She wiggled her nose at me as if to suggest I was a lying son of a bitch about the house and she was right.

It was that bad. Even after a year of trying to make changes and cheap improvements, it still looked like shit from the outside. The inside wasn't much better.

It had been fine for me. All I needed was a roof, a toilet, a fridge and some heat.

But for Nora, and the Child Protection Services who checked in on her quarterly, it was definitely not okay.

What the hell was I supposed to do? I needed money to make real changes. Money I didn't have, now that every spare dollar I did have went towards taking care of Nora. Paying babysitters whenever I could so I didn't have to take her out on the water with me. Plus saving up to buy a car.

Now, my house, my life was going to be judged by the one person who I never wanted to see this place.

That whole summer we were together, I never once brought her here. Every "date" we'd had, had been on the boat, or at the beach, or in a car. It had worked for both of us since she'd been keeping me a secret from her life, and I'd been keeping my life a secret from her.

Of course she'd asked about where I lived, but I kept putting her off.

There was no putting her off now.

I heard the back of the truck bed squeak open.

"Okay. Let's do this." I said, more to myself than Nora.

I got out of the truck and made my way toward the back, where she was scooching her butt off the end of the truck in that wedding dress that was riding up her tanned thighs.

Thighs I had memorized. This woman had legs that went on forever.

I had taken them as proof of a loving god.

I offered a hand and she took it. Her slim fingers and soft skin dwarfed by my beefy callused hands. These hands didn't fit together. They made no sense.

She hopped down onto the grass and together we made our way to the passenger seat to get Nora. She needed a front sitting car seat and Ness was right, she should be in the backseat of a car. But back facing and in a truck was what I had, until I saved up enough money for the right car seat and a car.

I was a champ now at the buckles and making sure the harness thing didn't touch her face. She raised her arms to me, and for a second I had an image of Vanessa doing the same with her father at some point. Lifting her arms in anticipation of being carried. Safely. Securely.

Only to have that same person one day turn around and slap her across the face.

No wonder Vanessa was so fucked up. It wasn't a pass for what she did two years ago. She was still a liar and that was on her, but when you grew up in a fucked-up family, it had an impact on your life.

Growing up, it was just me and my dad. My mom died when I was too young to remember her. My dad never felt the need to re-marry, although there had been a couple of girlfriends along the way.

Then the storm.

I didn't like to go there. Bad memories were supposed to be left in the past. It made it easier to live in the present.

I plopped Nora on my hip while she watched Vanessa with total fascination.

She probably thought she was a fairy princess come to

life. Had I done what parents around the world had, and set Nora down in front of a TV to watch *Frozen* to give myself a solid hour of *me* time? Yes, yes I had.

Now the kid was addicted to Disney princesses and it was all my fault.

Even with her hair a mess, her mascara smudged under her eyes, her cheek red and swollen, Vanessa Dumont was still the most beautiful woman I'd ever seen.

"So this is it? The Barnes Estate," Vanessa asked.

It was an old joke between us. Most of the town called her summer home the Dumont Estate. So, I'd referred to this shack as the Barnes Estate.

It was a traditional Cape Cod style house. White with black shutters. Except the white paint was chipped in spots and the black shutters were missing some slats.

That's what a nor'easter did to a home on the New England coast. It ate her up.

"A'yup," I said in my best Maine twang.

"You want me to take her?"

For a second I thought she meant taking Nora away. From this beat-up old house, the bench seat pick-up truck and me.

Instinctively, I hugged her closer against my chest.

Then I realized Nora was still staring at Vanessa and Vanessa was only offering to carry her while I led us all inside.

"No. I got her."

"Okay," Vanessa said. Then she hiked up the skirt of her wedding dress and made her way across the grass that was mostly dead patches, and up the steps to the porch.

"Watch out," I barked. "There are some rotted boards to the right."

She looked down and saw the weak spot and nodded.

Her three inch heels looking absolutely ridiculous as she navigated her way to the front door.

"It's not locked," I said, coming up behind her, Nora in my arms.

The front door opened into the main living room with the old, but recently vacuumed, carpet. The furniture was equally worn, the gray couch, the brown recliner. But the coffee table was dusted. I didn't have money for new, but I kept things clean.

Now that Nora was seriously on the move, clean was key.

Clean, but not necessarily neat. Nora's shit covered nearly every surface of free space. Blocks, stuffed animals, all the books I could afford. There was a bouncy thing she'd basically outgrown. I could get rid of that, but the idea of throwing out anything she might decide to use again always froze me with indecision.

I mean, what were you supposed to do with all this shit? Upstairs she already had a small dresser stuffed to the gills with onesies she'd outgrown, but throwing out her baby clothes just felt wrong.

Once I was inside, I felt the push off. Basically her hand straight to my neck, her knee to my kidney. Nora's cue she was ready to be unleashed. I set her down and once the kid found her sea legs, she was off and running. She had no time for lap cuddles anymore. She. Wanted. To. Play.

This time when I set her down, she didn't immediately start running around like a lunatic searching for the toy that would occupy her interest for a few seconds before she was up and looking for the next toy.

This time she stopped and looked up at Vanessa.

"Bah, bah?" Nora said.

Vanessa shook her head. "I'm sorry, I don't understand."

"Bah, bah?" Nora said, a little more clearly.

Ness looked at me, her expression concerned as if she felt ashamed for not understanding a baby.

"It doesn't mean anything, Ness. It's what she says for everything. I keep trying to get her to say something else, and nothing. Kid only knows Bs."

Nora was handing Vanessa her stuffed rabbit, so Vanessa took it. That seemed to make Nora happy.

For one second. Then Nora was holding out her hand again.

"What does that mean?" Vanessa asked me.

"She wants it back," I told her.

Vanessa looked confused. "But she just gave it to me."

"You're really trying to get into the mind of a baby?" I asked her. "This is what she does. She gives you things, then she wants them back. And if you don't turn that rabbit over in three, two, one..."

"Ahh!" Nora scrunched up her face and tiny little fists.

"Hey," I said, loud enough to get her attention. "Not cool."

She pointed at Vanessa.

"She's still new to the game, kid."

Vanessa quickly handed her back her rabbit and then Nora was off looking for the next toy.

"Follow me to the kitchen. I'll get you your ice pack."

"Should we leave her?" Vanessa asked, looking over her shoulder.

Nora had plopped on her butt in front of a stack of blocks. She would build them up until she thought they were high enough, and then she would knock them over. Then she would laugh her ass off. The kid was into destruction.

"The stairs have a gate. Everything down here is kid

proof. She'll wander into the kitchen when she's done knocking over her blocks."

It was a small galley style kitchen in the back of the house. Stove, refrigerator on one side. Cabinets and sink on the other. There was a small table tucked in the corner with Nora's high chair and my chair catty-corner to each other.

"Sit," I told Ness.

"You must not entertain much," she noted, sitting down at the small table.

"Nah, dinner parties all the time. I make those fancy horse de-vors."

"That's not how...oh, you were kidding."

Yeah, my sense of humor was not for everyone. But Nessa used to love it, like the darker and stranger my jokes, the more she would laugh. It was one of the things that used to make me happy – making the princess laugh. I'd always had the sense that under that sunny smile, and kind of vapid blonde act she'd perfected– that she'd been sad. Like grieving.

It was one of the things that bound us together.

Fuck. This was the shit I wasn't going to think about.

I pulled an ice-pack from the freezer. I had plenty of them because some part of me always needed icing. Life on the ocean meant getting knocked around.

"Here, catch." I tossed her the pack, because I didn't want to do that thing where I pushed her hair back off her face and gently brought the ice up to her cheek.

She, of course, didn't catch the ice-pack but let it drop to the floor. Vanessa Dumont was the least coordinated person I'd ever met. That apparently hadn't changed in two years. She bent over to pick it up and then pressed it against her face, sighing with pleasure.

She looked ridiculous in that dress in my beat up kitchen.

But she also looked very, very alone.

I crossed my arms over my chest and leaned against the stove.

"So tell me why your father wanted you to marry that guy so bad."

She shrugged; half her face covered with the pack. "What motivates my father to do anything? Money."

"He doesn't have enough of it already?"

"I guess not," she said softly.

Not that any of this was my problem. I didn't care about her, her father, or her future.

Now who's lying?

"What are you going to do now? Go back to modeling?"

She laughed. "Turns out I wasn't very good at it."

"Fuck that. You're beautiful." It was a fact. Not a compliment.

"Pretty, yes. Not striking. Not interesting. They all decided my face was boring."

"Who did?"

"Designers. Photographers."

"That's a thing they can decide?"

She shrugged.

I grunted. The last thing Ness was, was boring. "You think your dad is really going to cut you off?"

"I think he's done it already."

Not my monkey. Not my circus. Just keep telling yourself that.

"So? What comes next? You got some friends you can crash with somewhere? South of France or whatever..."

Her smile was the saddest fucking thing I'd ever seen. "I think you promised me a trip to the bus stop."

I grunted again. No friends, then. There hadn't been a whole lot of friends around that summer we spent together either. *Fuck. Me.*

"I know I have no right to ask this-"

"I'm not marrying you," I said, reminding her and myself that I wasn't in the hero business anymore. "Anybody else, but not you."

She blinked, and if anything, got a little paler. "I didn't...I wouldn't ask again...I was only going to ask if you had some sweat pants or something. So I could get out of this dress."

"Oh. Right." Now I felt like an idiot. A mean idiot. "Wait here, I'll see what I can find."

I left the kitchen to head back into the living room. Nora was happily building up her blocks. I got to the stairs and hooked one leg over the gate, then the other. This whole Nora walking thing was inconvenient as shit, but I imagined in another few months when she had it mastered, she could figure out stairs.

Upstairs there were two bedrooms and one bath. In my bedroom I had a queen bed, that I'd left unmade, because fuck it, sometimes I didn't want to make the bed. I was rummaging through my drawers where I found the soft sweats and a t-shirt I slept in these days. No more sleeping naked for me. Nora usually woke up once during the night and needed to be settled down.

Then a thought occurred to me and I opened the bottom drawer.

There, in the back, I found Ness's old sweater. The green one with the buttons. It was that fancy material – super soft. She'd left it in my truck that summer, and I, being a fucking idiot, had kept it. I'd sniffed it until it stopped smelling like her.

What a sap.

Yeah, not giving that back to her. She'd read all kinds of shit into that if she saw it. I stuffed it back in the drawer and shut it.

I tried not to think about what Vanessa said. About getting out of her wedding dress.

I tried not to think of what she would look like wearing my clothes, nothing underneath.

I tried not to wonder what would happen after I dropped her off at the bus station.

Where the fuck was her brother anyway? I knew he was hooking up with Lola Pappas these days. Lola was too nice to waste her time with an asshole, so if he wasn't an asshole, then he should be helping out his sister.

That was a better plan. I would find him first. Let him step up and do the right thing. I didn't need to be involved in any of this family shit, but I also wasn't going to drop Vanessa all alone at a bus stop.

Clothes in hand, I jogged down the steps. Carefully, I made my way over the gate. When I got to the kitchen, Nora had found her way onto Vanessa's lap.

Nora wasn't a lap kid. At least she wasn't with me anymore.

"Peekaboo," Ness crooned, then lifted the part of the long dress she'd put on Nora's head. Nora laughed like this was the funniest thing that had ever happened to her, and Ness put the lace back over her head.

"Bah!"

This time Ness easily translated that word. It meant *again*.

"Peekaboo!" Ness said as she lifted the lace and silk. Nora was now snot giggling. She was losing her little baby mind because she had her very own princess in her house.

A princess who looked like Ness and played peekaboo like it was the only thing she wanted to do.

Don't do it. Don't do what you're thinking.

But - and this was a huge but – if Ness did live here and take care of Nora, I could make more money, faster. I could get out on the water earlier. Stay later. It wouldn't be permanent, just as long as the season.

Everything inside me said. This. Was. A. Mistake.

Nora shrieked with joy, and now Ness was laughing, and the two of them were locked in their own little happy world.

"Fuck me," I blurted. "Okay, I'll save you."

Without missing a beat, Ness turned her head toward me and said, "Don't use the F-word around Nora. And yes, thank you."

3

Roy

"Let's set some ground rules," I said, looking at the two of them sitting at the table.

Ness smiled, looking at me out of the corner of her eye. The same look she used to give me that summer, right before she'd kiss me. But I absolutely wasn't thinking about that. "You do love your ground rules."

"None of that."

"None of what?"

"No... flirty eyes."

"I don't have flirty eyes, Roy. I just have eyes."

"There's nothing between us. Nothing." Yeah, that killed the flirty eyes. "I'm doing this for the kid. She needs...more than me. And I need help."

She nodded, even as she pulled Nora more snuggly into her lap. The kid was getting tired. That's how it went. She woke up like a live wire, but by three in the afternoon she was done for. A one hour power nap and she'd be raring to go until bedtime.

I didn't have a set time for that. She basically just let me know when she was beat.

"I can't afford day care, or a nanny, or any of that shit. You can stay here, take care of her and I'll feed you."

"That sounds like a deal," she said. It was a better deal for me. If I remembered right, she barely ate.

"This is temporary, Ness. It gives you time to get back on your feet. Gives me a chance to make the most money I can this season."

It would probably look good to CPS, too.

Nora was passed out now, basically adding her drool to that cheese sauce down the front of Ness's dress. Not that Vanessa seemed to care. She was casually running her fingers through Nora's soft curls, almost like she didn't even realize she was doing it.

"You're a liar and I don't forgive you," I told her, putting the knife in her side. "For that bullshit two years ago."

"I don't expect you too."

Then I twisted the knife. "I don't like you either."

Her blue eyes, wide and wounded, met mine. "Okay. I understand."

The silence in the kitchen was cold, and I wondered why I felt like a fucking asshole for just laying down the boundaries. For keeping her hero complex bullshit about me in line. This was a girl who could create rose-colored glasses for her *father*. There was no telling what she would do for me. This was a business arrangement between the two of us, nothing more.

"What happened between us, two years ago? We don't talk about it. Like it never happened, okay?"

"You don't think... maybe we should clear the air?" she

asked, and I could see all those pretty excuses, those lies forming behind her wide blue eyes.

"Nope. I was grieving my dad and you were...what did you call it? Slumming it?"

"Simon said that, not me."

"Well, you certainly didn't correct him, did you princess?"

"You didn't used to be so mean," she whispered.

"I've always been mean, I just wasn't mean to you."

She nodded and pressed her nose to Nora's head.

Crap. I felt mean.

"Verity told me you had a cousin who died. I didn't know you had any other family besides your dad," she said.

I grunted. I hated that Vanessa had some of those pieces of my life. I'd lost my dad the summer before I met her. Back when we were spending time together, I'd spilled my guts to her. And she'd been so...fucking sweet about it all. She hadn't rushed in with all the platitudes everyone else had been giving me for a year. She'd been quiet and she'd listened, sitting next to me on a blanket on the beach, like she understood heartache. Like she knew what it was to be alone and scared.

She'd been one of the reasons I'd started living again. Imagining a future instead of just banking days on the ocean.

And the whole time she'd been lying.

No, this wasn't some happy reunion. I wouldn't let it be. This was two people temporarily helping each other out of a jam.

"Apparently my mom had a brother. I didn't know him or his daughter."

"What was her name? Nora's mother?"

"Diane," I answered, and then because I felt like there

were a lot more questions coming, I rattled off the facts I knew. "She was nineteen. Dad wasn't in the picture. She had the sense to make a will after Nora was born and named me as the guardian."

"What happened-?"

"Suicide," I said tightly, the word hard to spit out. The woman who lived in the apartment next door had found her. Nora had been crying for hours, and finally the woman couldn't take it anymore. The door hadn't been locked.

Diane must have figured someone would come eventually.

"That's awful," Vanessa whispered, and wrapped her arms more securely around the kid. Like she could protect her from the past.

"Yeah."

"So is that how CPS is involved?"

"Yes. Nora was sent to foster care until they found the will and contacted me. Just because Diane named me as a guardian legally, the state has jurisdiction over an orphan and a responsibility to make sure she's placed in a safe environment."

"What would have happened if you hadn't taken her in?"

"I did," I said. There hadn't been a question, really. She was family. Family took care of family.

"Yes, but if you hadn't?"

I shrugged. I hated thinking about this. Hated it. And now I was mad at Ness for making me think about it. "Don't know. I guess the state would have made her available for adoption."

Where she might have had the opportunity to go to a loving family with a mom and dad. Maybe even a couple who had other kids, who would give Nora siblings.

A nicer house. A safer car.

Would she be better off without me? Was I the worst possible choice for her?

A scowling fisherman, eking out a living on the water, with a rundown house and no prospects for a mother anywhere in the picture.

Until the Disney princess ran away from her own wedding.

I *hated* thinking about this. Maybe this whole Vanessa living here was a mistake. Because she poked and prodded and asked questions and made me think about the shit I hated thinking about...

"So what happens now?" Vanessa asked me, and I took a deep breath and pulled myself together.

"We put Nora down in the crib. It's important she sleeps in her bed. That's what the book says."

"Okay."

"You can shower and change. Then when she wakes up we'll need to go find your brother."

"He's probably worried," Vanessa said. "I didn't take my phone when I left."

"Why didn't you just go to his place?" I asked her. It seemed like the logical choice.

She sighed. "He's got Lola now. They...they're really in love. Like in love, in love. It's not that I don't adore them, I just thought maybe I could solve my own problems for once. Then I saw your notice at The Lobster Pot and thought maybe that was a way out."

I shook my head and pointed at her so she understood. "I am not your way out. You don't want to stay with your brother right now, fine, you stay here and help me out with Nora, but that's it."

"You've made that very clear, Roy. But I have some ground rules, too."

Well, that was a surprise. "Hit me."

"You can't change your mind."

Outside I could hear the neighbor's dog bark. The other neighbor's dog answered. They better not wake up the kid.

"Vanessa-"

"I'm serious. You can't say yes now and no later. You can't decide I'm not what you thought I was and kick me out. You can't decide I'm too much or not enough-"

"Vanessa." I said, in the firmest voice I had. That summer she'd spiraled like this too. But so did I. It was part of the grief thing we shared. Though, it was weird I never knew what her grief had been about. "Look at me."

I waited for her big blue eyes to meet mine.

"I won't." She didn't believe me, and I thought about all the ways the men in her life had fucked her over. "I promise, Ness."

She nodded and a chill ran down my spine. It felt like we'd somehow spoken vows.

"Can you cook?" I asked her. Maybe I should have led with that one.

"No."

"What about minor repairs around the house?"

"Uh...I can swap out a toilet paper roll. Does that count?"

I pinched the bridge of my nose. "Do you know anything about kids?"

"Nora likes peek-a-boo and her hair smells nice," she bent down and gave that head a kiss.

"It's the shampoo," I grunted.

This. Was. A. Mistake.

And I couldn't change my mind.

∿

Vanessa

I WAS in the back of Roy's pick-up truck again. Except this time I was dressed in a pair of baggy sweat pants, a t-shirt that fell almost to my knees, and a pair of crème colored Jimmy Choo heels.

There had been no shoes in his house that worked.

That there were no spare women's clothes just lying around the place, shouldn't have made me happy. But it did. Two years ago when I made the choice to go back to Simon, I'd let Roy believe the worst of me and I'd put him firmly in the rear view mirror.

I couldn't think about him, or ask anyone in town about him, because it all hurt too much. In fact, I'd stayed away from Calico Cove as much as possible. Only returning this summer for the wedding.

And only because my brother asked me to. He'd been planning to win over the girl he'd loved his whole life – Lola.

I'd agreed because part of me wanted to see Roy one more time before I'd committed myself to my fate.

Was it pathetic that I took just a little solace in the fact that he didn't have some random woman's clothing in his house? Yes. Words did not describe my pathetic-ness.

Roy pulled us into the parking lot of my brother's building. The idea was to get all of the clothes I'd left at Jackson's place, let him know I was safe with Roy, and then get down to the business of being Roy's...whatever I was.

Roy parked and came around the truck to get Nora out of her seat. She was all wide-eyed curiosity. Not crying or fussing. Just a thumb popped in her mouth. Her curls blowing around her head.

Roy should have looked uncomfortable with this baby girl. Instead he carried her like a lobster trap. Like she was just an extension of his arms.

I scootched my butt across the edge of the truck bed and carefully hopped down, making sure I was solid on my shoes. Then I led them into the building. We got on the elevator and I hit the button.

"He might not even be home yet," I said. "But he hides a spare key for me behind one of the paintings in the hallway."

"Why not just give you a key?"

I blinked. Because Jackson hadn't. Not in all this time. He'd only left a key where I could find it, if I needed it.

Because he didn't trust me.

Jackson couldn't totally trust that my loyalties weren't with Dad or Simon. I'd been stupid in the past, telling Simon things about Jackson's business. Not because I was deliberately trying to hurt Jackson, but because I wanted to believe Simon and I were on our own team.

Only we weren't. Everything I told Simon about Jackson's business; he shared with my Dad. That's where Simon's loyalties were.

While I'd been trying to create that stupid fairy tale out of thin air.

I didn't answer Roy about the key. It was just one more embarrassment.

The elevator doors opened and I said, "It's this way. Last door at the end of the hall."

I got there first and knocked. I'd only give it a second before using the key. It wasn't likely Jackson would stick around to do damage control after the wedding that wasn't, but he might have felt a certain amount of responsibility for cleaning up my mess.

As much as Jackson tried to distance himself from the family, he'd always been a really good brother to me.

The door opened immediately, and Jackson hauled me into his arms and lifted me off my feet. "I knew you would do it! I knew you'd never marry that asshole! Swear to God, Vanessa, I've never been prouder..."

He saw my face and set me down.

"What happened to your face? Did you fall?" He took in the odd clothes I was wearing and the looming man standing behind me. Jackson scowled. "Who are you?"

"Roy?" this came from Lola, who was standing behind Jackson, trying to peek over his shoulder. "Roy, did you find Vanessa?"

"She found me," Roy said.

"Thank you for bringing her home. We've got it from here." Jackson pulled my hand and it reminded me of Dad pulling on my arm. I jerked my hand back.

"Roy's with me," I said. "If you'll let us in, I can explain."

Jackson and Lola shared a look. One of their many looks. These stupid love looks of theirs were a part of the reason why I couldn't marry Simon. If my brother could find love, maybe I could too?

"Sure, come on in," Jackson said, stepping aside. I stepped past him and Jackson got a whiff of me. "What is that smell?"

"Fish," Roy said, even as he hefted Nora up in his arms. "My truck smells like fish."

We had to maneuver through some building materials, as Jackson's condo was being used as storage while the diner was being redone. Larry the Lobster from the diner was in the living room as well as the old cash register.

Lola gave me a hug. She always smelled like French fries and maple syrup. It was a delicious smell. "I've got your phone and stuff. Your purse."

"Oh, thank god," I whispered and grabbed the Positano tote she held out to me. I had some cash. Not a lot. The cards would be useless by now. But my phone...

"It's been buzzing for hours," Lola said.

I had hundreds of messages and snaps. My Insta was blowing up too. And all of it...

She was always such a flake.

Why would she run out on Simon? He's fucking hot.

I fucked him two weeks ago. He said she's totally repressed #notsuprised

She's sweet. Someone should have told her.

A hundred bucks they're back together in a month #dramamuch

I heard her parents were talking about a conservatorship #freebritney

I turned the phone off and set it down on the edge of a table crowded with mail. I was going to conveniently leave it there. Forever.

"It's bad?" Lola asked.

"About what you'd expect," I choked out.

"Honey," she whispered. "Your face. Come with me and we'll get you an ice pack."

Why was everyone so obsessed with ice?

"I'm okay," I swallowed. What did I say? How did I account for the bruise? I could just say it was an accident. I tripped and fell. Roy helped me up. I decided I would be his wife/not wife for a while.

Pretty simple.

Only it wasn't. Not really. My father had hit me. Hit me to hurt me. To make me obey. To punish me.

I was going to need some serious therapy to unpack all this garbage, but not right now. Right now, all I needed were my things.

Except Lola wasn't having any of that. Still dressed in the pink summer dress she'd worn for the wedding, she grabbed me by the hand and shoved aside a box of tiles to make room for me on the couch. The very cool couch I'd picked out for Jackson when he'd first bought this place.

I could pick out furniture. Comfortable. Cool. Fashionable. Serviceable. I knew what looked right together. I knew what colors worked in a given space. I'd helped Jackson with the interior design of his Shells Family Restaurants and Lola with the renovations for Pappas', now that the diner was officially hers.

But those weren't like... skills.

"Jackson, get some ice and a glass of water," Lola told him. "Roy, you need anything?"

"No."

Lola turned back to me. She'd always been so kind, even when we were kids. Opening her life for Jackson and me when I was around. I totally understood why Jackson planned his epic seduction this summer.

"Tell us what happened."

"I think you were there," I said with a small laugh. "I bolted. I runaway-brided that shit."

"Yeah, you did," Jackson said, and high-fived me over the edge of the couch.

"But why?" Lola asked. I owed them an answer. The two of them had thought I didn't see Simon for what he was, but I'd always known.

"Everything really fell apart when I found out he'd cheated on me on the day of the engagement party..."

I heard the grunt from where Roy was standing.

I couldn't imagine what he thought of me, but I knew it wasn't flattering.

"Then you two fell in love," I smiled at Lola. "Even after all the shit that Jackson put you through, and I guess, I thought, there might be hope for me after all. So I just couldn't marry him."

"There's always hope," Lola said softly, taking my hands in hers. Jackson brought over an ice pack and handed it to me. Seemed kind of pointless now. The bruise was there. The swelling would eventually go down.

He pressed a glass of water into my hand and I put the pack on my face.

"So?" Jackson said, leaning on the back of the couch behind Lola. "You ran out of the wedding, then what happened?"

I took a sip of water, then another. Stalling. Creating another story. "I...well, I went to The Lobster Pot and Verity gave me some lobster mac and cheese. I spilled some on my dress and..."

Just say the easiest thing. Avoid the conflict.

"I tripped on the train of my dress and hit my cheek. Roy found me and offered to drive me back here."

"Fuck. That. Shit."

All eyes shifted to Roy and Nora, who was sucking her right thumb even as she was petting Roy's stubbled cheek with her left hand.

"Roy," I hissed, trying to communicate without explanation that he shouldn't say anything.

"No, Ness." he said with a dark scowl. "You tell him the truth or I will."

"Tell me what?" Jackson said, looking between me and Roy.

"Dad actually found me-"

Jackson stood and pointed at my cheek. "He did this?" The energy in the room got dark and weird. "He did this to you?" he shouted.

Nora startled at the harsh angry sound and began to cry.

"Dude." Roy glared at Jackson and patted Nora's back. A little too hard, I thought. Like he was trying to get her to cough up a chicken nugget instead of soothing her. That made her cry too.

"It's okay, kiddo. He's just an ass," Roy said to Nora, who ducked her head in the space between Roy's ear and chin.

"Roy," I said, my tone was sharp. "Language."

"Okay, everyone calm down," Lola said, a little too loudly because she was trying to be heard.

Now, Nora was wailing, and three adults in the room made it happen.

"Shit," Jackson said. "What do we do?"

Roy closed his eyes and took a deep breath like he wished he was anywhere but here.

"*Shhh, baby Nora,*" he... *sang*? Well, talk sang, but still more singing than I'd ever think Roy Barnes was capable of. "*When she gets scared I pretend I'm in a cartoon and I talk to her like this and it works...*"

It was working. She wasn't wailing anymore. Just crying. Was Roy Barnes some kind of baby whisper-er? And was that perhaps the cutest thing I'd ever seen?

"Is this a joke?" Jackson asked, and Roy glared at him as Nora's face clouded up again.

"*Okay,*" Lola stepped in with her own sing-song voice. "*For the baby. We're all going to talk in our best Disney princess voices while Vanessa tells us what happened.*"

Right. Disney voice.

"*Dad found me and tried to get me to go back,*" I sang. "*I said no and he slapped me across the face. Now I'm going to help Roy with baby Nora...while I figure out the rest of my life.*"

Snow White couldn't have done it any better.

Jackson pinched the bridge of his nose. "Vanessa, what the hell?"

Lola smacked him and Jackson sighed.

"*Vanessa,*" he sing-songed. "*What the hell?*"

Lola burst out laughing. I did too, I couldn't help myself – my life was literally in the toilet, but this was funny.

"*I don't have any money, or a place to live-*" I sang.

"You'll live here with me," Jackson cut me off. "With us."

"*Where? Jackson?*" I asked, pointing around the house. The place was chaos central. Between the renovation of Pappas' Diner and the new bar he was building, the condo was half building supplies.

"We'll figure it out," he said stubbornly.

"No, I'm not moving in," I said quietly, firmly. No singing. "You and Lola just moved in together and I'm not going to be a third wheel. Roy needs help with the baby and I...I need some kind of purpose."

"Roy can hire a nanny," Jackson said quietly.

"No, he can't," I whispered back.

"Vanessa," Jackson said, clearly struggling to hold on to his temper. "You can't just live with some stranger, taking care of his kid."

"Roy isn't a stranger," I said.

When I looked at Roy, he immediately avoided my gaze. I'd told no one about him. About our summer together. Not even Jackson. He'd been my secret and I hadn't wanted anyone telling me what a mistake I was making.

Because in a life full of mistakes, Roy had felt like a non-mistake.

"What's going on?" Jackson asked, his eyes darting between me and Roy.

"Roy and I met two summers ago. When I left Simon..."

Roy grunted in protest.

"We were...well, we know each other. It will be fine."

Jackson gave Roy a hard look. One that Roy returned. Finally, my brother sighed and shook his head. "Vanessa, it's not going to be fine. Our father did that to your face. He went nearly apoplectic when you took off. This wedding means more to him than just you getting married. I don't get it."

"It's financial," I said quietly. "Simon's family is investing in Dumont Holdings."

"What does that have to do with you?" Roy asked.

"They wouldn't invest unless they got something in return."

"You're telling me our father *sold* you?!" Jackson asked.

I flinched and squeezed my hands together. "Can we not talk about this now?" I asked. Not in front of Roy. It was all too embarrassing. "Look, I knew what I was doing. I agreed to it."

"Why?" Jackson asked. "Why would you agree to that?"

Tears clogged in my throat and I stopped talking, I wasn't doing this in front of Roy. I had to have some kind of pride.

"Can we please stop talking about this?"

"Oh, honey," Lola took my hand in hers. "You know that's messed up, right? Jackson, you need to give her some space, okay?"

Everything was messed up right now. None of this seemed real. This morning I looked like the perfect bride. Now, I smelled like fish and my clothes were too big for me and I had a giant bruise on my face.

"Dad's not going to let this go," Jackson said to Lola. "Mom was talking about Vanessa having mental health issues."

"What does that mean? Like they could have her committed?" Lola asked.

"They could do anything with enough money," Jackson said grimly.

"You don't think this is over?" Roy's perma-frown was a little more frowny than normal. They were quite a picture: sweet little Nora, all innocence, patting the scruffy face of a man who looked like he was ready to bust heads.

"No," Jackson said carefully. "I don't. I think the best thing we can do is get Vanessa as far away from our father as possible."

I shook my head. "Jackson, I don't have any money. Dad will cut me off from any accounts. I'm sure he's already put a hold on all my credit cards. I don't even have access to my clothes or jewelry. And all of our own money is tied up in our investments and renovations for the diner and the bar."

"We can put those off," Lola said.

"They've already started," I countered. "You can't just stop now. Eventually, we'll see a return on the investment, but in the short term, Roy is my best offer."

"Vanessa, I'm serious," Jackson said. "I don't know how unstable our father is right now. How far he might go to force your hand. Don't forget, Simon has his own reasons for doing this, and no offense, it's not out of any great love for you."

"None taken," I muttered.

"Your father can't force her to marry the fuckface or do any of that other shit if she's married to someone else," Roy said.

"Uh, yeah," Jackson said. "Sure, I guess."

"I'll do it," Roy announced.

"Do...what?" Jackson asked.

"I'll marry her. Legally."

"Roy," I breathed. "You don't have to do this."

"I promised, remember?" he said. That vow in the kitchen. He wasn't going to change his mind. Tears threatened again and I turned away, pressing my fingers against the ducts in my eyes so I wouldn't cry. Not in front of him.

"We can get a marriage license pretty quickly, then we'll have the judge make it legal," Roy said more to Jackson than me. "Then your father can't do shit. We'll get married so you're protected, and CPS will be all over the happy family image. It's win, win."

Right. He got something out of this, too.

"Are you okay with this, Vanessa?" Jackson asked.

Was I okay with it?

Roy was going to save me. Legally now too.

"*I guess,*" I sang.

4

Three Days Later
Roy

"Let's get a few things straight now," I said to Vanessa under my breath.

"Here we go," she said. "More rules?"

We were standing in a lobby area just outside the judge's chambers in the municipal building in the center of town. We'd filed our intentions yesterday and gotten our marriage license, but we had to wait a day to book an appointment with the judge.

Vanessa had packed up everything she'd left at Jackson's place and moved it to my house yesterday. She didn't have much there, mostly pajamas. Jackson had tried to go back to the Dumont Estate to get more of her things, but his asshole father called the cops on him.

"That's right."

I kept my voice low so that our witnesses, Jackson and Lola, couldn't hear us. Both of them were currently occupied by keeping Nora happy with a dancing stuffed bunny.

I gave it two minutes before Nora's interest wore off.

"Okay," she said.

Vanessa was swimming in a pair of white capri pants and a sleeveless blue blouse she'd borrowed from Lola that were too big for her thin frame. She was wearing the high heels, which were the only shoes I'd seen her in besides a fuzzy pair of pink slippers.

Her hair was down, loose and bouncy.

She was fucking gorgeous. Which for some reason only made those ground rules more important.

"This is just a... what do they call those..."

"A marriage of convenience," Ness said.

"Yeah. That."

"Gotcha." She glanced over at me. "You nervous, Roy?"

"No," I lied. I ran my hand down the front of my second-best shirt.

"You look nice."

I scowled at her, which made her smile. Swear to god this girl was cracked.

I admired how cool she was being. I was freaking out and she was calm and steady. But I guessed if she was willing to sign her life away to Scumbag Simon, living with me for a few months wasn't such a bad deal.

"That thing you said at your brother's house?"

"I said a lot of things."

"About how your father sold-"

"He didn't sell me," she insisted. "He just...needed me to do it. For the family."

"It was that summer, wasn't it? When he came here looking for you?"

She nodded and showed her first sign of nerves, chewing on her lips. I tried to keep the question back behind my teeth, because I had no business trying to figure out why she left me. That was old business, and it was only going to make me angry.

"Why did you say yes?"

She blinked. Again. Faster. Then she turned with the kind of smile that took my breath away. "The money, silly. Why does anyone do anything?"

Exactly. And now I was angry.

Except... was she lying?

Which was par for the course with this girl.

"The ground rules are," she said, putting us back on track. "You're keeping me safe from my Dad. I'm helping you out with Nora. Period. The end. We are not friends."

"We're not friends," I repeated. "We can be civil and that's it."

She looked at me like she didn't believe me. More flirty eyes from her as she teased me. "You can be civil?"

"Sometimes."

She nodded. "You'll barely know I'm there."

That was doubtful. The house only had the one bathroom, and there was already blond hair clogging the sink. Products filled the counter space, like lotions and tinted moisturizers and lip gloss. My God, the fucking lip gloss!

But so far, any time Ness was around, Nora was out of her mind with happiness and that was what this was all about.

I shot a glance to Nora who was still watching the stuffed bunny Lola was making fly around in the space between them.

"What's that?" I asked, pointing at Nora's head.

"What?"

"The purple thing."

"It's a hair bow. It matches her shirt."

"Where did she get it?"

Vanessa shrugged. "I bought it at the pharmacy yesterday when I was picking up my shampoo and stuff. It's cute."

"Nora doesn't need cute."

"Every girl needs cute."

I growled. "Look, I don't have any extra money for bows and shit. Nora doesn't need accessories. Got it?"

She crossed her arms over her chest, and for a second I thought she was just going to nod along. Instead she lifted her chin.

"No. I don't *got it*. I used my own money, Roy," she said. "And Nora smiled when I showed it to her. So as long as it doesn't cost *you* anything, I get to make Nora smile when I want."

I opened my mouth, then shut it. She was using her tiny store of cash for Nora's freakin' smile. How the fuck was I supposed to argue against that?

Behind us, the judge's assistant popped his head out of the chamber door.

"The judge will see you now," the young man said with a polite smile, then stepped back inside the judge's chambers.

At the far end of the hallway the outside door opened with a bang, and in walked one fuckface and one scum-of-the-earth father.

They looked like they'd just come from a tennis court. Fuckface had a sweater around his neck. Swear to God, I should punch him for that alone. And scum-of-the-earth father wore pink shorts with little blue crabs on them.

Those two clearly didn't get bullied enough as kids.

"There you are!" Dumont shouted. His face turning the color of his shorts. "I have to read about this nonsense in the paper, Vanessa? Have you lost your mind?"

"Vanessa," Simon said, like he was bored. "What are you doing? First the drama at the wedding, now this?"

"What are you doing here?" Vanessa asked. The cool and calm girl was gone and in her place was the runaway bride. Pale and looking for a place to hide. It made every protective instinct I had go apeshit.

Dumont sneered. "Stopping this nonsense. Marrying a... fisherman? Vanessa, what are you thinking?"

He said the word fisherman like I said fuckface. However, I was going to keep my cool because I wasn't going to upset Nora and end up singing to her in front of these two assholes.

"Vanessa," Simon sighed. "You've had your fun. It's time to come home. I mean really. Am I supposed to be jealous? Of this guy?"

Fuckface moved his chin in my direction. Then his eyes narrowed, and I could almost hear the click in his brain.

"Hold on a second," he said. "I know you. Were you... oh my god," he started laughing. "You're the fucking local she was slumming it with two years ago."

All right. This was over.

"Lola, Vanessa, Jackson, take Nora inside the judge's chambers," I said.

"Why? What are you going to do?" Vanessa asked.

"Have a real quick conversation with Fuckface and Father of The Year."

"Roy," Jackson said, coming up behind me. "Trust me, you don't want to cause any trouble. There are cameras in this hallway and my dad is a litigious asshole."

Dumont smiled like he was proud that he didn't know how to fight his own battles like a man. "Your threats of violence against me won't work in a municipal building filled with legal professionals as well as police officers."

"Only two things are going to happen," I said, and stepped in front of Vanessa. If her father thought he was getting his hands on her again, he was more stupid than his shorts. "Either Vanessa is going to change her mind and leave with you-"

"That's not going to happen!" she insisted, as she stood behind me on her tip toes.

"Or, you're going to have to go through me to get to her."

"Through both of us," Jackson said, backing me up. Which was nice.

Simon laughed like a fucking knob. "Where the hell are we? The Wild West? That's my fiancé. She's obviously had a mental breakdown of some sort. She needs professional help. Jackson, why are you encouraging this?"

"She doesn't want to marry you, Simon. Because you cheat on her and you don't love her."

Simon's face turned sour. "I haven't loved her or been faithful to her for five years. What's suddenly changed?"

"Me," Vanessa said quietly. "I've changed."

Oh, man, I had no business being proud of this woman. But here I was. Proud.

"You heard her," I said.

"This isn't the end of it," Dumont said. "You'll be hearing from my lawyer."

"She'll be legally married to me and your lawyer won't be able to do a thing about it," I said.

"My children," Dumont snarled. "My heirs. The future of the Dumont fortune. Where did it all go wrong?"

I had thoughts about that, but I was tired of talking. I'd said a lot of words today. Had to say a bunch more in front of the judge.

"Vanessa, really?" Simon said, trying to look around my shoulder to her, but I stepped in front of him. "Do you know what the world is saying about you, right now? Your friends are dining out on this all over Insta and Tiktok."

"Then I guess they're not my friends," she said quietly.

"We had a deal, remember?" he asked, his eyebrows raised. "When you came back after that little vacation on the wild side with this caveman. You said I could...what were the words you used...?"

Behind me I could feel the cold chill of her embarrassment.

"Don't," she breathed, but only I could hear her. I refused to be curious. I refused to care.

"Satisfy myself, elsewhere. That's what you said. So this tantrum about me being unfaithful feels a bit disingenuous," Simon said. "You said you wanted a family and security. That's what's on the table."

I looked over my shoulder at her. "What do you want Ness?" I asked.

Because it wasn't a guarantee she would stay. She'd left me once to go back to this guy for those very reasons. Chose the money and the lifestyle over anything I had to offer.

Which that first time was at least me, along with my whole heart.

Now all I was offering was a run-down home, a shoe-string living, some legal protection and a kid who was prone to ear infections.

My heart was officially off the table.

"It's over Simon." Then she laughed. A sad, soulful laugh. "What am I talking about? There was never anything there, to be over. From you or my father. I didn't understand that a few years ago. I do now. I know what's real. Jackson and Lola...that's real."

"Well *c'est la vie*," Simon said. "That's French," he explained to me like I gave a shit.

"Oh. Thought that was *fuckface.*"

He gave me that look that the summer people some-times did. Like I was beneath him or somehow unworthy because I didn't have as much money.

What a load of horseshit. Like money has anything to do with the character of a man. This man cheated and lied to the woman he was supposed to care about. Made Vanessa feel less than worthy and deserving of love. Her father fucking slapped her in the face.

Two men with money, who had no character. No honor.

"Have fun slumming it, Vanessa," Simon said with a smirk, then he turned and left the lobby area.

Dumont Senior stood there for a little while longer. Like he couldn't figure out what his next move should be.

I could practically smell his desperation.

I realized now what Jackson meant, desperate men did desperate things.

"I'm sorry," the clerk from earlier popped his head back out the door. "Is there a delay? The judge is on a tight schedule."

"No delay," I said.

"You're making the biggest mistake of your life, Vanes-sa," Dumont said, resolved it seemed, to her decision. "I'm writing you out of the Dumont will today. You'll have no mother, no father, no money, no car. Nothing to speak of."

"She'll have me," Jackson said.

"And me," Lola added, linking her arm inside Vanessa's.

I said nothing. She wouldn't have me. This wasn't permanent. When we each got what we needed out of the deal, Vanessa Dumont would have to learn how to stand on her own two feet. Make a living. Be an adult in the world instead of someone's spoiled child.

"Let's get this done," I said, and Vanessa led the way into the judge's chambers.

She said I do.

I said I do.

The judge said I could kiss her, but I didn't.

It was done.

"I'M REALLY sorry about my dad," Vanessa said as we walked back into my house. The ceremony had only taken ten minutes total. Jackson and Lola had wanted to take us out to eat afterwards, but this wasn't any kind of celebration. It was a business transaction and nothing more. I'd said I needed to get Nora back home and everyone had let it go.

Things had gotten emotional at the courthouse and the very last thing this marriage needed was more emotion.

"Watch the step," I reminded her as she navigated around the worn-out boards. I really needed to get that fixed. "And stop apologizing for your father. He's responsible for his own actions."

I pushed open the door and Nora did this thing when she was being carried but suddenly saw her toys, where her legs started running in midair. Like she couldn't get down to the ground fast enough to get to those toys.

Cracked me up every time.

"I need to make you a list," I said over my shoulder on my way to the kitchen. Vanessa didn't follow, so I turned and found her sitting down on the floor, legs crossed and offering Nora a toy.

"What are you doing?" I asked her.

"Playing? Isn't that what you want me to do?"

I frowned. Did I?

I wanted her to watch the kid, feed the kid, bathe the kid, change the kid's diapers. Those were the things I did. The kid had toys to play with.

"Yeah, I guess. If she likes it."

Vanessa's smile got me straight in the gut.

I knew that smile. All cheeks and teeth and bright blue eyes. That smile used to make my heart beat harder. It filled me with this sense of hope. Like the world wasn't as dark and heavy as it seemed. For a summer that smile made me believe in...everything again.

I fucking hated that smile.

"Of course she likes it," she said. "Who doesn't like playing?"

"Grownups who have actual responsibilities," I fired back, and watched her smile fade. Good. No more smiling. "I'm going to make a list of things you need to do. I have to get back on the water tomorrow so it's going to be your first day with her alone."

I rummaged through a junk drawer in the kitchen and found a pad and pen.

Jotting down Nora's schedule, my schedule, and some other things that would be useful around the place. Like grocery shopping and laundry. Maybe some manageable repair work. When I was done, I'd filled the page double sided and stomped back to the living room where Vanessa was still on the floor wearing what she'd worn to the court house minus her shoes.

That's when it hit me. She had nothing. Like absolutely nothing.

A useless wedding dress, stupid high heeled shoes, a couple pairs of pants and borrowed shirts and something she called *sleep shorts* and tank tops.

I didn't want to spend one minute thinking about what she slept in.

I knew Jackson gave her some money, but I also knew she didn't have any plans to take more.

"Where's your phone?" I asked her.

"I got rid of it."

Yeah, just got rid of it. Probably a new iPhone 7000 or whatever.

"I can't leave you here alone with Nora without a phone."

"Right. Sure," she shrugged. "They sell flip phones at the pharmacy."

"I can't just buy you shit."

I was loud enough that the two of them were startled out of their game of catch the stuffed bunny.

"All my savings are going to the car," I said with a frown.

I was pissed and I didn't even know why. She'd been a model for fuck's sake. She knew how to walk around in high heeled shoes. It was just now, seeing her barefoot, I realized they probably hurt her damn feet.

"You need shoes. And a phone."

"I can pay for those things. Honestly, Roy, I don't need much-"

"Seriously?" She was the definition of high maintenance.

She nodded. "Okay, I guess I deserved that, but only time will tell if I start demanding jewels and designer clothing."

"Here," I shoved the list in her direction.

She stood. Her long legs unfolding made her look like a gazelle pushing herself into her full height. She read the list and bit her lip.

"You got a problem with any of that?"

"No?"

"Just...do what you can do. I don't expect much more than you keeping the kid alive when I'm not around."

"I won't let you down, Roy. Not after what you did for me."

"I didn't do it-"

"For me," she interrupted. "I know. It wasn't for me. It was for Nora and I'm going to try as hard as I can to do right by her. Do you need to tell CPS about our marriage?"

"I don't know. They usually come by like once a month, I've never called them."

I was deeply terrified of the fifty-five-year-old woman they sent around with her thick glasses and chunky necklaces.

"I can call them," she volunteered. "Introduce myself. Or not? Whatever you think is best?"

I glanced down at where Nora was looking up at both of us. Counting now on both of us. I'd lived with the pressure of that expectation every day now for over a year. For the first time, however, I was able to share it.

And felt just a little lighter.

"It's just after noon, I'm going to head down to the docks and get the boat ready for tomorrow. I'll grab you a phone," I told her. "Don't fuck this up, Vanessa."

"Aye, aye, Captain Roy." She gave me a small salute, the note still in her hand.

I grunted because it was the only thing left to say.

5

Vanessa

"This doesn't look right, Nora."

"Bah!"

"I agree."

I held her in my arms as I looked down at my handi-work. See, a lot of people might take a different approach to Roy's chore list. They might look at the items listed and think to themselves; *let's start with a few easy things. Have some accomplishments. Present Roy with some solid efforts and maybe enjoy a word or two of praise.*

Me, I went the other way. Which was so very typical of me, I should have known I was making a mistake. I mean that was what I did. I broke things. I dropped things. I screwed up Jackson's plans, my dad's plans, Simon's plans. I ruined my mother's dinner parties by bringing up the wrong topics.

I broke hearts. Badly. Well, at least one heart and it felt like he wasn't ever going to forgive me for it.

Messy Nessy was me. I was her.

Unless I showed Roy, and maybe myself, I could change.

Which was why, in my brain, starting with the hardest thing on his list first seemed like such a sound strategy. Show no fear. Etc.

I held Nora in my arms even as I gingerly put the toe of my shoe on the board I'd just nailed down over the rotting boards on the porch.

Fix boards on porch.

It was as far out of my comfort zone as a thing could be, but seriously, when I broke it down, it was just nails, hammer and wood.

All of which I'd found in the shed behind the house. It was clear he intended at some point to fix it himself. The nails and hammer were stored in a proper space. Five boards were stacked on a work bench. All I had to do was relocate all of that to the front porch, place the good boards on top of the old boards and hammer the nails hard. While Nora watched from the play pen I put up in the yard.

She did not love that play pen.

Now there was this weird inch lift on the porch. I kind of messed the nails up so two were crooked and bent. And when I pressed on the boards they didn't really feel any more secure than what was already there.

I looked at Nora, "You think he'll be mad?"

"Bah!" she said, then yanked on my hair.

"Or maybe he'll be impressed I tried something hard."

"Babababba."

"You're right. Who am I kidding? Hookay. Well, we can't go shopping because Roy has the truck. My first attempt at home repair seems like a failure. Should we try our hand at laundry?"

"Bah!" she clapped and I tickled her belly. Then she laughed and I laughed with her, because listening to Nora laugh made it impossible to be sad or worried about anything. Even my wreck of a life.

"Okay, laundry it is...wait, what's that smell?"

I checked my shoes to see if I'd stepped in dog poop. But they were clean.

Had an animal died somewhere?

And then I felt an earth-shaking rumble in Nora's diaper.

"Nora!" I gasped. "Was that *you*?"

I couldn't imagine this smiling, happy, beautiful little girl being responsible for that smell.

"Nora? Did you poop?"

The girl had the decency to put her head down on my shoulder in shame.

"Wow," I gagged. I was holding poop. I mean Nora wasn't poop, but there was poop in her diaper, which was squished up against my forearm, so technically there was poop on my arm and... wait, was it, was it leaking out of her diaper?

"Ohmygod, ohmygod, ohmygod."

I held Nora away from me, just under her arms, which she didn't like at all and started to cry. She was wearing the purple dress I'd put her in this morning for the wedding, only now, runny brown poop was dripping down her leg onto the porch. It was all over my arm.

I gagged again. One more time.

Nora cried harder.

"Okay. We can do this. Step one. Let's get you inside."

I needed a water source and headed towards the kitchen sink.

Then I thought about poop in the kitchen sink and immediately changed my mind. I took the stairs fast because there was only so long I could hold Nora this way. I set Nora down on the bath mat so I could turn the bathtub water on, and started freaking out about what temperature it should be for a kid.

Then she made a face of extreme concentration and the smell got worse.

"Oh, Nora," I sighed, the reality of the situation hitting me all at once. "Shit just got real."

THERE WAS a knock on the front door and then the sound of the door squeaking open. Oil door hinges, that was on Roy's list, too. "Hello?" A woman called out. "Roy, you home? My mom wanted me to drop off cupcakes for you guys."

Oh, thank God. Someone else to deal with this.

"Help! Please help me!"

I sounded pathetic. I *was* pathetic. Nora was crying in the tub, I was covered in poop. The bath mat was going to need to be thrown away and I didn't know what to do to make any of this right.

Did I clean her and then clean myself? If I was covered in poop wouldn't I get Nora more poopy? Did her stomach hurt? Was that why she was crying? Was that why she'd turned into a poop fountain?

Or was the water too hot? Too cold? If she pooped in the bath – what was I supposed to do then? Burn the house down?

A second later, a curly, dark-haired head popped into the bathroom. My savior had dimples and was wearing a Let Them Eat Cake t-shirt and a baffled expression.

"Uh...is everything okay?"

"No. Everything is really not okay. I am covered in poop. Nora hates the bath, and really hates this rubber ducky." I put the rubber ducky next to her and Nora screamed and heaved it out of the bath like it was her mortal enemy. "I don't know why she's crying, but when I put her on the toilet she just cried harder... and... please tell me you know what to do."

"Hey, Nora," the woman cooed as she came into the bathroom. She wore black tights and a pair of Doc Martins along with her t-shirt. My savior looked like a cute punk baker.

I loved her with my whole heart.

"I'm Vanessa Dumont," I said lamely, and she looked at me out of the corner of her eyes while she dipped her hand under the running water. I hadn't stoppered the tub. Instead I'd tried to rinse Nora's bum under the faucet, but she started screaming when I did that.

"I know who you are, Vanessa. There isn't anyone in Calico Cove who doesn't know who you are." The water must have been fine because she took a washcloth that had been hanging over the towel rack. "Hold her up, would you?" she asked and I grabbed Nora under the arms and upright in the tub. My new best friend soaped up the cloth and gently cleaned Nora's bum.

Nora whimpered.

"It stings, huh, sweetie?"

"It hurts?" I asked, horrified.

"Yeah, she's got a little diaper rash. I've told Roy to lay off the fruit juice."

Nora had a new toy that she was bringing up to her mouth, but my hero quickly grabbed it out of her hand.

"No, Nora," she said. Like a magician she had Nora

cleaned and rinsed. Then she grabbed a towel, and scooped the little girl up into her arms. "No toys until we get everything disinfected. I'm Mari Smith by the way. Stephanie's daughter. She did the cake for your...uh."

"My not-wedding," I said dully. That's right. Now I remembered. Five tiers of Lemon cake with vanilla buttercream frosting covered in a waterfall of pink and gold roses. "It was so beautiful. I'm sorry I never got to try a piece."

Mari laughed. "Oh, it was delicious. They called me to come pick it up and we ended up cutting it up and giving out free samples to anyone who came to the bakery that day."

"I'm glad it didn't go to waste then."

Mari looked down at me, with a naked Nora in her arms, who was now at least poop free and not crying. There was something in Mari's expression. Like I wasn't what she expected me to be. Only I didn't know how to be anything else but me, so she was just going to have to deal with it.

"Let's get some cream and a diaper on you little girl," she said as she carried Nora out of the small bathroom.

"I can do that," I insisted. I knew how to put on a diaper. After putting one on backwards, Roy gave me a quick lesson. I was kind of a pro at it now.

Mari shook her head. "Uh, no, you can't. I hate to tell you this but you are one of the things that needs to be disinfected."

I glanced down at myself and gagged.

For whatever reason Mari and Nora found that hysterically funny.

"I've got Nora, you get a shower. Then we'll get some cleaner to clean out the bathtub. Sound like a plan?"

I nodded. "Thank you. Thank you so much."

"You're welcome. And once you're cleaned up and Nora's

settled down you're going to tell me how the hell the Runaway Bride of Calico Cove ended up in Roy Barnes' house covered in poop, right?"

"It's a long story," I said, my shoulders slumping.

"Those are usually the best kind," Mari said.

"So you made these?" I asked Mari.

"My mom makes them. I do all the decorating."

"So the roses? On my cake?"

"All me."

Nora, worn out from all the activities of the day, had dropped off like a champ for her nap. Meanwhile, my limited wardrobe was currently in the laundry machine, so I was wearing one of my silk robes that I'd recovered from Jackson's place. It was my favorite, green and short and silky. We were sitting at the kitchen table, each of us with a mug of tea while I was trying not to stare at Mari as she devoured one of the cupcakes.

Chocolate fudge with chocolate chips in the chocolate icing on the chocolate cupcake.

Chocolate. I hadn't had chocolate in so long...

"You know, you could have one," Mari pointed to the plate of cupcakes on the table.

I shook my head. "I can't."

"Why? There's plenty. Nora can-"

"She shouldn't eat that!" It was my mother's voice coming out of my mouth and I immediately hated it.

"Well, obviously not a whole cupcake. I think Roy just gives her a little piece."

"That's so much sugar."

"You're talking to the daughter of a baker... my sugar intake was always off the charts and I turned out just fine."

That made me smile and she nudged the plate my way.

"I'm not supposed to..."

Eat.

That was the word I was looking for. I wasn't supposed to eat. I was supposed to stay thin for modeling, then for the wedding, then for the wedding pictures. There was always some reason not to indulge.

Because that's what my mother called it. Indulging...like food was a treat I needed to monitor.

"You know what?" I said. "Fuck it."

I took the cupcake and sank my teeth into it in one massive bite. I'd never had sex as good as this cupcake. That was a fact.

"Thisisdelicousumph" I said around cake and icing and chocolate chips.

Mari laughed. "Yeah, my mom is the best."

I swallowed and refused to feel guilty about the second bite. "How long have you worked together?"

We had already covered my story.

Runaway Bride.

Superhero Roy.

Me helping out with Nora until I figured a few things out.

Mari really didn't question it too hard. Like why Roy would be motivated to save me and I didn't elaborate about our past.

"I went to New York for Art School-"

"Wow!"

"Well, I didn't graduate. I came home after one year and I've been working in the bakery ever since."

"You didn't like it?" I asked.

"It just didn't work out," she said, picking a chocolate chip off the top of the cupcake and putting it in her mouth. There was a kind of stillness in her, the same stillness that I'd recognized in Roy that summer we spent together.

She was in pain.

And she did not want to talk about it.

"Well, what you make is still art," I said. I remembered her designs at the bakery. The things Mari could do with fondant were magical.

"Hardly," she laughed. "It's like really good craft work."

I took another bite of cupcake and shook my head. "I still think it's art and having a talent like that is very cool."

"You totally helped my mom with her display window. Don't you remember? That summer you were here a few years ago. You just breezed into the bakery and started making all these suggestions."

"What?" I asked.

Except, I did remember that summer. The bakery had this huge bay window that they hadn't been utilizing. I walked by it a million times before I just went in and suggested building a platform in the window and making it into a display case.

"That wasn't anything," I argued. "She just needed to figure out that window."

"Well, it worked. Foot traffic increased by like ten percent after that."

I shrugged, about to dismiss it again when I heard the front door open and a resounding

"What the fuck?"

I dropped the cupcake and left the kitchen to let Roy know the baby was sleeping.

"What did you do to the porch?" a very annoyed Roy asked me. "I just about broke my foot-"

"Shh. Nora's sleeping and she's had a day let me tell you."

"What the fuck are you wearing?" he asked, his voice even lower.

"That's what I was trying-"

He stepped closer, close enough I could feel him. The heat from his body. His breath. his eyes going up and down the length of my body, lingering where the robe ended, halfway down my thighs.

"What are you trying here, Ness? If you think I'm going to fall for some weak ass seduction you've got planned, by prancing around the house in a robe with your ass hanging out, you're delusional. We both know how it would end if I actually touched you and I am sure as shit not that desperate. If I wanted what you're pretending to offer, I know to go looking for it somewhere else."

This was what it felt like to get stabbed. Over and over. Deep cuts, short cuts.

Cuts, cuts, cuts, cuts.

"Uh, hey, Roy."

He looked up over my shoulder, clearly surprised by the presence of Mari in the kitchen entrance.

"Mari, what are you doing here?"

Watching me get humiliated? I turned away from both of them, tying the robe tighter around my waist. *Where was a snowsuit when you needed it?*

"Mom heard about the wedding, so I stopped by to drop off some cupcakes. I found Vanessa covered in Nora poop so I stayed to help. I'll...just be going then."

"Mari, seriously, thank you so much," I said, as she walked around us toward the front door. I couldn't meet her eyes. I was still in bloody pieces all over the living room.

Mari smiled slowly. "Hey, next time you're in town, stop by the bakery. I know my mom would love to see you again."

My heart leapt like I was at yet another new school and someone asked me to sit at their lunch table.

That felt like life progress.

Except as soon as the front door closed, it was just me and Roy and those things he'd said.

"You got pooped on by Nora," he said, clearly contrite.

"My clothes are in the dryer right now. This was all I had."

"You need more clothes, Vanessa," he said tightly. "You can't be walking around the house *in that*."

Suddenly, I was pissed.

"What's wrong with this?" I asked, swinging my arms out. "Yes, it's silk. Yes, it's short. But we both know you're not interested in what's under it. Isn't that right, Roy? Didn't you just remind me how completely inadequate I am at sex? Check it off the list, just one more thing for me to be bad at. The walking definition of irony, every guy wants to fuck me and they don't even know I suck at it!"

"Nora's sleeping," he reminded me.

I rolled my eyes at him. He could stomp around and swear, but I needed to be quiet. I'd left that kind of bullshit at my parent's house – I wouldn't stand for that here.

I gave him the finger and his eyes went wide with surprise. That's right, I thought, I'm not pushover Vanessa anymore.

The buzzer for the dryer went off in the back of the kitchen. I went back to get my clothes, and to get away from him, but he followed me.

"What happened with Nora?" he asked.

"She had really bad diarrhea. Mari said you shouldn't give her so much fruit juice."

He ran his hand through his hair with a heavy sigh.

"Should we take her to the doctor?"

I crossed my arms over my chest and his eyes dropped to my boobs almost like he couldn't help himself.

"Eyes up here, you're not interested, remember?"

He turned away, going to the sink for a glass of water. "I usually give it twenty-four hours before I panic. Did she have a fever?"

I shook my head. "Not when I laid her down for her nap. She wasn't hot."

"Then we'll just watch her."

"And stop giving her fruit juice."

He nodded and it felt like a victory.

"I picked up a phone for you," he said, and put the bag I hadn't noticed in his hand, down on the kitchen counter top. "It's nothing fancy. You can call and text and that's it."

I thought of the all the people blasting me on social media. "I'll survive. That it?"

"I already programmed my number," he said.

"Good. Did you set your contact name to Jerk-face?"

He sighed and I figured our conversation was over.

I turned to the stackable washer and dryer tucked into the corner of the mud room, just off the back door. I reached up to empty the dryer, doing my best to keep my ass covered by my robe.

"You did laundry," Roy said, coming up behind me.

"Mari showed me how to do it and really it's not that hard. One cold color load, one hot white load. I was worried about the poop but Mari said it all cleaned the same."

"It does. Not the first time I've done a poop load. The front porch though..."

I turned with the basket of laundry now between us.

"I thought I would try the hard thing first," I said, lifting my chin.

He shook his head, like I baffled him. "Why?"

"Maybe I wanted to impress you," I said. "So, you know, first half day with Nora and it went just awesome, thanks for asking. Between the poop and you embarrassing me in front of my new friend and the porch I'm going to have to try and re-fix..."

He put his hand on my shoulder and I shut my mouth and held my breath. Don't make it worse, I thought. Please don't say something mean.

"Roy," I whispered. "It's been a bad day. Can we keep the critique-"

"Hey," he said gruffly. "You survived your first shit show and Nora is sleeping soundly...so yeah, I'm impressed."

It was probably criminal how good that made me feel.

Almost like eating a chocolate cupcake.

6

One Week Later
Roy

"Okay, this is how it works," I said, with my hands on the grocery store cart as we stood just outside the sliding doors of the Hernandez Family Market on Harbor Road.

"Roy, it's a grocery store, I think I know how it works. You walk in, you pick out stuff, then you pay for it."

I gave Ness a glare that told her I wasn't done talking.

Her eye roll said *okay, fine.*

So far Ness had been making sandwiches and soup for dinner, which wasn't bad, but a man could not live on PB and J with a side of Campbell's forever. Also, we were out of PB and J. We needed supplies. Supplies in Calico Cove meant the Hernandez Family Market.

The scene of Nora's multiple crimes.

"Nora doesn't like the kid seat in the cart. I think the metal bothers her thighs. Also don't even attempt to get one of those oversized toy carts. She hates it. I think she feels trapped in them and I don't blame her. Plus they're germ farms. Kids are always gnawing on things and shit. She'll want to be held or she'll want to be let down to run loose. Only that can't happen."

"Why not?" Ness asked, scrunching her face into the kids stomach so that Nora giggled delightedly. "Nora loves to run."

"Because she steals shit."

Vanessa blinked at me, then looked at Nora, who looked decidedly innocent.

"Seriously?" Vanessa asked, surprised. "Nora, do you take things you're not supposed to from the grocery store?"

"Bah!" she announced without an ounce of guilt.

"Puts stuff in her pants, under her shirt. She's a freaking kleptomaniac in the making, Mr. Hernandez is cool about it now, but he won't be when she's older. So that means she needs to be watched at all times. It's just easier to hold her. Only don't get too close to the shelves. Got it?"

"Aye aye, Captain."

I scowled. "Cut the captain crap."

That had been one of her little jokes that summer. It reminded me too much of our past and I wanted to stay focused on our present. Which was getting through this store without Nora getting busted for theft.

"Follow me and keep your eye on the kid at all times."

We entered the store, and immediately, I knew this was a giant mistake. We should have gone to the big chain grocery store over in Portland, no one would know us there. But here...*shit.*

It was like everyone stopped talking, stopped chatting, stopped minding their own damn business and turned in our direction. Gossip had gotten around town.

Former model, semi-famous heiress, The Runaway

Bride of Calico Cove, Vanessa Dumont ~~and~~ had taken lobster fisherman Roy Barnes up on his ad.

Nothing to see here folks.

I leveled everyone who was looking at us with a hard stare which made most people back off.

"Hello Roy!" Madame Za called out. The town's fortune teller didn't scare easily. She was wearing some gold caftan dress, and her fingers were weighed down with rings.

She smiled and wiggled those jeweled fingers at Nora who was fascinated by them.

I had to make sure she didn't try to steal them.

"I heard about the wedding," Madame Za said. "You must be Vanessa."

"I am. And you are..."

"Madame Za," she announced, and then handed Vanessa her card. "I do aura readings, fortune telling, palm readings and generally anything you need to know about your past, present and future but were afraid to ask."

"Oh. Cool."

Taking a step back, she looked at us. First me, then Ness, then Nora.

"Hmm... the three of you have a very powerful aura. A connection." She gasped. "*A past!* I see siblings, maybe, in a past life. Or maybe..." she narrowed her eyes, cocked her head as if she could see the bullshit better. "Nora was your father?"

"All right," I said, pushing the cart past Madame Za. "We gotta get moving."

Madame Za sighed heavily. "Oh, Roy, always so grounded in the here and now. One of these days you will open yourself up to the universe."

"Not likely."

"Vanessa, love, come by to see me anytime for a reading." Madame Za pressed her hand against Vanessa's arm and Nora made a dive for those rings.

"I will," Vanessa said, prying the baby's fingers off the jewelry.

"You shouldn't encourage her," I muttered to Ness, as soon as we were out of earshot.

"What, she was nice? Besides, she wasn't wrong. We do have a past. We did have a connection."

"Yeah, well, that was a long time ago." I pushed the cart down the first aisle.

"It feels like a past life," she said with a little laugh.

I picked up three Honey Crisp apples, Nora's favorite, and threw them in a bag.

"We need to give her more vegetables and grains to stop the poop," she said. "I looked it up on YouTube."

"She hates vegetables."

"I think *you* hate vegetables and you're projecting." She picked up carrots and something that was green and then another green thing.

"She's never going to eat it."

"You'll see," she said. "So does it feel like a past life to you? That summer?"

After a week of making no conversation that wasn't about Nora or the day's schedule or whether I wanted grape jelly or strawberry jam, she wanted to talk about our past?

In the freaking grocery store.

"I don't think about it."

"Oh. I think about it all the time."

I jerked. Cleared my throat and grunted to keep from saying the words that had no business being said.

"It was the best summer of my life, Roy," Vanessa said quietly. "You probably don't want to hear that, but it was."

"It was all a lie, remember? You were with Simon the

whole time," I reminded her, pushing the cart toward the bananas. "And you ended it. So, you don't get to miss it."

She sighed. "I don't think that's how it works."

Vanessa was holding Nora, but Nora was doing her leaning thing to try and snag a banana. So Vanessa just reached over and gave her one. Nora would have that thing squished in no time and Ness would learn a hard lesson with banana in her hair.

"Why?" I asked bluntly.

She blinked. "Why what?"

God damnit. Now I was sucked into this nonsense. I blamed Madame Za.

"Why did you do it? Why did you go back to him then? Why didn't you go back to him now?"

I wasn't even sure who I was referring to. The fuckface or her father.

Why am I asking this again? She told me already it was for the money. Except I think she was lying. Doesn't matter, I don't care. I swear to God I don't care.

Except suddenly, in the middle of this market – it was all I cared about.

She turned her gaze to Nora who was now squeezing the banana with both of her little hands, the skin starting to split. She was grinning like a maniac. The girl really did love destruction.

"Oh, Nora, no..." she said. But it was too late. The damage was done. Nora now had mashed banana hands, and, as predicted, she was trying to clean the mess off in Vanessa's hair.

"Never mind," I said, plucking Nora out of her arms. "Get stuff you like. I'm going to take her to the bathroom to clean her off. Never hand her fruit in the store."

Vanessa nodded. "I'm sorry..."

"Stop fucking apologizing."

"No, I'm sorry for that sum-"

I walked away without letting her finish. Stupid mistake, bringing up the past. There was no point.

In the end, Nora managed to steal a packet of taco seasoning from aisle four and a Blow Pop from the check-out line.

All things considered, not her worst day.

Vanessa

"AND THEN THE hero said to the little girl that she needed to stop stealing stuff or she would go to jail."

I crossed my arms over my chest and bit my bottom lip to stop from laughing. There were few things more endearing in this world than standing in the doorway of the bedroom I shared with Nora, while Roy Barnes made up a bedtime story about a thief for a young kleptomaniac.

He didn't let me do bath time with them. He said the bathroom was too small and it was a job for one person. But really I think he wanted to make sure he had his time with Nora now that he was gone during the day.

He pressed his lips against Nora's soft hair and said, "Good night, princess."

I swallowed the lump in my throat. Had my father ever done that? Had he ever held me on his lap and whispered soft words and gave me soft kisses?

I didn't know, but I think somewhere in my head I'd pretended that he had.

Roy backed out of the bedroom and caught me in the hallway.

"Sorry, I was just..." I pointed towards the bathroom that was all steamy from my shower. I showered at night, and Roy showered in the morning before leaving and then again when he came back.

"Yeah," he said, looking at my damp hair and the towel I had clutched around my chest, then down at his hands. I felt myself go bright red.

"I didn't plan this," I said, in case he was thinking this was another robe incident. "It's just a tiny-"

"I know," he said fast, stepping around me as best he could in the tiny hallway. "She's already out. You can go change, or whatever."

He went down the creaky stairs and I quickly changed in the dark. Nora had a little crib and I had a single bed that must have been Roy's when he was a kid. It was so old it was practically a hammock, but I wasn't complaining.

I changed and considered just going to bed, but it wasn't even eight yet. There was nothing to do but go downstairs and tough out what was becoming the most awkward part of the day.

Our nights alone together.

Roy didn't have a TV. He said his broke a few years ago and he never bothered to replace it. He listened to music, read a lot of books and showed movies to Nora on an old laptop.

Honestly, the lack of TV was almost a deal breaker for me. But then one day last week, I loaded Nora into her stroller and we went to the library. And...wow. There was so much there. We checked out puzzles and books and games for Nora. Then I wandered over to the adult section of new releases. I'd been about to grab some novels when I noticed a slick, brand new coffee table book about interior design. I asked the librarian if she had more like that and *there was a whole section.*

And I could check them out for free!

Honestly, libraries needed to promote themselves more.

There was an old recliner in the corner of Roy's living room, which I'd claimed as my own. It wasn't very comfortable, but I'd stolen one of the throw pillows I'd bought for Jackson's condo when I was visiting the other day and that helped.

It wasn't like I could sit on the couch with Roy. I'd be so nervous and self-conscious, I'd probably burst into flames.

I was searching my stack of library books for inspiration for both The Starboard Tavern and the last touches of the Pappas' renovations. We were down to the details and the fun was always in the details.

"Too cliché?" I muttered.

"Huh?"

Roy was sitting on the couch. The laptop next to him was closed and he was reading a book that he'd just shut. I hadn't realized I'd said anything out loud.

"Sorry," I said. Then I remembered he didn't like that either. "I mean, not sorry. Sorry, not sorry is what I mean. I was just talking to myself."

"'Bout what?"

"Jackson wants me to help with the interior design of the bar he's building."

"The thing they're building behind Pappas'?" he asked.

I nodded. "It was never going to be any sort of competition for the diner, but Jackson ultimately decided on a tourist bar. Something different from the One-Eyed Gull, which has more of the local vibe. So I was thinking maybe this...but I'm worried it's not the right vibe."

I unfolded my legs from the chair and brought the design book over to Roy. Plopping down next to him on the couch, I pointed to a picture of a coastal bar, with strung up lights and clean bright fixtures.

"What do you think of that?"

"It's a bar," he said.

I rolled my eyes. "Okay, look at this one versus this one," I said, turning the page to a bar that looked more like a traditional Irish pub and carefully folding them so you could see both images without creasing the pages.

"Different," Roy grunted.

"Yes, obviously, but which one do you like?"

He shrugged. "Doesn't matter. Which one has better beer?"

"You're not helping."

"Not trying to. This stuff, the design shit, that was always your thing."

Was it? Always *my* thing? There were times I felt like I didn't even know myself that well. Like I was this lump of moldable clay always trying to shape myself into something another person wanted me to be.

What my mother wanted:

Thin. Attractive. Quiet.

What my father wanted:

Obedient. Loyal. Useful.

What Simon wanted:

Pretty. Brainless. Social Climber.

What Roy wanted:

Babysitter. More peanut butter on his peanut butter and jelly sandwiches.

At some point I had been all those things, but now so much of that was gone. At some point this arrangement with

Roy was going to end and then there would be no one who needed me to be anything.

Which meant I was going to have to figure out who I was supposed to be.

I looked at the two pictures and started to see ways I could combine the two. Something cozy but with a beach aesthetic.

"So, do you come up with the look and then find all the shit and order it?"

"No," I said, laughing a little. "I mean, I do some shopping, but Jackson sources all the materials and orders them. He's the money. I'm just ideas."

"You're good at making things look good."

I sighed and he bumped my elbow with his. "It was a compliment, Ness."

"Thanks." I closed my book and then looked at the book he had in his lap. "What are you reading?"

He sighed and I knew that sigh. That was Roy taking time to gather his thoughts, sift through them, decide what he thought was important. What he was willing to share.

Roy lifted the book so I could read the title.

A Parent's Guide to Raising Kids Right!

"Wow, they make books for this? I should have gotten my parents this for Christmas," I teased. "You're a good dad, Roy."

He grunted.

"I can't understand caveman, Roy. Use your words, please."

"Sometimes...I mean it's been over a year, but I still don't feel like it's real. Like she's mine. I feel like I'm just watching her until someone raises their hand and says, wait that's my kid. I'll take her back now."

"Can that happen?" I asked, because even though I'd

only been part of her life for a little over a week, I couldn't imagine my day without her. That was probably a terrible mistake, to fall so hard so quickly. But she was just a sweet smiling baby who stole things. How could I not?

If I was nervous about her being taken away after knowing her for only a week, Roy must be terrified.

"What if you adopted her?"

"I'm not her dad."

"Not her biological father, but you're the guy taking care of her."

He looked at me, hard. "I hadn't thought that far ahead, I guess."

"You should," I said.

He shrugged. "Shit happens, Ness. I know that better than anyone. You can't ever count on forever. It's a ridiculous concept. Everyone goes away. Eventually."

It was hard to refute that. His mother had died when he was a child. His father died tragically at sea and I...well I made the wrong choice, once upon a time. In this quiet house that I'd tidied and cared for, where we laughed when Nora danced to the songs on the radio – I wanted him to know the truth. Well, a truth. Some little bit of truth about me. About us and that summer.

"Love," I said.

"What? Tell me you're not going to feed me some crap line about how love conquers all."

I shook my head. "No. You asked me what changed earlier today. Why the last time when my father asked me to come home was different than this time. The last time...he told me he needed me. That only I could save the family. I didn't agree to the marriage because I wanted money. I just wanted my dad to love me. To make me important in his life. To matter to him. It had nothing to do with Simon. That's why I could walk away this time. Because I know now any affection he might have had for me...it was totally conditional. I have to live my own life. But ...if you do get to keep Nora forever, just always let her know she matters to you."

"Ness," Roy whispered.

"You'll see how strong it gets, Roy," I said, reaching out and putting a hand on his thigh. It wasn't like me. I wasn't a touchy-feely person. And I certainly wasn't trying to seduce him. I just needed him to feel my words. "You'll see how she looks at you, how much she needs you, how everything about you is fascinating to her. That bond is strong, and as long as you take care of it, then no one can take that away from you. There. My cheesy speech is over."

I started to pull my hand back but he caught it.

"Why didn't you just tell me that?" he asked.

"Back then?" I asked. "How? When? I went down to the dock to tell you I had to leave. Simon found us and said all that hateful stuff and you issued your ultimatum. It was them or you. I couldn't have both. I knew that. I just figured it was a clean break that way. If you hated me, then maybe it would be easier to get over you. Stupid, really."

"I thought the worst of you, Vanessa," he said roughly. "You didn't even want to try and change my mind? Stand up for yourself a little?"

"We both know that's not my strong suit."

"That shit with your dad. That's on him. Not on you."

"Thanks," I said, and smiled at him. Some of the stiffness we lived with every day leached out of the air and it was just us sitting there.

"It was a good cheesy speech," he said, a small smile tugging at his lips.

I don't know why, but I suddenly felt very proud. There was a time I'd made Roy Barnes happy, and it had felt like such an accomplishment because he'd been so fundamentally sad.

I had thought I'd lost that power forever, but maybe not. Maybe fate had brought me back here to make Roy Barnes smile again.

At the very least, I could try.

7

Two Weeks Later
Vanessa

"Can you say avocado?" I asked Nora, as I cut up pieces to put on her highchair tray along with Cheerios and grapes. Grapes that I'd cut in half like Roy had shown me so we didn't get nervous about her choking on them.

"Bah!"

"Oh, so close. Avo-ca-do."

"Bah!"

"Forget about it," Roy said as he came into the kitchen, already dressed for the day to head out on the water.

There were ominous dark clouds out this morning, which had me a little worried, but I felt silly asking him about it.

Roy knew the water like most people knew the back of their hand.

I held up the back of my hand to study it. Had that freckle on the corner under my thumb always been there?

"Kid only knows *bah*, that's the way it's going to be. She's too cool for language and we just need to roll with it."

I tried not to think about how him using the word *we* felt on the inside.

Temporary. Not forever. Short amount of time. We are not a we.

The words were on a circular loop in my head.

"We have to teach her words, Roy," I said. "She can't just grunt her whole life."

"Works for me."

I blinked at him. "Was that... was that a *joke?*"

He turned away, but not before I saw that smile again.

"She certainly isn't going to say avocado as her first word. I don't know why you keep pushing the vegetables when she won't eat them."

"Avocado is actually a fruit," I told him. "And the baby cookbook I checked out of the library says it's good for her and for her poop."

"When you say baby cookbook it sounds like you're cooking babies."

I laughed, and he did that thing with his eyes that made me think he was laughing on the inside. He was full of jokes this morning.

"Can you say dada?" I asked.

"No!" Roy barked. "No... I'm not dada."

"You want to be Dad?"

"I'm Roy. That's it. I'm Roy, she's Nora."

Why was Roy being weird about Nora calling him Dada? I mean, for all intents and purposes he was her father.

"Can you say Roy?" I asked Nora, just to see if I could make Roy smile again. He didn't.

"Bah!" Nora bashed her fists on the highchair, sending a bunch of Cheerios to the floor. I bent down to pick them up individually.

"How many times do I have to tell you, wait until she's done eating to clean up. Otherwise you're just going to get annoyed when she starts flinging the O's around."

"I don't like to step on them," I replied, even as I scooped up a bunch and tossed them in the trash. "If I crush them, it's harder to get all the dust up."

"It's your time, I guess. Hey, I'm gonna be late tonight."

"Why? Because of the weather? It looks bad out there." So much for being cool about it.

He snorted. "It's a bunch of clouds. Some hard rain at best. The wind's coming out of the south, so nothing major."

"Okay." I felt marginally better.

His eyes narrowed as he looked at me and took in my expression. "Don't you worry for me, Ness. I don't want it or need it."

"That's not exactly how worry works, Roy."

"I'm serious. Do *not* care about me, Ness. I don't want the guilt associated with being mean to someone who frets about me."

"You could be nicer," I pointed out.

"But I'm not going to be."

Right. Because it was all getting too easy.

The routines were starting to fall into place. Like this morning. Feeding Nora, getting his to-go mug filled with hot coffee, prepping his lunch. Turkey with a sick amount of mayo because he was done with PB and J's. He was smiling more. Cracking jokes. I'd checked out a cookbook from the library and was getting better at dinner every day.

He went off to fish and Nora and I did our thing, which was mostly play and nap and go to the library. When she

napped, I tried to do one thing on the chore list, but sometimes I had to lay down too because life with a toddler was
exhausting.

At night, it was all about Nora. Playtime, bath time,
bedtime. Then the quiet after the storm. When she was
asleep and I was folded into my not so comfortable chair
with my design pad and library books, and Roy either read
or worked on his laptop from the couch.

Once I asked him what he was working on and he said
he was watching porn. I never asked again.

He always went up to bed first. I said goodnight. He
grunted in reply.

Then for a time I could be alone. I liked the quiet of the
house when everyone was asleep. I could pretend for a
second it was mine. That this was my place and these
people were my family. A harmless little fantasy I should
probably squash.

Yes, it was getting a little too easy.

"So why are you going to be late?"

"Poker game. Once a month. Usually, I bring Nora, but it
would be nice to just play without having to worry about
her."

"Oh, sure. Yeah. That's what I'm here for. You go play
poker with the guys and I'll watch Nora."

"Not sure what time I'll be home," he said. Only there
was a little awkwardness when he said it. And my Spidey-
senses went on full alert.

Was he lying? Maybe it wasn't just the *guys*. Maybe there
would be women there too. Which of course was fine.
Women were allowed to play poker. How stereotypical of
me that I imagined a bunch of grumpy old fishermen sitting
around a table. All of them with cigars hanging out of their
mouths.

Or maybe I was completely off base. What if *poker* was code for something else? Like sex.

What if Roy had a standing monthly date with a woman he had sex with.

"If I wanted what you're pretending to offer, I know to go looking for it somewhere else."

I felt a flush creep up my cheeks. I couldn't very well object if that's what this was about. He was a man. He had needs.

He had *serious* needs. None of which I could satisfy even when I was trying. Even when he was desperate to let me try.

So there was nothing I could say about it now.

This marriage wasn't real. He wasn't mine.

"Okay. Have fun playing...*poker*."

"I will."

"Don't..." I struggled to come up with a poker euphemism for sex. "Go *all in* unless you wrap it up."

"What?" he squinted.

"I'm just saying you should practice safe poker."

"Ness, I swear to God, there are days I'm convinced you're from another planet," he grumbled as he grabbed the to-go mug I'd filled up and the lunch I'd packed for him and headed out the door.

I heard the roar of the truck's engine come to life and then the rumble of thunder in the distance.

"I'm not going to worry and I'm not going to think of him having S.E.X with another woman tonight," I told Nora.

"Bah! Bah!"

And another round of Cheerios found their way to the floor.

～

Later That Night
Roy

"I check," Mal said.

"Ditto," Bobby said.

"Bet," Fiona announced, and the table groaned.

There was a Queen on the River. That usually spelled disaster for the men around the table.

Fiona, who ran the dress shop in town, usually kept to herself. But she found out we had a monthly poker game and wanted in. It hadn't taken us long to learn two things about her:

She had the best poker face on the planet, and she loved queens. Not kings, not aces. She always liked to play the ladies.

"Three dollars."

"Out." I tossed my cards to the dealer.

I'd felt guilty enough telling Ness about poker tonight, I couldn't risk being careless with money. I was ruthless with her on the household budget, but I made allowances for my entertainment. It was only sixty bucks once a month, but still. She'd wanted to buy a t-shirt for Nora that said Daddy's Little Girl and I'd shut her down hard for the unnecessary expense.

That's why she must have been looking at me funny when I told her about tonight.

We were at Mal's house tonight, which was always cool. He had a special table just for poker he set up in his fancy living room, because people who had money could do shit like that. The sky was dark outside the big windows that looked out at the lighthouse and the ocean beyond it. He had a table set up with food. Nothing fancy, though we were all hoping once he and Jolie made it official she might cook up some tasty snacks.

Our normal crew was Matt, who ran the ferry out to Piedmont island, Bobby, our town's newly elected sheriff, Levi, an ex-photo journalist who we all sort of wanted to be when we grew up, me and Mal. And most recently Fiona.

Mal had also asked Jolie's dad, Arthur, to play, but those two were still working out their issues. Their issues being that Mal had broken Jolie's heart before he realized what a colossal ass he'd been and begged her to forgive him. Arthur was still holding a grudge.

Speaking of. "When is Jolie coming home?"

Mal smiled and it did weird things to the scar on his face. Like every part of his face cracked open and was rearranged. Like the act of being happy changed him all the way through.

"Three weeks, six days, and," he looked at his watch. "Ten hours. She's flying into Boston and then she's home for good."

"She's going to need new clothes if she's thinking about opening her own restaurant," Fiona said. "Chef's jackets are fine for the kitchen, but she'll want to set herself apart when she's front of the house."

"Noted," Mal said. "Oh. And I fold."

"Ugh," Bobby groaned. "Don't leave me out here alone with The Shark."

Our endearing nickname for Fiona.

She chomped her teeth a few times just to show Bobby she was a good sport. Or because she was threatening to eat him. It was hard to know with Fiona.

"And you, Roy?" Mal drawled. "I don't pay much attention to town gossip but I understand congratulations are in order?"

"Nothing to congratulate," I said. Of course everyone here would know. It's not like you could keep secrets in a town the size of Calico Cove. Everyone knew everyone's business. "Vanessa and I have an arrangement, that's all. She's helping me with Nora is all."

"Ah," Mal crooned. "So a beautiful young woman runs away from her own wedding and you offer to marry her as part of a child care arrangement. Why do I feel like I'm not getting the full story?"

Bobby snorted, leaning his big body back in his chair. "Because you don't know the half of it. Roy and Vanessa Dumont were a thing a few years back until she crushed his soul under the heel of her fancy Choo Choo boot."

"Choo Choo?" Fiona asked, with absolute scorn on her perfect face.

"The fancy boot?" Bobby looked around like he needed support from us. "What are they called, something Choo. Whatever," he waved it off. "Vanessa Dumont broke Roy's heart."

"I'm going to tear off your arm and beat you with it," I told Bobby.

"Can't," he said, with a huge guileless smile. "Assault on a cop is a serious no-no."

"Are you joking?" Matt asked me. Matt was a real local's local. He'd been a high school track star and had been given full rides to dozens of schools, but he never went. Stayed in Calico Cove and ran the ferry just like his dad. He was probably ticked this was the first he was hearing about us. "You and Vanessa Dumont?"

"You didn't know?" Bobby asked Matt.

"No one knew," I growled. "Except you, which was clearly a mistake."

"Was this a dirty little secret situation?" Levi asked,

waggling his eyebrows. He wore his dark hair back in one of those man buns, which should look stupid as fuck. But on him looked kind of cool. It was annoying.

A dirty secret. That shouldn't have hurt as much as it did.

"I was," I said honestly. "For her."

"Ah," Levi said. "Daddy's little rich kid slumming it with the local. I remember those days."

I fucking hated that word. Slumming. Simon had said it that morning on the dock when I found out the truth that Vanessa had been cheating on Simon, with me. I'd thought it was love and she was... slumming. I remembered being unable to believe it, but Vanessa didn't fight him. Or correct him. She'd just stood there saying nothing.

Because she was doing what her father had asked her to do.

It was all a fucking mess in my head now and I did not like fucking messes in my head. I liked things simple. Basic.

Nothing about Vanessa was basic.

"Were you the rich kid or the local?" Bobby asked Levi. Levi's story was deeply shrouded in mystery. Bobby had been trying for months to get more details about his past.

"Far from rich," Levi said, and left it at that. "You know, just noting, it's clear you were keeping Vanessa from meeting your friends, too."

It wasn't like I'd hidden Vanessa. Exactly. I was just an intensely private person. She'd been the one who didn't want to hold hands in town. Who only wanted to hang out on my boat or in my truck or alone on the beach.

But Bobby was a good friend and I had to tell someone about Vanessa. So yeah, he'd known we were together back then.

Hell, it was his tux I'd borrowed the night of Vanessa's

stupid engagement ball. He understood why I had to go to the ball without giving me a hard time about it.

"Okay, wait a minute. You and Vanessa Dumont. Of the actual Dumonts?" Fiona studied me and I scowled back at her. Then she shrugged one shoulder. "Yeah, I guess I can see it."

"You can?" I asked, before I could stop myself.

"She's beautiful and sweet. A damsel in distress and you're a grouch with a hero complex. Makes perfect sense to me," she shrugged.

"I'm confused," Matt piped up as he shuffled a second deck of cards. "Are we playing cards or are we talking about Barnes's love life?"

"I do not have a love life," I snapped. "It's an-"

"Arrangement," Mal finished. "Yes, we heard you the first time." Though his lips twisted up into a smirk.

"Hey, better talking about his love life than what we usually talk about when Roy's here," Bobby said. "Which is baby poops, formula brands, and that stupid parenting book he's always reading."

"*A Parent's Guide to Raising Kids Right!* is not a stupid book. It's helping me figure shit out when it comes to Nora." I said. "Besides, you got a problem with me talking about my kid?"

"No. I love kids. But you could take a break on the poop stuff," Bobby said. "Okay Fiona, I'll bite. Three bucks to call. Show me that queen you can't possibly be holding."

Bobby was correct. She wasn't holding *a* queen. She was holding two of them, which knocked his two-pair hand out of the water. Fiona carefully scooped up the chips.

"How long do you imagine this arrangement lasting?" Mal asked, clearly not done with the topic.

"I don't know. A couple of months."

"Or the rest of his life," Bobby said and laughed at his own joke.

"Give me your gun," I told him. "I'm going to shoot you now."

"Can't. Witnesses."

Fiona's face softened then. "You have feelings for her."

"Had. Past tense. Now she watches Nora and I keep her daddy from kidnapping her. That's all. It's an-"

"Arrangement," everyone said in unison.

"Yeah," I said. "That."

When I pulled the truck up to the house, I put it into park and sat there for a moment. The front porch light was on. That bulb had been dead for as long as I could remember, but Vanessa had added it to her chore list. She'd bought extra bulbs, gotten the ladder out of the shed and replaced it.

So she could leave it on for me when I came home.

I hated to admit it, but it was pretty fucking convenient. And just plain nice.

Fuck. We needed to re-establish the ground rules. I didn't want her worrying about me, or doing nice things for me. I didn't want to see glimpses of the Vanessa I used to know.

What I really wanted was to hold onto my grudge and be mad that she chose her father over me, but fuck...I understood it. All that girl wanted was her father's love and he dangled it like a carrot.

Getting out of the truck, I heard the thunder rumble above. A midnight storm could mean a rough Atlantic tomorrow, which always made fishing a challenge.

As soon as my foot hit the first porch step, the front door swung open.

Light poured out from behind Vanessa, making her look like she glowed. Which naturally pissed me off.

"Why are you up?" I snapped. "It's late."

She crossed her arms over her stomach, her hair falling down around her back. She was in her sleep shorts and tank top, and from here I could tell her breasts were loose under that tank.

I thought I'd gotten used to it. Her bedtime clothes. The legs that went on forever, the waist that was small enough I could wrap my hands completely around it.

After she'd left, I tortured myself with pictures of her in magazines. Weird clothes, strange make up, shoes I didn't know how she walked in. All I ever saw was her. Like she was playing dress up and the joke was on us. It's probably why she didn't make it as a model. She could never really sell the drama she was wearing, because she, Vanessa Dumont, shown through all of it.

"I...I know you said you were going to be late. But the storms were bad and... well it's not like you texted to tell me everything was fine and...I didn't even know if you made it to...*poker*."

"Why are you saying poker like that?"

"Like what?"

"Like *poker*," I said it with air quotes.

"Am I?"

I climbed the steps to the front porch, we'd fixed the mess she'd made of it the first day. Now that I had someone here who I could trust Nora with, it was easier to get shit done around the house.

The reality was, Vanessa made everything a little easier.

Except one thing. Me.

She backed up into the house and I followed her inside, closing the front door behind me.

"So I guess you made it through the storms fine."

"It was nothing and I told you not to worry."

She shrugged. "I told you it doesn't work that way. I can't just say – Roy said don't worry, so don't worry."

She looked so fucking vulnerable, standing there in my living room. I tried to put myself in her shoes. She was cut off from the very expensive lifestyle she was accustomed to. No fancy clothes. No shitty friends. No summer estate.

No parents.

I knew what it felt like not to have that connection. It was fucking lonely, and I'd left her with that every day.

She's going to bond too much with Nora.

It wasn't a sudden concern. It was a fact. When this all ended, and it would end, there was going to be collateral damage. More so on Vanessa, than Nora, because as young as Nora was, eventually she'd forget Vanessa was ever part of her life.

Or maybe not. After all, I hadn't forgotten Vanessa.

"I'm sorry I didn't come home and check in after I got off the boat."

"Thank you," she said, and I could see the relief on her face. It made me want to cup her cheek, an old habit I used to have with her. Cup her check, cradle her head in my big, callused palm. Force her to look me in the eyes. Wait that important second until I had all of her attention.

"Why were you saying poker funny? And that whole thing before about practicing safe poker..." My eyes went wide as it dawned on me. "You thought I was out getting laid."

"No." She was clearly lying.

"You thought I made up poker night to spare your delicate feelings."

"You wouldn't do that," she said, as if just realizing it herself. "If you were going to be with another woman, you would just say it. That was stupid of me."

Shit. We had a whole different ground rules situation to figure out. "I'm fucking married to you, Ness."

Cheating didn't sit well with me, regardless of what our "arrangement" was.

"But we both know it's not real. I can't...I mean you should get to be with...whoever you want to be with."

"Like your fuckface of a fiancé did?"

Vanessa's lips turned down and she wrapped herself up tighter, arms around her stomach. "It wasn't all his fault."

"He cheats on you and it's your fault? Seriously?"

"Roy. You know..." her eyes searched mine. "You know what I'm like. With sex. There's something wrong with me. So yes, he was with other girls. Lots and lots of other girls."

"Ness, there's nothing wrong with you."

"Roy, come on." This brave smile she had on her face made me angry. It also made me want to kiss her

I sighed. It had been a long day and really none of this was my business anymore. Ness, wasn't my business anymore.

Except she was also my wife.

So I let myself do the *thing*. The thing I promised myself I would never do again. I cupped her face in my palm. Like a puzzle piece clicking back into place, we fit. Her blond hair cascading over my fingers. Her smooth cheek against my rough hand. Her eyes, glued to my chin.

I had to wait for that one second, until she realized she couldn't avoid me and her eyes lifted to mine. There she was. Eyes on me.

A lightning bolt went through my whole body.

"I know I gave you shit the other day, but that was just me lashing out. I know your weak spots. All of them. Some-times this...anger kicks in and I go for the jugular. I'm sorry."

"It's okay-"

"But it's not. And we both know it."

I felt her smile against my palm and I wanted to touch her lip with my thumb. But even I knew that was too far. That was going a step into really dangerous territory.

"There were times we were pretty great together," I said.

She'd loved kissing. She'd make out with me until our lips were swollen and I was one accidental hand brush against my dick from coming in my pants. But the second I'd tried for anything more, a hand up her shirt or down the top of her pants – she went stiff and things got awkward.

"It's okay," she'd whisper against my mouth. "You can... it's okay."

Like she had to psych herself up for it.

Only I wasn't into doing anything she didn't want to do. At first, I'd thought maybe she was just a skittish virgin and I had all the time in the world to get her used to the idea of having sex with me.

It had been frustrating, sure, but in the end, just being with Vanessa had been better, more satisfying, than fucking any girl I'd known before.

Then I'd learned the truth.

"Be careful, Roy," she said quietly, bringing me back to the present. "You're almost being nice to me."

"Can't have that."

I should let her go. Tell her to go to bed. Dismiss her with something mean and cutting that would put us back in our separate corners.

But it was late and quiet and all I could hear was the sound of her breathing.

Don't do this. Stop. Right. Now.

How could I listen to that reasonable voice when I could smell her, clean from her shower? And all I could feel was the softness of her skin, her damp breath against my wrist.

"You liked kissing," I whispered, my eyes on her mouth. And she'd liked words. I remembered that. "You would have let me kiss you for hours if that's what I'd wanted. You trembled any time my tongue touched yours for the first time. And you made that sound in the back of your throat. Half grunt, half groan. You still make that sound, Ness?"

"I...I don't know."

"Remember that time I asked you to show me your tits?"

"Roy-"

"No, I asked you to show me your tits and you lifted up that bikini top and your nipples were so hard. So hard and pink and fucking perfect. I didn't have to pinch them or suck them into my mouth. I only had to look."

"Roy," she said, closing her eyes.

"If I look down right now, Ness, would your nipples be hard little pebbles?"

She gasped, and so I had to look. There, under the tank top, two hard little pebbles. My grip on her head tightened instinctively and I lifted my hand to brush my thumb over one hard peak. I watched her, waiting for that moment when she slipped out of her body and back into her head. But it didn't come. Trembling, she stood there, letting me touch her again and again until she was panting.

"This is how I remember you," I told her. "Just like this. So hot and beautiful and fucking begging for it. You just didn't trust me. If you had trusted me, I would have shown you how good it could be..."

And...she was gone. Mouth closed. Eyes open. She'd gone back up into her brain.

"I trusted you," she said.

"No you didn't. Not really. If you had, you would have trusted me to take care of you instead of going back to him."

I understood her reasons for picking her family over me. I did. The shit with her dad, I totally got it. But she still lied to me. She still played me. *Used me.*

Vanessa's sexual damage could be laid at Simon's door and it wasn't my business anymore.

"Go to bed, Ness. I'm not going to fix what I didn't break."

She blinked a few times, pressed her hand over her heart, and then turned, running up the stairs like someone was chasing her.

While I stood in the living room and told myself that she wasn't mine to chase.

She never was.

8

Vanessa

I was sitting at the counter at Pappas', while Lola and Georgie, the diner's cook and Lola's good friend, made cooing faces at Nora in her high chair.

"Can you say George-gie? George...gie?"

Georgie was wearing large hoop hearings that Nora kept lunging for.

"Bah! Bah!"

"Roy's convinced that's all she's ever going to say," I said, as Lola reached in to tickle Nora's ribs.

"Nonsense, she'll be talking up a storm in no time," Lola said. "Can you say, Lo-la. Looo-la?"

"Bah!"

"See, that's close," Lola said.

I laughed. It was nice to get out of the house. Roy had left early for the water this morning with his to-go coffee mug and packed lunch, without saying so much as a word to me. Which, whatever, we had a lot of quiet mornings. But after last night...

My nipples went hard again at the memory. The memory of last night and all those other memories of kissing him. He was right, I had loved it, and for a minute last night when it seemed like he was going to do it again, I'd been so excited. So happy. Like coming home after a long and terrible vacation.

I'm not fixing what I didn't break.

I'd gone from being his toothache to being a broken thing. I sighed, and tried to shake loose the memories. All the memories. Every memory.

Lola and Georgie shared a look. "Okay. What's happening?" Lola asked.

"Nothing is happening."

"Girlfriend, that is not a *nothing is happening* sigh," Georgie said. "That is a *something is happening with my grumpy husband* sigh if I've ever heard one."

"It's nothing," I said. But my nipples were making a liar out of me.

"You get the deets, honey," Georgie said, nudging Lola with his elbow. "I have to get back into the kitchen."

He left, and it was just me with Lola on the other side of the counter. The restaurant was quiet in the lull past the breakfast rush and before the lunch crowd showed up. Jackson would come in with the lunch crowd for a sandwich and some time with Lola.

"Do you want to talk?" Lola asked me gently. "I mean I know this can't be an easy time. You're living with Roy, you're taking care of Nora, you're cut-off from your parents. Seriously Vanessa, it's okay to be freaking out. Jackson and I are figuring out how to live together and share space. It's not easy - and we adore each other! I know you said you knew Roy, but talk about an adjustment."

"Actually...that's sort of been the easiest thing. Nora is really kind of simple. She lets me know when she's hungry, or poopy, or needs a nap. I just sort of help her out with the things she can't manage on her own. And Roy's gone most of the day, but he's not fussy about what he eats or how put together the house is as long as it's clean."

"You sound so zen."

"Well, can I tell you a secret?"

"Anything."

"I like it way better at Roy's house than I ever did at home. There is no one judging me. I don't have to attend all my mother's *events*. Plus, I ate..." I looked around like my mother might be hiding in one of the booths. "Spaghetti with meatballs and...and...well, I didn't tell Roy this, but he likes Oreo cookies and I had one. Okay, I had two," I confessed. "THREE! I HAD THREE OREO COOKIES!"

Nora started at my raised voice, but when she saw I wasn't upset, she immediately joined in the chorus.

"Bahbahbahbabh!"

Lola shook her head a little sadly. "What your parents did to you both...it's not right."

"No. I can see that now. Anyway, I'd be happy to be Roy's wife/not wife forever if it weren't for the whole... he hates me thing."

"That's just Roy, he hates everything."

"Well, he used to like me. Like... a lot." My face went hot as I remembered that day on his boat when he had me lift my bikini top. Maybe he just liked my tits? No, even as I thought it, I knew it wasn't true. Roy was a good-looking guy, he could see all the boobs he wanted. He'd wanted to see mine.

Lola bent over the counter, her chin propped up by her fists. "Yeah, about that. So when did you know Roy?"

It had been a secret at the time. My secret from my family, but I think Roy's, too. Other than his friend Bobby, I don't think there was anyone who knew we'd been as close as we were.

But I had to talk to someone about Roy.

"It was two years ago. Simon and I were...on a break. Well, that's not true. I thought I was done with him forever, *he* thought we were on a break. It doesn't matter." I waved it off, even though it was the only thing that really mattered. The crux of the whole thing. "One day I was fighting with my mother over the break up and I'd just had it. I left the house, stole Jackson's boat..."

"Not the Craftsman! He loves that boat."

I smiled. "Oh, I know. Anyway, just outside the harbor I ran out of gas."

"Let me guess," Lola said, a knowing look on her face. "Roy saved you."

"Roy saved me," I acknowledged.

To this day, I could remember Roy's angry face when he'd pulled his boat up next to mine. I'd never heard cursing like he'd cursed at me that day. For not paying attention to fuel levels, for making him tow me back to the docks and ruining a perfectly good day of fishing.

He had not been happy with me, but for some reason all his grumbling didn't scare me like it did when my father yelled at me. I knew right off the bat Roy Barnes was all bark and no bite. He'd helped me. Made efforts to make sure I was okay. Me. A total stranger to him, but I mattered as a person. And he was upset I'd put myself in jeopardy.

The next day I had our housekeeper Danie make him a pie to say thank you, and took it down to the docks.

"We just got to talking," I said. "He'd just lost his dad a couple of months before and I could see he needed a friend."

"Yeah," Lola sighed. "Losing his father was tough on Roy. They were so close. And Roy is Roy, it wasn't like he would let anyone in town do much for him. So you just became friends?"

I nodded, then averted my eyes as I brushed my hair behind my ear.

"Vanessa...what aren't you telling me?"

"We didn't have *sex* or anything, if that's what you mean." I whispered the word sex and put my hands over Nora's ears at the same time.

Because I couldn't. Because I didn't like it. Because I was broken.

You liked it when Roy touched you last night.

I did. I always liked when Roy touched me, I was just too afraid to go any further and be a disappointment to him. Like I was to Simon.

"Got it," Lola said. "You weren't intimate. Then what happened? Why do you think he hates you now, which...I mean... he clearly doesn't."

"Oh no, he does."

"Vanessa," she said, giving me her cut the crap look. "He married you. I don't care what history you have, Roy would never marry someone, or bring someone into Nora's life, if he wasn't certain you were a good person."

"He thinks I lied to him." I handed Nora a french fry covered in ketchup. She licked the ketchup off and smashed the french fry in her fist.

"Bah," she said and I handed her another one.

My mother would be appalled.

"Lied to him how?"

"Roy thinks I was still with Simon that summer and just slumming it with him."

"Have you told him that's not true? You were broken up."

"Does it matter?" I shrugged. "I went back to Simon. There was no future for me and Roy. He asked me to choose and I chose."

And he didn't want to fix what he didn't break. It was only fair. So there was no point trying to make things right.

"We get along fine," I said. Mostly.

The bell over the door rang, announcing a new customer. I turned to see a smiling Jackson walk through the diner. He didn't stop moving, just made a bee line around the diner's counter to kiss Lola.

Like he'd been holding his breath all day and was about to pass out from lack of oxygen. That's how much he needed Lola's kiss.

"Hey, babe. I've missed you," he said on an exhale.

"Since this morning?" Lola laughed and patted his chest, although she didn't look in any hurry to leave his embrace.

"Yeah, is that weird?"

"No, I missed you too."

"Coughpatheticcough" I mock sneezed. I mean really. All this love in front of a Runaway Bride Wife/Not Wife...it just wasn't right.

"Hey Ness, I'm glad you're here," Jackson sat beside me at the counter. "I actually wanted to talk to you about business."

Oh no. That could mean one of our investments with the Calico Cove Investment Bureau paid off big and he was going to hand me a bunch of money.

If I had money, then there was no reason to stay married.

If I had money, I could leave town.

If I had money... I had to go.

"What business?"

"Lola and I are taking a road trip. Lola hasn't been away from this diner in...well, ever, and she needs a break. Georgie is going to run things in her absence. But I don't want to stop the momentum we've got going with construction of the new bar across the street. Could I put you in charge as a project manager there? We're about ready for you to start working your magic anyway."

Magic. My brother was so full of shit. I loved him for it.

"Magic?" Lola asked.

"Nothing," I said. "I just start picking out some pieces I think will work in the space. General aesthetics."

"You mean interior design?" Lola said.

"No, I didn't go to school for that. I just...you know, see something and I know when it will look good." I didn't source anything or negotiate with manufacturers. I didn't worry about budgets or supply chains. I did the easy part. "It's just ideas. I've been looking at some designer books, so I'm ready."

Lola smiled. "Yeah, I'm pretty sure that's what interior designers have. It's called *an eye*. And you have a really good one. Look at what you've done for me."

Lola lifted her hands out. Sure I helped pick out the paint, the new counter tops, the seat covers. But most of that came from the original Shells Family Restaurant design.

Which I'd put together years ago.

"You're making it a thing," I said, embarrassed by this attention. "It's not a thing. Mostly it's an obsession with shopping."

"Lola's got a point, Ness," Jackson said, looking at me thoughtfully. "Maybe you should think about it."

"Think about what?" I asked, completely confused.

"Going back to school for interior design. Make it official."

I snort-laughed so hard, Nora lost interest in her ketchup covered fry to check on me. "Me? School? Hello, I'm Vanessa Dumont. Have we met?"

Jackson lifted his chin. "Look, I know you hated school-"

"Understatement," I cut him off.

"But this would be different," Jackson continued. "You would be studying something you love. Ness, I don't need you to have a degree. I'll take your talent as is. But if you're thinking about the future, and independence from Mom and Dad, Roy too, for that matter. Maybe your own interior design business could be something you put your energy into."

No way. There was simply no way. No to school, no to my own business. I helped Jackson out with his projects. I worked with him on the CCIB to invest in places we both agreed were solid investments.

I couldn't do anything on my own. The idea was ludicrous.

Roy would probably have a laughing fit.

I ran my hand over Nora's head. Her soft hair falling through my fingers. Her face was covered in ketchup and she was currently pushing some of it up her nose.

"This is where my energy is right now," I said. "This is what I need to be doing."

∼

Later That Night

Roy

SHE MADE BURGERS. With bacon. And cheese.

They were delicious.

"You made these?" I asked, checking again. "You didn't order these from Pappas', and like, pretend they're yours?"

"No," she said, daintily wiping the corner of her mouth with a napkin. "But Georgie gave me some pointers and let me borrow one of his burger smashing spatulas."

I grunted and took another bite.

"They're good, right?" she asked.

"They're fucking delicious." I said. She'd burned the tator-tots, and insisted on making a salad that Nora and I were not interested in, but these burgers were really good.

Vanessa smiled at me, which I refused to acknowledge, and took another big bite of her burger.

This whole wife/not wife thing had some major advantages. One of them was not cooking. These past few weeks, Vanessa had been checking out cookbooks from the library. Half the food she made was burned, or a little raw or filled with vegetables. But half the time it was really good.

And I got to watch Vanessa eat like she'd never had real food before. She ate like she kissed – with total enthusiasm.

She groaned as she bit into her own burger and the sound went straight to my dick. Then again, since the other night, everything she did went right to my dick.

Touching her like that – talking about her fucking nipples? What was wrong with me? It was hard enough having her in my house day in and day out. If we started touching each other, if we crossed over into *that* space, separating again was going to be twice as hard.

Focus. This is temporary. An arrangement. That's all.

"Hey, is it okay if I take Nora with me into town to oversee the construction at the new bar? I'll make sure she's safe, but Jackson wants me to make sure the project is moving forward."

"Sure... is that a thing you do too? Along with the design stuff?"

"Well, I've done it in the past with some of his properties. Mostly, I only take over when it's time to do the finishing touches though."

"Yeah. I get it now. You're his interior designer."

"No." She said it like I was an idiot for suggesting that. "I'm a person who likes to shop for light fixtures and tiles. I'm not a *designer*!"

"Why are you getting so touchy about it?"

"I'm not."

I took another bite of my burger, waiting her out.

She sighed and pushed her hair back behind her ear. "Jackson thinks...it's a stupid idea, I don't even know why I'm talking about it."

"You're not yet. Spit it out."

"Jackson thinks maybe I should go back to school for interior design."

"Why is that stupid?"

"I sucked at school, remember? I spent my life in summer school making up for the fact that I sucked at school. The very idea of trying something like that again..."

She shuddered.

That was the thing about Vanessa. She could charm the snake away from a snake charmer. She could light up on command and make everyone around her smile, happy just to be in her company.

But all of that was on the surface.

"Isn't that what you already do?"

"I do ideas. Interior design is like... budgets and math and negotiating with manufacturers and solving problems. I can't do that."

Right. Inside she was empty of all the building blocks her parents were supposed to have laid down as a foundation. Things like confidence and independence and competence.

A Parent's Guide to Raising Kids Right! said for every one thing you tell a kid they've done wrong, you've got to tell them ten things they did right, in order to keep up that confidence level. It was a balance.

Which meant Vanessa needed to hear a hundred thousand good things to balance out all the crap her parents had doled out over the years.

Only she wasn't getting that from me. No, I was just piling on the crap because once upon a time she stomped on my pride. And my heart.

Yeah, she'd lied to me about having a boyfriend, and yes, she'd made me think what we had was special. Possible. But in the end, I was the one who had given her the ultimatum.

Her old life or me.

I was the one who wanted her to give everything up for me. She'd been, what? Twenty-two? Twenty-three?

Only here she was now, without any of her fancy shit, completely cut-off from her parents and her old life, and she seemed perfectly content.

She clearly did not harbor a second of longing for fuckface.

What if she'd made a different decision two years ago? Would we be here now, only this marriage wouldn't be fake? Or would she have grown to resent me? Resent the fact that

I forced her to walk away from the only life she'd ever known – before she was ready to do it on her own.

One thing was true, though, I couldn't keep taking my swipes at her. Making her feel like garbage for the stuff she couldn't control. The truth was, I'd fallen in roses when she took my flyer off the wall of the Lobster Pot. She was that good with Nora.

The kid was in heaven with her very own Disney princess Mommy.

Plus, she made a killer cheeseburger.

Okay, so what did *A Parent's Guide to Raising Kids Right!* say when a kid was already fucked up and lacking in any confidence?

Building blocks. I needed to work on showing her how capable she was.

"Tomorrow we're going to Portland," I announced.

She blinked at me. "Why?"

"Thanks to you helping out, I've finally got enough money saved. We're going to buy a used car."

"We?"

I nodded. "Here's the kicker, you're going to do the negotiating."

"Me?" she squeaked. "No way. I can't buy a car. Especially something like a used car where you have to haggle."

"It's called adulting. You're an adult. You should try it."

She pouted, and it almost made me want to pull her into my lap. Tell her never mind, I would take care of everything for her, but that was the last thing she needed.

"You really want to put me in charge of buying your new car?"

I'd saved for months for this car. Absolutely every cent was going to count. This was going to take all the skill of someone who knew every trick the salesman was going to throw at us. It was an incredibly foolish idea putting a car-buying-virgin in charge of this transaction.

But Vanessa Dumont needed a win from someone other than her brother.

I said none of this. Instead, I said, "A'yup."

9

The Next Day
Vanessa

"We've been over this," Roy said. "Are you ready?"

"You just get up and say, thanks but no thanks," I repeated back what Roy had taught me.

"That's right. Thanks, but no thanks. We have to show these people we're willing to walk away."

We were in his truck, parked at the first used car lot of the day.

Carl's Used Cars was highlighted by two big blowing balloon stick men. I didn't understand how those things were supposed to encourage people to come in and buy a car. They were ridiculous. This whole thing was ridiculous.

"I think this is a mistake," I said.

"It's not."

"No, seriously Roy, I once paid double the price for Lizzo concert tickets."

"Well, that's not-"

"By accident! And one time I bet four thousand dollars on a horse because its name was Sir Horse-a-Lot. The horse lost, Roy."

"Four thousand?" he asked, looking a little pale.

"Also, I invested in a high-end cat hotel and spa," I told him.

He pinched his nose and closed his eyes. "Please tell me you didn't."

"I did. You know what cats don't like?"

"Spas?"

"Spas, Roy! The cats flipping hated it. I'm going to mess it up."

He pressed his lips together. "You might."

"Roy!" I cried. "Why do you want me to mess this up for you?"

"Because I don't think you will," he said calmly. "This is important. You know that. I think you're going to do the right thing."

Ugh. His faith was making me angry.

Suddenly, I was missing Nora. She was something I knew I could do well.

Roy had debated whether Nora might serve as a valuable prop. Pulling at someone's heartstrings to give us a better deal on a car. At the end of the day, he didn't like the idea of taking her on the longer drive into the state's capitol without a proper child seat. So, we left her with Mari and Stephanie, who were like two baby-crazed aunties with flour in their hair.

"You ready?" he asked.

"No!" I cried, but it was too late. Roy was getting out of the truck and I had nothing to do but follow.

Lying in wait for us was a man in his mid-forties, salt and pepper hair and a big smile, ready to greet us.

"Hello folks! Great day to buy a car, isn't it?"

"Thanks, but no thanks," I said back.

Roy looked at me and shook his head. "You sort of want to save that part for the end."

"Oh, right. Yes. Of course. Yes sir, we would maybe or maybe not like to purchase a used vehicle. Please. And thank you."

Roy groaned, but our friendly salesman, who had introduced himself as Carl, didn't seem to mind. He led us around the lot showing us exactly what Roy had asked for. A reasonable four door sedan with airbags, low mileage and a good safety record.

I, of course, wanted something pretty. I mean, essentially it was going to be my car. Roy would have the truck, but this was what I would use to drive Nora around all day while we did chores. Two hot girls, getting shit done. We needed something with style.

"Ooh, what about that one?" I said, pointing to the red convertible.

"No."

"Right. Four doors. Practical." I found one that had a racing stripe. "What about that one!"

"No."

"Why not?"

"Because racing stripes signal to cops that you're prone to speeding. Bobby told me that once."

"But I don't," I said. "Like to go fast, that is."

"White, black or sliver. Those are the only colors we're considering. They hold their value better."

"Boring," I muttered under my breath, and Roy gave me a swat on my ass.

We both stopped. It was something he used to do all the time. Nothing harsh or serious, just a tap on my ass when I was being bratty, to remind me I was being bratty.

That summer we'd been together I'd been extra bratty, because I kind of liked it when he smacked my ass.

It was a little thing that said he was my man and I was his woman. He smacked my ass and I rolled my eyes at him and it was all very playful. Also, a little hot.

"Ness, I'm sorry," he said quickly. "I shouldn't have done that."

I shrugged as we moved on to a new row of cars. "You never used to apologize before."

"That was different," he said.

"Why?"

"Because you were mine then."

As soon as he said it, I knew he regretted it.

Except there was something about being out in public with me that made him want to break all his *no talking about the past* rules. Maybe he felt safer this way. Like the strangers around us offered him some type of protection.

"Only you weren't," Roy frowned. "You were still his, weren't you?"

"Hey folks, I think I found the perfect car," Carl called out from two rows away.

Roy turned away from me, but I reached out and grabbed his arm, to stop him.

"Forget I said anything," he said.

"No," I snapped. "I'm not letting you do that. You didn't want to talk about the past, but you're the one bringing it up all the time. So here is the truth. I broke up with Simon. He cheated on me and I stopped seeing him. I didn't call, text or email him. I thought...no, I *believed* we were done and that was before I met you."

Roy pinched his nose. "That day on the dock when he showed up, he said your *little break* was over. How the hell else was I supposed to interpret that?"

"You could have asked me," I said, folding my arms across my stomach. "We could have talked about it. But you took his word over mine-"

"I didn't take his word over yours," Roy interjected. "It's that what he said, made sense."

I tried to remember what Simon had said exactly. That whole day was a huge blur of embarrassment and pain. "That I was slumming it?"

"Yeah."

"You thought I was slumming it?"

"It made sense."

"More sense than I just really liked you?"

He glared at me.

"That's why you demanded I pick? My old life or you. You wanted me to show you, you didn't mean anything to me."

He glared harder.

"Everything is so black and white with you, Roy," I said, shaking my head. "You're lucky. Nothing in my life has ever been so simple. I didn't lie when I met you. I was not with Simon when I met you. I'm not a liar. I'm not. And I sure as hell didn't think I was *slumming* it. Which is a gross thing to think or even say about you."

He looked at me, then dipped his chin in acknowledgement.

That felt good. That felt like a win.

"Folks," Carl called again. "You're really going to want to see this car. It's the best deal on the lot."

"We better go look at the car," Roy said.

"Yes," I said, feeling a little lighter. "I've got some haggling to do."

~

FOUR HOURS LATER, we were back at Carl's after having walked away from every other used cars salesman in Portland. I had the *thanks but no thanks* down pat.

"Carl, it comes down to price. It's a great car, but you're going to need to meet us half way," I said.

This, I realized, was not entirely unlike modeling. Back then, I would make up a character in my head and then just play her as I walked down the runway. Or looked into the camera. My role for today, I was a busy new mom who didn't have time to waste and wasn't interested in bullshit.

"I've already taken as much off as I can," Carl argued with a smile. Always with a smile. "I have a family to feed. I need to make some money from these cars."

I shook my head. "Roy, phone him."

Roy immediately knew what I meant. I didn't have pictures on my basic phone, but I'd made sure Roy had a background picture of Nora on his. He hadn't even known how to do it, until I showed him.

Obediently, he held up his phone, now filled with cute shots of Nora, with my favorite one as its background. A picture of Nora cuddling her stuffed bunny.

"Look at that face, Carl. This baby girl needs a car she can drive around in safely. You want to make that happen, don't you?"

"She's a very cute kid, but I've given you my best price."

I looked to Roy, who said nothing. Not one word. We communicated strictly through his eyebrow raises. Don't ask me how I was able to interpret one lifted brow, from one arched brow, but I was.

This time though his brows were completely neutral. He was letting me make the call. Did I think I had gotten the best price out of Carl today? He'd already come down a thousand dollars. I wanted him to come down another thousand. Roy had said anything we saved over what he'd budgeted was gravy.

"Sorry, Carl. Thanks, but no thanks. Come on Roy, we've got to go get Nora. It's getting late."

Roy walked over to the glass door. The whole office was glass, which I thought was weird. Like what was the point of an office, if everything was see-thru.

I was just stepping past Roy, who was holding the door open for me, when Carl said the magic word.

"Stop. "

Roy's eyebrows were ecstatic.

"Okay, you win," Carl said. "I'll take off another five hundred dollars, but that's it. That's as low as I can possibly go."

That was two wins in one day.

~

Roy

"AND THEN I WAS LIKE, sorry, can't do it. You're going to have to take a little more off the top, Carl."

We'd stopped by Mari's apartment over her mom's bakery to grab Nora. We were standing on the landing outside the door and Ness was giving the play by play of her badass negotiations. With only tiny little embell-ishments.

This woman looked good with swagger.

Vanessa had driven the car back to Calico Cove and I'd followed in my truck. The whole time watching her dance in her seat behind the wheel, singing along with whatever she had on the radio.

"What kind of car did you get?" Mari asked.

"Just a Mazda," I said.

"It's not just anything!" Vanessa said. "It's awesome. A perfect car for a great price."

It was hard work not smiling at her enthusiasm.

Underestimating Vanessa was too fucking easy. To be convinced she was all one thing because she looked the part. Former model, socialite Dumont heiress, rich, beauti-ful. It was easy to underestimate her, because she so easily underestimated herself.

There was so much more to her than her looks and her sweetness. I knew that once, but I'd let the angry and bitter me forget it. And she let me. She let everyone who met her put her in a box of their choosing.

Oh, you all need me to be this one thing? Okay, I'll do that and shut the box up behind me. Sorry to disturb you. Please and thank you!

"Sounds like you killed it," Mari said. "Took no prison-ers. Sealed the deal. Told Carl to stuff it!"

"Or she just bought a car like a normal adult," I said, trying to reign in the ridiculous.

Vanessa smiled at me. "Yeah, I did. Just like a normal adult. They call that adulting, Mari."

"Oh, I suck at adulting," Mari said. She wore a Gryffindor t-shirt covered in smears of pink frosting.

"We got to get the kid home," I finally said. Nora was

rubbing her eyes and we still had to bathe her. I'd already moved the car seat from the truck to the backseat of the Mazda, so we were all set to go.

"Yes, we do," Vanessa agreed, stroking Nora's head as the kid plopped it down on her shoulder. Why did the kid always look so comfortable in Ness's arms? Like somehow it was the place she was supposed to be, when they shouldn't have fit at all. "She's going to be asleep before we pull out of the parking lot. Thanks again, Mari, for watching her."

"No problem," Mari shrugged. "We had a blast. Oh, and hey, if you could come by the bakery to help us figure out some fall and holiday window ideas? No big deal if you can't, but mom and I are like totally boring. We want to do something with punch."

I looked at Vanessa to see how she was going to deflect.

"Yep, I'll be by tomorrow," Ness said, like earlier today she hadn't turned herself upside down to scoff at the idea that she should go back to school for Interior Design.

It had worked. *A Parent's Guide to Raising Kids Right!* had worked. "I'm checking up on the construction at the bar, but I can stop by when everyone goes on lunch break."

"Cool, cool. Night guys."

Vanessa made Nora's hand wave goodbye.

Together we made our way back to where the truck and the car were parked next to each other.

Vanessa opened the back door and set Nora inside her now totally secure, very legal car seat. A sense of satisfaction hit me. I'd worked hard to save for this car. I'd sacrificed for Nora. Put her first and it felt good. Maybe I'd gotten my own lesson in adulting today. Because I couldn't remember the last time I'd felt more fulfilled than this moment right here.

"Okay, here you go," Vanessa held out the car keys.

"Why are you giving them to me?"

"So you can drive Nora home. I'll take the truck."

"You can drive Nora home." Even as I was saying it, Vanessa was shaking her head.

"I...no. What if I got into an accident?"

"It's two miles to my house."

"What if she starts choking and I can't reach her?"

"What is she going to choke on?"

"I don't know!" She cried. "I could have the window down and a piece of gravel could fly in and land in-"

"Vanessa."

"Freak accidents happen all the time, Roy!"

"Were you planning to walk to the bar tomorrow?" She walked from my house to town all the time because I had the truck, but it was only about two miles. The bar, however, was on the other side of town. Five miles at least, there and back.

"I suppose now that we have the two cars, I don't have to but..." her sentence trailed off as she looked into the back seat of our new used car. Nora was already fast asleep.

"You can do this," I told her. It was just one more step she had to take. One more building block that needed to be put in place.

She twisted her hands together. "I don't think I should. We're okay walking."

"Ness, I followed you all the way back into town. You're a safe driver. She's secure in her car seat. I get it. I was scared shitless the first time I had to take her somewhere."

"You were scared?"

I nodded. "I drove five miles per hour and cursed out anyone who passed me. But we made it. The kid and I... we've been making it. You can do this."

She looked down at the keys in her hand, then again at Nora, and nodded.

"You have so much faith in me," she said. "I'm going to let you down."

"You won't."

All of this was an exercise in trust. Leaving her with Nora that first day I'd gone to fish without the kid had been brutal. But the second day had been easier, and the day after that even easier. Now, I felt secure every morning when I went off to work that the kid was in good hands.

I wanted Vanessa to have faith in herself.

"Okay. I'll drive her."

Vanessa walked around to the driver's seat like she was getting ready to launch into space. She got in carefully. Checked her seatbelt a few times. Checked the mirrors even though she'd done that at the dealership. She started the car and put her hands at ten and two.

I got in the truck and started the engine. Then I watched as she oh so carefully left the parking lot and turned on to Main Street. She drove slowly the whole way home, and there wasn't any car seat dancing. I didn't pass her. Just let her do her thing how she needed to do it.

Next time she drove Nora it would be better, until eventually it would become second nature.

At home, she pulled the sleeping kid out of the seat, but I rushed up to take her. Sleeping Nora was a lot of dead weight.

"I've got her," I told Ness as I took the kid in my arms.

"Should we wake her up for her bath?" Vanessa whispered as she followed me into the house.

"Nah, the book says you never wake a sleeping baby. We'll just get her in her PJs and you can give her a bath in the morning."

"Okay."

I stopped suddenly and felt Ness bump into my shoulder from behind.

"What?" she asked, which I knew meant, why had I stopped.

It just hit me again. That feeling. The house was neat as a pin. All of Nora's toys were stored in the toy chest. Everything was clean and dusted. Together Vanessa and I were going to put the kid to sleep. Then we would come downstairs and I would sit on the couch and she would sit in her chair. We'd talk about our successful outing today and it all just felt like...

Family.

"Here," I said, giving her the kid. Vanessa looked surprised, but she didn't hesitate. "Just change her and put her down."

"Where are you going?"

"Out," I said.

"Yes, but..."

"I'm going out," I snapped. "We spent the whole day together, Vanessa. I just need a minute."

It hurt her, but I didn't have time to explain or apologize. I had to get out of this house. I had to get away from her and the kid. This feeling I had was suffocating me.

This feeling that I had something back, that I thought I'd lost forever.

10

———

The Next Day
Vanessa

Went to work early. Be home late.

I crumpled the note in my hand and tossed it in the garbage. And then immediately wanted to pull it out to see if I could read some kind of secret message in his handwriting. Even I wasn't that pathetic.

"Bah!" Nora banged her hands on her tray.

"That's right," I said, and put the pieces of scrambled egg on her high chair tray. "I don't care what he does."

Nora laughed.

"I didn't wait up for him last night, did I?" I asked her, sitting down with my cup of coffee.

Nora blew a raspberry.

"He told me not to do it. That he didn't want it, and so I didn't." I shrugged, sipping my coffee.

Last night, I'd put Nora to bed, took a shower and went to bed early without once thinking about why Roy had left so suddenly.

Okay, that was a lie. I thought about it like two hundred times on a constant loop until eventually I fell asleep.

Yesterday had been a good day. We'd had fun. I had finally gotten to tell him my side of the story about Simon showing up that summer. I haggled for that car. I'd driven Nora home on my own and no one got hurt.

So many wins.

We should have been celebrating, and instead he'd run out of the house like someone was chasing him.

Then he just skipped out on our nice little morning routine and left without coffee, breakfast or his lunch. Wasn't he going to be groggy, hungry and grumpier than usual?

Not that I cared.

It was his way of reminding me this was all temporary. Probably a good reminder.

I cleaned Nora up without the little *cleaning up* song she loved so much. Got her dressed in her clothes without the *getting dressed* song. And I resisted the urge to make it up to her with the *buckling in* song while settling her into her car seat.

She looked at me like she was disappointed in me.

"Honey," I said. "We can't get used to this. Because he's right. We're only temporary."

She pressed her fat little baby hands to my cheeks and I couldn't resist.

"Okay, fine. You win. *It's time to buckle our belts, buckle our belts, buckle our belts,*" I sang.

～

I PULLED up in front of The Starboard Tavern. The front doors were wide open and the big front windows had been put in. I knew the floors were in progress and that the bar that nearly ran the length of the space, which Jackson had custom made, was already installed.

"Okay, Boop, let's see how this is coming along."

All the structural stuff was done, so none of the guys coming in and out of the building were wearing hard hats. But maybe I should check on hard hats for babies? Was that a thing?

It was all right. We'd be in and out.

The rough ins for the bathrooms were scheduled to be done by the end of this week and that was what I was primarily checking on for Jackson. Also, I wanted to look at the space to see if I was heading in the right direction with my coastal bar, Irish pub mash up. I hoped so, because the idea was kind of lighting me up. So many cool choices for fixtures and tiles. I found these bathroom mirrors with cat legs and I thought they'd be perfect for Calico Cove.

Maybe I should consider a future in interior design?

It's just the thought of school made every lingering insecurity come back to haunt me. I'd been horrible at school. The best private schools in the country and one abroad, all the best tutors money could buy, and none of them could help me.

I'd barely gotten a high school degree. I wasn't entirely sure my dad hadn't bribed my teachers.

No one even contemplated I might go to college. No one seemed to think I had any talent other than looking pretty. Especially me.

No, the expectation for me, Vanessa Dumont, was to marry wealthy.

Only now, I was married to Roy Barnes, lobster fisherman. I'd burned my old life to the ground and every bridge back to it.

Not even a shadow of guilt lingered inside. Not a whit of regret.

"Do you think this means I'm growing up?" I asked Nora, who was in my arms as I stepped along the plywood planks that were laid over the mud and dirt until the landscaping was finished.

Nora shook her head. But I knew it was because she liked the way her swaying hair felt as it brushed against her cheeks. It was her new thing.

"No, huh?" I said, and tickled her belly until she giggled. "I'll show you. Watch me be the boss of these guys."

"Hey! What the fuck are you doing in here?"

I started at the loud voice and Nora didn't like it either. This wasn't like Roy's grumbling cursing which we had both gotten used to, this was angry shouting.

"I...uh..."

The man who yelled crossed the floor in five heavy steps. He was big, bearded and had a belly that folded over his worn jeans. His nose was thick and he had mean, squinty eyes.

Just like that my confidence dried right up.

"I'm...um...I'm here to..."

"What?" he barked. "Spit it out. I haven't got all day."

Nora ducked her head in the space between my shoulder and neck and I held her there.

I swallowed. "I'm Vanessa Dumont," I finally managed.

"So?"

"This is my brother's bar. He sent me to check in on things."

The beefy man rolled his eyes. "I'm Stu. The foreman. Checking on things is my job."

"Yes, I know you're leading the team, but my brother wanted me to check and make sure we were on schedule."

"*We*?" he laughed. "Sweetheart, you're not a part of this. So why don't you run home with your little baby and stay out of it. I'll let your brother know how things are going. Okay?"

"But he said...I was supposed to check the progress of the bathrooms specifically."

"Bathrooms are fine. Now, this is no place for a kid. Or you, in a pair... Geezus, are those fucking high heeled shoes? Honey, go the fuck home."

"I don't have boots," I muttered, but he'd already turned his back on me as if I didn't exist.

No one was looking at me, and it felt like if I pushed it, and demanded to see the bathrooms, things would get ugly.

Jackson might be disappointed, but if his foremen was giving him updates...

Stu was right, this was no place for me or for Nora. Even if I had on boots, I still didn't belong here. I don't know what Jackson was thinking. Of course no one here would take me seriously. Yes, I'd worn my heels with my jeans, because right now they were my only actual shoes outside a pair of flip flops and slippers, which I thought would have been worse.

With Nora in my arms, still quiet, clearly not liking the vibe of the bar either, we made our way down the wood planks and back to the car. I settled her into her seat and got behind the wheel.

Her eyes were in the rear view mirror, looking at me solemnly.

"Guess I'm not doing such a good job of growing up after all."

"Bah, bah."

I hated it when I could understand her so clearly.

Roy

I PULLED the truck up to the house and parked it. Vanessa's silver Mazda was already pulled up in the driveway. I wondered how their trip into town had gone.

Leaving before five am had been the coward's way of not having to face Ness. Which meant I'd put a ridiculous amount of hours in today on the water. I was sore, dirty and exhausted.

My arms were practically numb. All I wanted was a hot shower and something filling to eat.

I thought about Nora and bath time and bedtime. How would I have ever managed a day like today if it weren't for Vanessa? It wasn't a coincidence that without having to worry about Nora on the boat, I was bringing in more lobsters.

More lobster meant more money.

So I had Vanessa to thank for that too.

I needed to apologize. For being a dick last night and for being a no show at breakfast.

The truth was, pre-Nora I always hit the water before six am. You wanted to bring in the best haul, you had to be out on the water hustling. Over the past year though, that changed to work with Nora's schedule. To let her sleep until she was ready to wake up. Change her, feed her. Make sure she was set up for the day, before I was set up for the day.

I'd done it, sure. But now that I had help, I could see it

had cost me. Not just in money...but I hadn't been able to take the time to really enjoy the kid.

She was my responsibility. I would die for her. I'd moved heaven and earth to make a place for her in my life.

But I don't know that we'd had a lot of fun along the way.

Vanessa was having fun with the kid. I could see that by how much the kid searched her out. Any time Vanessa left the room it was like a little bit of the light went out for Nora.

I told myself this was temporary, but if I really was going to do right by Nora, did that mean temporary looked a little something like seventeen years?

Fuck. Me. That meant I had to go seventeen years without fucking?

Without fucking Vanessa.

I'd had dry spells, but seventeen years?

I had to get some shit right in my head, but the first part of that was apologizing.

I walked inside the front door and could hear their voices coming from the kitchen. Once again it struck me. How orderly everything was. How there was a spot now for all of us.

I walked into the kitchen and leaned against the doorway. Vanessa's back was to me and Nora was fixated on whatever Vanessa was feeding her.

"This is sweet potato. Can you say sweet potato?"

"Bah!"

Ness tried again. "Po-ta-to." She then proceeded to swoop a spoon of mash into the kid's mouth. I always loved this moment. When Nora took the time to determine what was in her mouth and if she did or did not like it.

She braced herself on the arms of her high chair bent

over the tray, opened her mouth, and didn't so much spit, as she just let the orange mush fall out.

"Boop," Vanessa groaned. "What is it with you and vegetables?"

"She's picky," I said. Vanessa jumped, startled. Nora banged on the tray and smiled at me with all her little baby joy.

Yeah, kid. It had been too long since I'd seen you too.

"Hey," Vanessa said, her tone muted.

I took the empty seat on the other side of Nora's highchair.

"What's for dinner?"

"Spaghetti and meatballs. I know we just had it, but it's easy."

"And good," I agreed.

"I tried making my own meatballs this time so they're a little uneven. But it's crazy, if you just buy all the stuff to make them, it's actually cheaper than buying the store bought ones. So I thought I would try."

I got up from the chair and made my way over to the stove. Sure enough, when I lifted the top off the pot on the stove I could see meatballs swimming in a red sauce. One was almost black. One was the size of a tennis ball. Another the size of a golf ball. But she'd tried because she knew we were on a tight budget.

Vanessa Dumont had never been on a budget in her life.

Now she was attempting to make homemade meatballs.

"There's already a dish for you in the microwave. You just have to heat it up," she said, then turned her attention back to Nora.

I opened the microwave, saw the paper towel covering the dish. So the sauce wouldn't get all over the walls of the microwave. It was a trick I'd had to teach her after she learned what putting an uncovered bowl of soup in the microwave would do after a few seconds.

I hit the button for a minute and put my head down. I couldn't put this off anymore.

"Ness," I said.

I could hear the damn gruffness in my voice. This was what she did. Just like that first summer. She'd gotten under my skin so quickly, it was like she had worked her way inside me before I even realized there was an opening.

"Yes, Roy?"

"I'm sorry about last night," I said, looking at the microwave timer counting down instead of her. "I just... needed some air and didn't want to talk about it. Okay?"

"Okay," she said quietly. "I was a little worried about you today without coffee or a sandwich or anything."

"I picked up a sandwich at Pappas'. It's what I used to do. Before Nora. I'd get up as early as possible, stop by Pappas' for coffee and an egg sandwich. Then hit the water."

"Oh. I guess you can go back to doing that, right?"

The microwave dinged and I opened the door. I took the steaming plate out, grabbed a fork and sat down at the table. Nora was still making a mess of her highchair. Smearing the orange sweet potato around like it was paint and her tray was a canvas.

Vanessa had made homemade meatballs and sweet potato mash for the kid. I mean... it was amazing.

"Nah," I said after my first bite of meatball. It was dry as fuck and tight as leather, but I smiled as I ate it, because Vanessa had tried. Maybe that was something I needed to do.

Try.

"No?"

"Nah, I didn't like missing...I didn't like missing Nora in the morning. Day's too long for that shit. Right, kid?

"Bah!" she exclaimed from her seat.

"Can you say bah?" I asked her.

"Bah!"

"That's fucking amazing," I smiled.

"Roy, language. Or I swear you'll regret it when her first real word is F.U.C.K."

"It's a solid first word. Super versatile too."

She rolled her eyes and that made me smile. Apology behind me, I tucked into the spaghetti and when I was done, Nora was done playing too. Bath time was our time, but for some reason it felt wrong to leave Ness out.

"Come on," I said. "Help me with Nora's bath."

I watched her mouth open in a silent oh, but she quickly followed me up the stairs to the second floor. It was, as I knew it would be, a tight fit. With both Ness and me kneeling by the tub, our legs and shoulders brushed against each other, but I was determined to ignore it.

I turned on the faucet, while Ness stripped Nora, who was as eager to get into the tub as we were to put her in. The kid freaking loved the water. Loved splashing and playing with her toys. Except for the rubber ducky. She had a vendetta against the duck.

"Boop! No more splashing!" Ness said.

"I could have warned you," I said, even as I slid the soapy washrag over Nora's legs. I glanced over at Ness. "Where's Boop coming from?"

"Because of her favorite game," Ness said, smiling.

When it didn't connect, she covered her hands over her eyes and then looked at Nora, who immediately understood the game and tried to pry Ness's hands away from her face. Until Ness finally relented and spread her hands wide.

"Pee-ka-*boop*!" Ness said, and Nora plopped down in the shallow water of the bath and laughed until she snorted.

"Pretty sure it's peek-a-boo," I said, trying not to let the sound of that kid laughing fill me up.

"Oh it is, but she likes it this way better. Emphasis on the boop. Probably because it fits in with her b sounds." She sat back, her arms at her side, and I got a good look at what she was wearing.

God-damnit.

It was a white Pappas' Diner t-shirt. Another gift from Lola. The damn thing was wet and sticking to her skin, her tits and...yep, those were her nipples.

My dick went from exhausted to hard in a heartbeat. I remembered those nipples. One time, one time she let me kiss her there. Part of the whole lift your bikini and show me your tits event. It had been brief, but it was seared into my brain. I knew how they felt in my mouth. Knew how much she loved me sucking on them.

"You're....ah...all..." stupidly I gestured to her shirt.

She looked down at herself and clapped her arms over her boobs. "Oh shoot!"

I scooped Nora out of the tub and wrapped her up in a blanket, needing to get as far away from Ness as I could in that moment.

"Let's go kid," I said to a confused Nora. This wasn't normally how bath time ended. She liked to pull the plug out of the tub and watch the water drain. I would say "all gone" like seven million times and she'd say bah.

I had her snuggled against me and was heading to her room to dry her off and change her with Vanessa right behind me.

"I'm sorry. I didn't know. I only have one bra and it's in the laundry."

"It's fine, Ness. It's not..." I didn't even know how to finish that sentence. It's not a big deal? My dick thought it was a big deal. My brain did too.

This house was too fucking small.

I wouldn't look at her. Just dried Nora's legs and arms. I reached for a diaper and it was just there.

"Can I...?" she said, reaching past me like she might help. Her breast touched my back and I flinched away.

"I'm fine!" I snapped. I couldn't take this. "Just give us a minute, would you?"

I heard her stomping off and I was grateful for the space. No doubt she was changing into a snowsuit or something. I got Nora dressed and realized she was too keyed up to be put to bed yet. That was my fault. It was like she could sense my agitation.

"We'll go downstairs for twenty minutes, but that's it."

She nodded like she understood the terms.

Downstairs, I set her on the floor and let her go crazy on her toys. She was snug in her jammies, her hair still wet. Watching her helped calm me down.

A minute later Vanessa came down in one of my t-shirts that I'd lent her. She swam in it so I couldn't see her damn nipples, but it was only a minor improvement.

"How... how did it go today at The Starboard Tavern?"

"Awful," she flung herself into her chair. "Stu, the foreman, was mean to me. Kept calling me honey and sweetheart. He wouldn't even let me look at the bathrooms. I thought I would just let him fill in Jackson, but no. Jackson wanted to get an update from me. So I'm going to try again tomorrow."

All I heard was *mean to me.*

"You said the foreman's name was Stu?" I grumbled.

She nodded.

"Tomorrow, we'll go see Stu together."

"I don't need you to fight my battles for me."

"I'm not," I said.

"I have to start rescuing myself," she said.

I wanted to point out the meatballs and the car. How happy Nora was, and how much money I'd made today because she was keeping an eye on things here.

Because I realized with a sudden sinking feeling, that with all of those things - she was actually rescuing me.

Instead, I just kept my mouth shut, but I thought about what I was going to say to *Stu* tomorrow.

11

The Next Day
Roy

I t was the shoes. If a girl who looked like Vanessa walked onto a job site wearing those shoes, I'd tell her to get lost too.

"I thought you were going to get new ones, you said you had cash for that," I asked as we left the house. It was cold out. Fall had officially landed with a dark low sky. I'd dug a new winter coat out of a bag of hand-me-down kids' clothes Shirley Ling, my closest neighbor and mother of three young girls, had left on my porch. Shirley was cool. She didn't make it out to be like charity or anything. Just gave me the stuff her kids couldn't wear anymore.

Ness, however, wore one of my big sweatshirts that hung like a dress down to her knees.

She'd put on the high heels but I'd told her she had to

change. She put on the flip flops and I realized how ridiculous this situation was.

"I just haven't had a chance," she said.

That was a bald-faced lie.

I had a new pack of boxer briefs because my old ones she claimed were not fit to wear, and Nora had two new sets of pajamas because her old ones were too small. Pajamas, Vanessa insisted, should be brand-new because of all the pooping and peeing that happened in them.

We would fix that, after this. Vanessa might look down her nose at a shopping trip to the nearest Bullseye, but that's all I could afford. It was time to get her necessities, like an extra freaking bra and a damn pair of sneakers.

No, she wouldn't look down her nose, she'd only be bothered that I had to pay for her.

Which was another thing that was starting to tick me off.

Jackson was using Vanessa's help to design the bar.

Lola had used Vanessa's help to design the diner.

After the disaster at the bar yesterday, Vanessa had told me she'd spent time with Stephanie working on a new fall display for her front window. She said it had helped cheer her up and I could tell it gave her a shot of confidence.

However, that was work she should get paid for. At least some sort of consulting fee. She'd earned that money. Deserved it.

I pulled the family car up to the bar.

The fucking family car.

The gang was all here for this little outing. Nora was going to witness me being a badass firsthand. Probably a good warm up for when she started bringing boys home. Or girls. Whatever her preference, I wasn't going to like anyone she was dating because that mythical person might hurt Nora and I was not down with that shit, boy or girl.

"I don't know, Roy. I don't think this is smart. I mean, if they think I need *muscle* to have anyone listen to me, how is anyone going to take me seriously?"

"Look, I'm not going in there to swing my big dick around."

"Nice visual," she said with a little blush on her cheeks. Her eyes drifted toward my crotch.

"Hey, Ness, eyes up here."

She blushed even harder.

"I'm not going to say anything in there. This is your show. You do the talking," I told her.

"You're not going to say anything?"

"No."

She pushed a piece of long blond hair behind her ear. She wore it in a ponytail almost every day, it was nice to see it long and loose. "Oooookay. So you're just going to do what...stand there?"

I nodded.

"That doesn't exactly sound like a plan, Roy."

"Trust me."

We got out of the car and I scooped up Nora, who seemed to be happy with the outing. It occurred to me how, in so many ways, she'd been isolated by just hanging out with me. And sometimes Mari or Stephanie.

We were on the boat, we were at the house, or she was stealing stuff from the grocery store.

Across the road from where I'd parked, I could see the large park in the center of town. A big green field for frisbees or just kicking a ball around. One corner of the lot was full of jungle gyms, slides and swings.

I could see a bunch of moms chatting while their kids played. Those kids were a little older than Nora, but still.

"You think the kid needs friends?"

Ness stopped and looked at me. Then she looked at Nora.

"Uh...I don't know. I'm her friend."

"Nah, I mean kid friends. Should we be taking her to the park and stuff?"

Ness followed my gaze to the other side of Main street and the park full of kids.

"Oh, totally. Nora would love that. Maybe we can go after I check on the bathrooms?"

"Got plans for today, but yeah...maybe tomorrow."

"Aren't you going back out on the water today?"

"No. We have family plans."

"Oh. Okay."

Stupid. Saying family... calling us a family was dumb dumb dumb. I could hear ringing in my ears and I was about to explain myself, take back the word, but Ness just started walking towards The Starboard Tavern and all I could do was follow.

Together we entered the bar still under construction. There was the sound of buzzing and hammering. So loud Nora covered her ears. I immediately spotted *Stu*. He was exactly how Vanessa had described him, and looked the type to throw his weight around with someone half his size.

His chest was puffed out as he was speaking to one of the guys who was measuring for the molding around the floor.

"Don't fuck it up, that wood is expensive," Stu barked at him. His attention there, he hadn't spotted us near the doorway yet.

"Go do your thing," I told her.

She looked at me like I was crazy.

"You got this. Tell him you're going to check out the bathrooms as you were asked to do by the owner."

She shook back her hair and squared her shoulders.

"Uh...excuse me, Stu," she called out over the noise. "Stu!"

His head lifted and frowned. I could see him mouth the word fuck.

"Sweetheart, what did I tell you yesterday?"

"I don't really care what you said. Jackson wanted me to check up on the bathrooms and the progress overall, so that's what I'm going to do."

"Oh, did you bring your boyfriend with you?" he crooned, looking over Ness's shoulder at me. I fixed my death glare into place.

"No, that's my husband," she announced. It was funny the way she said it. Like by giving me a title, I was suddenly more important to the world. "We have plans after this, so I'll make this quick."

"Call her sweetheart one more time and I'll remove a finger," I said.

I said I wasn't going to talk, but yeah, couldn't let that one pass.

Stu was dumb, but he wasn't stupid. He quickly looked away from me and back to Ness. But that smirk was toned way down.

"We had a delay with the bathrooms," he said. "We got a box of broken tiles and had to re-order."

That was the real reason he'd pushed Ness out yesterday.

"Oh no. Have you gotten them replaced?"

Stu blinked. "No. That's ah... that's Jackson's job and he's on vacation."

"Well, I can do it," she said, surprising Stu, me and by the look on her face – herself.

"Uh. Yeah," Stu nodded. They exchanged phone

numbers so Stu could text her the right number for the manufacturer.

"I'll need the box too," she said.

"Yeah, it's over there." Stu pointed.

"Now, I need to give Jackson a more detailed report. The bathrooms are just over there?" She was walking away, not giving him a chance to respond. Total baller move. "I'll just take a peek."

"Boop!" Nora threw her hands in the air, having heard the word peek.

Ness clicked away in her high heels like a bad ass, pulling a pencil and notebook out of her fancy tote bag.

She disappeared around a corner and I was left with *Stu* and his crew. Everyone had stopped working to stare at me. I wasn't sure how much my badass reputation suffered with a kid in my arms.

Ness had put Nora in a dress today. It was pink.

"We got a problem?" I asked in my deadliest, coldest voice.

Everyone immediately averted their eyes and went back to work. Nora shook her head and patted my cheek, like she knew I was full of shit.

"Bah, bah, bah."

The hammering and buzzing came back in full force, and *Stu* made himself look busy behind the bar.

Ten minutes later, Ness came back out from around the corner, her pencil tucked over her ear in a way that made her look ridiculously cute.

Like Contractor Barbie or something.

"Okay, Roy, I've seen enough. I can write up my notes and give Jackson a solid update while he's on the road with Lola."

"Let's get out of here then," I said, and she took Nora so I could pick up the box of broken tiles as we made our way back to the car.

"That was bad ass," I told her.

"Language," she said. Then she beamed at me. "Yeah, it was, wasn't it?"

~

Vanessa

"Why are we stopping here? We already did our bulk shopping for the week."

Roy had pulled into the parking lot of the Bullseye. A one-stop shopping mega store just outside the town limits of Calico Cove. There wasn't anything the Bullseye didn't have. From toilet paper to toiletries to office furniture to eggs.

We bought Nora's diapers here because the bulk discount was worth the price in gas, but I preferred the Hernandez Family Market for day in and day out grocery shopping.

"You need more clothes."

I stopped, half in and half out of the car. "I don't have any money for that, Roy. You know that."

"I know it, and we're going to fix that. All these jobs you're doing for people, you need to get paid for that work, Ness."

I snorted. "For helping people pick out tile? That's nothing, Roy. I'm just offering advice."

"It's not nothing. You told me yourself. Stephanie's improved foot traffic into the bakery using your ideas."

I bit my bottom lip. "She did offer me money, this last

time...but it felt like, I don't know, maybe she was just feeling sorry for me. Besides, I was happy to help."

"You can be happy to help. You can also get paid." Roy got out of the car and I knew he would take care of getting Nora out of her seat. "I'll float you some cash until you can pay me back."

I sighed. The truth was, I did need a few more things. A pair of jeans now that we were fully into fall weather. A sweater, maybe.

Sneakers, socks, more underwear.

It was all going to add up.

Then I laughed at the thought. There was a time I would never have considered shopping for clothes at Bullseye. My mother, if she knew, would be outraged. Nothing I owned, or used to own, wasn't designer. I had a brand to uphold with my followers on Instagram, Tiktok, Pinterest. Appearances were everything, and how I dressed impacted what people thought of the Dumonts and the family name.

How funny to be walking across the parking lot, following Roy inside the Bullseye, knowing that all of that bullshit was... bullshit.

How I looked, how I dressed, was the least important thing in my life right now.

The store was massive, with big overhead signs announcing each section. Roy pointed toward the back of the store to the sign that read WOMEN.

"Are you sure we can afford this?"

"I'm sure you can afford it, once you start getting paid for your work."

I nodded. When I was at Stephanie's bakery, Fiona, from the dress shop across the street, had popped in. She was hoping I could stop by next week and give her a few ideas for Christmas window dressing.

It wasn't like I didn't know it was a job. For other people. I just didn't realize it was a job – for me.

We grabbed a cart, but Nora went full monkey when Roy tried to put her in the kids' seat. Roy was forced to carry her, lest our little kleptomaniac get at it again.

"I'll take the kid to the toy section. Let her steal a few things that I can just put back."

"Good idea," I said. "Let her think she's winning."

I dropped a kiss on Nora's head before they headed to the other end of the store, and then I got to work.

Practical. I needed to be practical.

So I stayed away from the cute jeans with the rips at the knees. Focused on hoodies and things that would keep me warm around the house, instead of the off the shoulder look I preferred with sweaters.

Sneakers, socks. Another bra, which would make Roy happy.

I was reaching for a five-pack of cotton underwear when I heard a gasp.

"Oh my God, I think it is."

"It can't be. Not here."

"No, I swear that's Vanessa Dumont."

I turned around to see two teenage girls gaping at me. One of them was clearly taking a video of me shopping.

Caught. At Bullseye. With discount cotton panties.

I just flicked my hair over my shoulder, in perfect model fashion, and gave them my best smile.

"Don't miss the sale on the panties!" I said, and blew a kiss for the video. Then I took my cart of very practical clothes and went in search of Roy.

I found him walking behind Nora, who was in the process of stuffing a plastic alligator in her pants.

Roy saw me and grunted. "You got everything you need?"

I looked at the cart and smiled.

"A'yup," I said in my best Roy imitation.

He scowled. "Not even close."

I glanced down at Nora and sighed. "Oh no, Roy. She put the alligator in her diaper. We're going to have to pay for it."

"A'yup," he said. "That's how it's supposed to sound."

We got up to the cash register and paid for everything, including Nora's diaper alligator, which the cashier took our word for.

All totaled, it was less than the Wolf and Badger jump suit I'd bought at the beginning of summer.

Of course it wasn't until we got home and changed Nora's diaper that we found a matching plastic lion she'd snuck in before the alligator.

Roy just shook his head. "Kid's got talent. Didn't even see her pick it up."

The doorbell rang and we both froze.

"You don't think it's the cops?" I asked.

Roy gave me a don't be ridiculous look, but we were sort of caught red handed.

"Probably someone selling something. Go give them the brush off. Just in case, I'll hide the evidence."

I left Nora in Roy's hands and made my way downstairs. There was a woman, probably in her fifties, standing outside the front door.

I opened the door and smiled.

The woman had horn-rimmed glasses and a big chunky necklace. She also carried a briefcase.

"Hello," I said. "Can I help you?"

The woman's forehead creased. "I'm not certain. I'm looking for Roy Barnes."

"Can I ask what this is about?"

The woman looked even more confused. "Can I ask who you are?"

That seemed rather cheeky. She was knocking on our door. I lifted my chin. "I'm Vanessa. Roy's wife."

"Wife," she repeated, her mouth falling open. "Well, that's very interesting because I was here last month and you weren't. Roy knows he's supposed to keep my office informed of any changes in the home."

"Shit!" Roy said, coming up behind me.

I was about to scold him for language when the woman beat me to it.

"We talked about that kind of language around a child, Mr. Barnes. It's not good for their vocabulary growth."

"Sorry," Roy said. "Vanessa, this is Mrs. Hughes. Mrs. Hughes, this is my wife Vanessa. We were going to call you when we got married, but..." he was going to say but he forgot and there was no way that sounded good. I wasn't sure who this woman was, but Roy's arm was rock hard with tension.

"We've just been so busy," I said, curling my arm around Roy's, trying to look like we were madly in love. "Newlyweds, you know."

"Well, it's nice to meet you. I suppose I can understand how calling my office might have slipped your mind," she said, pushing her glasses up on her nose. "I'm Ellen Hughes from CPS. As I'm sure Roy's informed you, I'm here to evaluate your fitness as Nora's guardians. Now maybe we should go inside and talk about this sudden marriage. Hmm?"

12

Vanessa

Roy and I sat on the couch together. I tapped my right foot on the floor so hard, Roy had to put his hand on my knee to stop me.

Blissfully unaware of the tension in the room, Nora played with her contraband toys on the floor. The alligator and lion roared at each other. Mrs. Hughes sat in my usual chair across from us.

"Nora looks happy and healthy, Roy," she said, making a note in her notebook. "I see you also got an appropriate family car."

"I did."

She glanced around the small living room. "Place looks clean. Orderly."

"That's me," I said, as if I was trying to impress a teacher. "I help with that now. So Roy can work."

"I'm sure that's a relief for Roy. He was working very hard as a single parent and a fisherman. I'm glad he has help." So far Ellen Hughes was pretty nice and I wasn't sure why Roy was so tense around her. It didn't seem like she wanted to take Nora away. "I do need to make a note in your file that there has been a change in the house. Usually there's a very extensive interview and vetting process for anyone who spends a significant amount of time with the child."

"Oh, well, I mean, you can vet me all you like," I said. "I'm not hiding anything."

"I'm sure you're not. Would you care to tell me how this marriage came together so quickly? I believe when I asked about anyone in your life romantically Roy, you said there wasn't anyone in the picture."

"It wasn't sudden," I interjected.

Roy turned to me, waiting for what I was going to say next.

"We've known each other for years. We dated. Two summers ago," I said hesitantly. "But I...well I had some growing up to do. I didn't realize what we had. How happy we made each other. I took it for granted and I've regretted walking away from him ever since. So I came back."

Roy's hand, the one still resting on my knee, gave me a squeeze.

"I see. Now you think you are mature enough. For marriage? For motherhood?"

I swallowed. "I'm trying to be. I'm trying to be everything I can be for Nora."

My case was helped by Nora toddling over to me and trying to give me the stolen plastic lion. "Bah?"

"We'll play later, honey."

"Bah, bah."

"Yes, I see your lion. Totally legit toy. Nothing wrong with it at all," I said.

Nora wouldn't stop, so I took the toy. Then handed it back to her when she reached for it. I did it three more times while Mrs. Hughes watched.

Mrs. Hughes sighed. "Roy, Vanessa...I'm not here to doubt your commitment to each other or to judge the speed with which you got married. I'm only here to make sure that Nora's best interests are taken into consideration. To that end, if she develops connections to people and then suddenly those connections are gone, it can have a significant impact on a child this age. Do you understand where I'm going?"

"I do," Roy said.

I felt a sinking sensation in my chest. Here, I'd been thinking about how much I would miss her when I left, not even really thinking how Nora would feel. How she wouldn't understand where I went, only that I was gone. I had abandonment issues with parents who never physically abandoned me. What would it do to Nora if I left?

I was sick to my stomach thinking about it.

"I just want to make sure that any decisions you're making about your life, you're also thinking about Nora too."

"I am. She's all I think about," Roy said in a firm tone.

Mrs. Hughes nodded, then made a few notes in her notebook.

"She's clearly happy and in good care. If you wanted to get a family lawyer and make Nora's position in your house permanent, I would gladly give you a recommendation."

"A lawyer?" Roy asked. "Why do I need a lawyer?"

"If you want to adopt her. I'm assuming that's something you want to do. If for no other reason than to spare you my surprise visits." She looked between us. "Is that assumption wrong?"

"No. Not at all. That's... that's exactly what I want to do," Roy said.

"Well, then I would caution you...if this isn't a real marriage, something maybe you're doing to look better on paper, a judge in family court will sniff that out."

"We're real," I said. Blurted, actually. "Totally real. Very real. The realest."

"You might want to work on that before you get in front of a judge," Ellen said.

~

Roy

"WHAT ARE YOU THINKING ABOUT?" Vanessa asked me, as we watched Mrs. Hughes drive away.

I grunted.

"Getting a lawyer?"

I grunted again.

"I know you spent all that money on the car, but with the season going so well it is possible. Plus, I can chip in, once the investments-"

"Stop." She was breaking my heart. Breaking my head.

"Don't you want to adopt her?" she asked, her voice so soft. Not that Nora would even understand what that meant. Besides, she was busy building her blocks so she could knock them down.

"Yeah. I do. I really do." It might have been the first time I said that out loud.

"It's not just about the money, is it?"

I looked at her. How had this gotten so real, so fast? We were temporary. I'd been saying that for over a month.

"Shit."

Ness folded her arms over her stomach like she did when she was nervous.

"Are you mad about what I said?" she asked me. "About us being real?"

"Lying never works in the end," I told her.

She bit her lip. "I didn't lie."

"Ness," I growled.

"Okay, maybe we're not real *romantically*. But, I am committed to Nora. I am committed to this marriage-"

"It's not a marriage," I cut her off. "It's a deal. There's a difference."

She raised her arms. "Really? What's the difference, Roy? Because I can't see it. We've got more of a marriage than I have ever seen between my parents. We live in this house, I take care of Nora, you make a living. We eat together, you have my back when I need it, I do your laundry. What is all that if not a marriage?"

I took a step closer to her, invaded her space just enough, that she sensed my energy.

"I'm not fucking you," I said, my voice low pitched. "That's the difference."

Her eyes went wide then flew around the room, avoiding contact with mine. She settled on that spot on my chin she always stared at when things got real between us.

"You don't want to," she whispered back.

"Don't I?"

"You think... you think it would be more real if we were fucking?"

I sighed. "I think it wouldn't hurt. I think...it would make things real."

Did I want that? Wasn't the idea of real between us too scary? Except I didn't feel scared.

"I'm not good at it. Remember?"

I could see her pulse beating in that spot where her neck met her chest. I wanted to lick that spot. I wanted to bite her earlobe and watch her whole body shudder. I wanted to teach her to be good at it. I wanted to show her what good sex feels like.

I wanted that too damn much.

"What are we doing, Ness?" I asked. This was supposed to be a marriage of convenience, but she was right. It felt just like...a marriage.

"We're living," she said, her tone strong. "You're not going to tell me this time with me here hasn't been better for Nora. If only to get her off that boat, Roy."

"And when you're ready to leave? When some of your investments come in and you've got enough cash to get out of Calico Cove and head back to your socialite life? What happens then?"

She looked down at Nora and then she looked at me. Her expression was surprisingly fierce and also a total turn on. "I don't want to go back to that life."

"No?" I said, calling her out. "You're going to tell me, you like your cheap jeans and panties by the pack? You like having to wash my smelly clothes and clean up Nora's poopy diapers? You like living in this small house and sleeping in an ancient twin bed?"

"Yes," she said. "To all of it! I'm good at it. I'm good with Nora. I'm good at laundry now. I can even cook things we all like. I want to take Nora to the park tomorrow and push her on the swings and I want to do it in my new cheap ass jeans. Because I want to be more than how I look, more than what

I wear. I've gained six pounds since I've been here. Six pounds that my mother would freak out about. My agent would lose his shit over. Photographers would tell me I'm gross! But you know what? I like food. I like eating. Fried things are delicious! I want to have that meeting with Fiona about her front window and I want to sort out the box of broken tiles. I want to stay. Stay where I am more than just a socialite. I'm something here. In Calico Cove. In this house. In your life. I have purpose and I like it."

"You done?" I asked her.

She nodded.

I wrapped my hand around her neck and pulled her toward me. I kissed her like I was a drowning man and she was the only source of oxygen in the land. I wrapped my hand around her ass and squeezed.

But she was stiff in my arms. Rigid. *Come on, I thought, come on. We've come so far, we can figure this out too.*

Then, a heartbeat later, I felt her arms come around my shoulders. She relaxed, not a lot, but enough.

I slipped my tongue into her mouth and was rewarded with a gasp, then her hot slick mouth. I never wanted to leave. The stroke of her tongue against mine, the taste of her, my fingers in her hair, tugging at it gently so I could move her the way I needed. So I could slant my mouth across hers.

I kissed her until she was putty against me. Until she was on her tip toes, trying to get as much of me as I was trying to get of her.

"Ness," I breathed, when I finally broke the kiss.

"More," she said, her mouth seeking mine, finding me, biting my lower lip as punishment for leaving her. God, I loved her like this. Hot and needy, living fully in her body with me in the moment.

"Bah!" Nora smacked my leg. Vanessa's too.

Crap. The kid. I'd forgotten for a hot second.

Nora looked at both of us, two toys clutched in either hand, her face set in a furious frown. What the hell was she thinking? That I'd basically devoured her Disney princess mother.

Nora lifted her arms and I swung her up. She wrapped one arm around my neck and the other one around Vanessa.

Geezus, a little on the nose kid.

"What just happened?" Ness asked me.

"I liked what you said. I like you being in my house."

"I like being here too. And... I liked the kiss."

"I know you did." I glanced down at those nipples, hard and needy against her shirt. Fuck it. If we were going to do this, we had to go all in. "Tonight you're in my bed, too."

"Roy-"

"No," I cut her off. "Don't give me that shit about being bad at it. I'm not even saying we have to fuck."

She bit her bottom lip. "Then what are we going to do?"

This was how I could keep her. I could show her everything she'd been missing with Fuckface. Fuck her into sticking around for seventeen years. Fuck her so good she didn't leave me again ever.

There was no question Vanessa had some issues around sex. Around her body. Around letting go and feeling good. It's like she learned all the bad shit about sex and none of the good.

A Parent's Guide to Raising Kids Right! Laid it all out like a blue print.

Teach her, praise her, encourage her.

That's what I was going to do. I was going to teach Vanessa how to fuck.

And goddamn, my dick, already hard from kissing her,

got even harder at the thought. I put Nora back on the floor to go back to her playing. I didn't want her anywhere near this heat between me and Ness. It could singe her.

"I'm going to show you what I like," I said roughly.

Her breathing got ragged. Yeah, that was another thing about Ness. She liked to please. She lived for approval and acknowledgement and praise.

"Okay," she whispered. "I can try."

Again, I wrapped my hand around her neck, pushed my thumb under her chin and tilted it up so she was looking directly into my eyes.

"You promise to try hard?"

Her eyes dilated. "Yes," she whispered.

"You do everything I want, like I want it, yeah?"

Her eyes dilated hard. "Yes, Roy."

"That's my girl. Now let's go feed the kid." Her smile was bright and it would all be so easy, to just get this thing I wanted. Her here for as long as Nora needed her. As long as she was happy. As long as I wanted her. But she had to know the consequences. This wasn't a summer fling. She couldn't fuck me around like she did two years ago. The ground rules were iron clad. I had Nora to think about.

"Ness?"

"Yeah."

"This isn't love."

Her smile vanished. "I know that."

"I'm serious, don't go making up those fairy tales of yours."

"I'm not. You don't love me. I hear you loud and clear."

"We take this step, there is no going back, but you have to know how it's going to be between us."

"I understand. I don't want to go back," she whispered.

"Then let's go forward."

13

Vanessa

To say I was nervous was an understatement. It was like I was floating over my body. I did all the normal things. Feeding Nora, putting food out for me and Roy. Roy took her up for the bath and I cleaned up. But I was non-stop obsessing over what happened at bed time.

My bed time.

The kitchen was clean, the dishwasher humming. I turned off the lights and stood at the bottom of the stairs listening to Nora shriek happily in the bath.

I couldn't make out the words Roy was saying to her, but I could hear the low timber of his voice like a touch. Like his hand on the back of my neck.

What was I supposed to do? Should I change into something sexy? I did have silk pajama shorts and a matching top. There was that robe he once accused me of trying to seduce him with. Would he like that?

Would I like that?

See, that's where things got messy in my head. I'd liked what he said earlier – he would just tell me what to do. He'd show me what *he* liked. I didn't have to think about it, I just had to follow his lead.

How hard could it be?

I heard the squeak of the step and I darted back to my chair. Fiddling with my design books and the notebooks I was using to write down the names and numbers of suppliers. Roy came downstairs and settled into his spot on the couch.

"Everything okay?" I asked. Was my voice weird? My voice was so weird.

"Fine."

He watched me and I watched him back, helpless to do anything else.

Was this it? Was he going to tell me what to do now?

What if I let him down, what if he decided, like Simon had, I wasn't worth the hassle? That he could find easier and more exciting women elsewhere. I should be okay with that. I had been okay with that for years with Simon.

Only there was no point in lying to myself. I wasn't going to be okay if Roy was with other women. I wasn't even okay with the idea that after I'd left him, there must have been women in his life. Women who knew what he'd liked.

I had to get out of my head.

"What are you thinking about, Ness?"

"Nothing," I said too quickly. "I mean, not nothing obviously. I'm...design...in my head I'm designing."

"Hmm," Roy said, and I could swear it came with a smile.

"Should we have a drink?" I asked.

"Do you want a drink?"

"I don't know... maybe? You know...loosen up."

"I'm okay."

"Me too. Totally." Maybe I could get this ball rolling. "Are you...tired?"

He stretched his arm out across the back of the couch, his muscles shifting under his shirt. His stomach was lean and his shoulders were wide, and that summer I used to run my hands from his fingers, across his arms, over his shoulders and down his chest over and over again. He let me do that to him for what seemed like hours. Without ever asking if he could touch me.

"Not particularly."

I couldn't do it. I couldn't sit here across from him calmly, while all this stuff was going through my head.

"I think I'm going to take a shower and just go to bed then," I announced. If he wasn't interested in doing anything tonight that was fine, but I needed something to calm me down and a hot shower would likely do the trick.

"My bed, Ness."

"Hmm?"

"When you're done your shower, you go to my bed, yeah?"

"Yep. Your bed. Because we're going to do this. This is going to happen. It is going *down*. I am ready. I am set. I am...ready."

"Ness, calm down. We're fooling around, not running a fucking marathon."

I went upstairs and got in the shower. I stayed under the spray of the shower head for what might have been hours. Or at least long enough for the hot water to turn tepid and my fingers to prune up. I was procrastinating, of course.

It wasn't like I was afraid of sex. Exactly.

I just didn't...like it.

That first time with Simon hurt and everyone who talked about sex said it would only be like that the first time. I did not find that to be true. It hurt every time we did it.

I went to an all-girls boarding school for a year. The stories went on and on about how amazing sex was. All the things they let their boyfriends do to them and they did to their boyfriends. Then I would be with Simon and it was just a few minutes of him grunting on top of me and...pain. Burning pain between my legs.

When I told Simon it hurt and I wasn't having orgasms, he said there was something wrong with me. I didn't get wet enough apparently. He said fucking me was like fucking tree bark.

That did not make anything better.

I did want kids and it was part of the deal with Simon. Thinking back on it, I wasn't sure how I thought it would go. I'd lay back and think of the queen or something.

God. What had I been thinking?

But I'd told Roy the truth. I wanted to be here. I wanted this to work. For me, for Nora.

For Roy.

I looked into the fogged mirror above the bathroom vanity.

"You can do this," I told myself. "Just do what he tells you and it will be fine. He doesn't have to know you don't like it."

As pep talks went, it wasn't the greatest, but it would have to do. I couldn't hide in the bathroom all night long. I wore my cute silk pajamas. Did my normal nightly skin routine which would make me smell like lavender. Then I left the bathroom and crossed the room to Roy's bedroom.

The room was dark, but with the door open I could see the bed. A queen, which given Roy's size, meant it would probably be a tight fit sleeping with him. When Simon and I shared a bed it was always king-sized and I could get as far away from him as I wanted.

Although, it might be nice to cuddle up against all that manly heat. To hear someone close to you breathing, snoring even, so you knew you weren't alone in the night. I didn't know what side he slept on, so I took the left side furthest from the door. Roy would probably want to be closest to the door in case there was ever an intruder.

He was that kind of guy.

I slipped under the covers. The sheets were the opposite of the Egyptian 1500 thread count cotton I had on my bed at home, but they were clean and soft. I knew because I'd cleaned them.

On a positive note, they weren't Star Wars sheets which were on the single bed in the room I shared with Nora.

I closed my eyes and decided if Roy kissed me again, we'd be okay. That was one thing I'd always loved. Roy's kisses were rough, like he couldn't be gentle with me and they had always given me butterflies low in my stomach. That summer we were together we would just kiss and kiss and I was so happy.

But then Roy would want more and I would shut down on him. I never said stop, but he always noticed and pulled back himself. He was never mad about it, not like Simon, who threw literal fits about it. I must have seemed like such a tease. Clinging to him, moaning into his mouth, but the minute he'd press his erection against me, I immediately went cold.

Not tonight. Tonight I was going to go with it.

That's when I heard his feet coming up the stairs. That

night a few weeks ago when he'd touched me, his hand
against my nipple, I'd listened for his steps and wondered if
maybe he would come in our room. Ask me to join him in
his bed.

I'd been both relieved and a little disappointed when
he'd gone to his own room alone.

Suddenly, he was there. Filling the doorway. Filling half
the room it seemed like.

I didn't say anything, couldn't really because my heart
was beating in my throat, like it wanted to pound out of my
mouth.

He just went about his business, like I wasn't even here.
Did he not see me?

I watched him pull his shirt off over his head, then he
unzipped his jeans and my body tensed.

Okay, this was it. Now he was going to ask me to touch
him or...would he want a blow job right out of the gate?
Simon said I was awful at that too.

Simon is not in this bedroom. Leave him in the past.

Roy still hadn't said a word and he was naked now,
except for his boxer briefs. I could see the significant bulge
at his crotch, he dipped his hand into his shorts and I
guess... adjusted himself?

That was hot. Why was that hot?

He left the bedroom, and a second later the bathroom
light went on. I could hear the faucet, he was brushing his
teeth. All so normal.

I'm going to have a heart attack.

Then he was back in the bedroom, shutting the door
nearly closed behind him. He pulled back the covers and
got into the bed, the mattress dipping so I rolled towards
him, our feet brushing. My knee against his thigh. I practi-

cally heaved myself back to my side, all but clinging to the edge.

This was a disaster. A total disaster and he hadn't even told me to do anything yet. There was no way to make this marriage real.

"Tonight," he said softly into the dark room. "I want to touch you."

"Touch me?"

"That's what I said."

I turned on my side and reached my hand towards him. "I'm not afraid, Roy. I can touch you and..."

He instantly caught my wrist in his hand.

"You said you would do what I wanted," he reminded me.

I nodded. "Okay."

"Turn on your side away from me."

I shifted on the bed and gave him my back. I could feel his heat moving closer to me in the bed and then his thumb was brushing over my belly button, exposed between the shorts and the top.

Just that. The weight of his hand on my hip, his fingers spread over my waist, his thumb making lazy circles around my belly button. Then he pressed his chest against my back and dipped his nose, so that it was against my neck.

"What's that smell?" he rumbled in my ear. I could feel his lips against my neck and I liked that.

"Lavender," I whispered. "It's my body lotion."

His hand moved down my hip, caressed by butt, then stroked my exposed thigh all the way to my knee.

"Is that why you're soft?"

I nodded.

His hand came back up and then he was stroking my

back, running his fingers up and down my spine, under the silky top.

"Do you want me to take it off?"

"Nah, I like dipping my fingers underneath the silk. Feels like I'm doing something naughty. Touching the princess with my callused fingers under all that silk."

"I'm not a princess."

His hand slipped into my shorts, his whole hand covering my butt cheek. "So soft," he murmured.

Oh yeah, I liked this. His fingers were rough but he was touching me so carefully. It was starting to feel like I was at a spa getting a really gentle massage. My shoulders. My arms. He threaded his fingers through mine and squeezed my palm. He did it forever, until I was limp and soft and quiet.

His hand slipped up under my top, fingers traced my ribs, slipped up and over my breast to my throat and then back down. Circling my nipple, but never touching me. Over and over until I gasped.

"You want me to touch your tits?"

I was silent, my entire body focused on his hand and my skin.

"Ness? You like this?"

He flicked my impossibly hard nipple. I gasped.

"Yeah, you like that."

"I do," I whispered. I wanted more. I turned slightly toward him to give him better access.

"Yes, that's a good girl. So good. Open yourself up to me, just like that." His hand spread to my other breast and this time he pinched the nipple. Not too hard. Not hard enough.

I could hear the breath leaving my nose.

Oh god, I was wet between my legs. I was never wet between my legs.

"Ness, lift your top up for me so I can kiss these pretty tits."

I didn't hesitate. Completely on my back I lifted the silk top over my breasts and might have even arched my back a little.

His mouth was hot and divesting. No warning, just him sucking me into his mouth.

"Roy," I panted. "Roy."

I needed more. More than his mouth. I squeezed my legs together, aching and desperate. I needed him to maybe touch me down there.

Except he released my nipple with a popping sound.

"Good girl. You're so responsive. Now kiss me goodnight Ness, like you mean it."

His mouth came down on mine and I thrust my tongue between his lips, drew the wet and heat into my own mouth. I breathed into him and sucked his breath back into my body. He was minty and fresh and hot. Wet and dark. He was like caramel candy and dark chocolate and everything else I'd ever been denied in my life.

He pulled away. "You did good, baby. Night."

Then he was gone, rolling away from me to his side of the bed.

Wait, what just happened? Wasn't I supposed to touch him? Give him an orgasm? And what about this feeling between my legs, shouldn't I explore it...

"You can't touch yourself, Ness," Roy said in the quiet of the room. "You do what I say, and tonight you don't touch yourself. I just want you to feel."

And that was it. I laid there with this pulsing between my legs and my nipples were still hard like little pebbles and I couldn't settle down. I was restless and frustrated.

Roy turned me so my back was against his chest, curled the long heavy arm over me and said, "Sleep."

So I did.

14

Three nights later
Vanessa

I knocked on Mari's door as I jiggled Nora on my hip.

"Remember, you tell no one about this," I told Nora. "Not even your new friends at the playground. I know how those boys in the sandbox like to gossip."

"Bah!" she confirmed.

The door opened and Mari greeted us with a huge smile.

"Hey guys, what's up? Was I supposed to watch Nora today?"

"No, I was hoping..." I didn't even know what I was hoping. "Maybe we could just talk. If I'm not interrupting or anything."

"Uh no, now is a good break time. Do you want to go get some coffee at Common Grounds?"

"NO!" I needed to tone it down. It's just that every ounce

of my body felt like it was on constant vibrate mode. "Sorry, I mean, actually I would rather talk somewhere private."

Mari blinked. "Okay, come on in. It's not much, but I can make us some tea."

"Tea," I agreed. "Would be awesome."

I stepped inside the apartment, and considering the magical wonderland of the bakery downstairs, Mari's apartment was pretty basic. Some old furniture and a TV. A bookshelf crammed with books and a galley kitchen with an open window over the ancient stove.

I took a seat at the round kitchen table and set Nora down in front of me. I shucked off the backpack I used as a diaper bag and got out two plastic toys, her stuffed rabbit and a spatula from home she was currently obsessed with.

When Mari brought me over my cup of tea, Nora was entirely engaged.

"So what did you want to talk about?"

I put my head in my hands.

"Wow. Is it bad?"

"No," I said through my hands. "Just awkward."

Mari lifted an eyebrow. "Girl stuff."

It wasn't like I wasn't used to these types of conversations in boarding school. It's just that I'd never really been one of the active participants. Happy to sit on the sidelines for that one.

When I was modeling it was never an issue. Models. Were. Not. Friends. We were always competing.

"Sort of," I said.

"You mean sex?" Mari suggested.

"Oh my gosh, don't say it," I said, reaching to cover Nora's ears. "At least spell it."

"You've heard this kid's vocabulary, right?" Mari asked dryly.

"Please."

"This is an extremely puritanical viewpoint and might be damaging in the long run," Mari said. "To both of you."

"Are you serious?"

"Fine. S.E.X. That's what you want to talk about, right?"

"Three days ago the social worker came to the house and she was like, you should adopt Nora but not if you're just pretending to be married. You could lose her and damage her because she'll have grown attached to both of you. Which she is. I mean, we are. We're attached. So Roy and I decided...we decided we're going to try this thing. Because it seems to be working out. But if we're going to do that, that means..."

"S.E.X."

"Right," I sighed. "Which...I'm not very good at and-"

"Wait," she cut me off. "Time out. No one is bad at S.E.X.
"

"You heard what Roy said that day in the kitchen."

"What Roy said that day was mean. And not like him at all. I didn't even realize you guys had...what? A past?"

I didn't want to talk about it back then, but I wanted to talk about it now.

"No, he was right, not just being mean. Simon told me in detail how bad I was at it. He said it was why he had to cheat on me."

Mari closed her eyes.

I winced. "I know, that sounds really bad. Like ditsy blonde bad. Like Cher in Clueless bad. Or Elle in Legally Blonde bad."

"Okay, you know both those blondes were really very smart."

I huffed. "My point is I ran away from Simon. Remember? I eventually figured out his cheating wasn't my problem."

"Okay, so let me get this straight. You and Roy want to try and actually make this marriage work but you're afraid to have se...to do *it* with him."

"Well, I was afraid, but then I was just going to suck it up, you know."

"Lie back and think of the Queen?" Mari asked.

"Yes! You read-"

"Historical romance. Lots of it," she said and took a sip of her tea. "Continue."

"Then Roy said I should just do what he told me to do and that has been working. I mean really, really *working.*"

"What is he telling you to do?" she asked slowly, like he was asking me to kill squirrels in the moonlight or something weird.

"Mostly," I said. "He just wants to touch me. Like touch me and kiss me. Last night he asked for a back rub."

"He asked you to rub his back?"

"No. He asked if he could rub mine. And-" I stopped, this was too far. Too much sharing.

"Oh, honey, you can't stop there."

"He talks. Constantly. Like, I swear to god, every time he says the words *good girl* I think I'm going to explode."

"Ah, I see. Mr. Barnes knows what he's doing," Mari said, a little smile playing around her lips.

"Yes, but it's been three nights of...stuff. Like not the serious stuff...like the baseball base stuff. I'm just freaking out wondering if I should try to initiate something more or find some way to tell him he can do more...I don't know how to have this conversation!"

"Okay, calm down," Mari said. "You're definitely keyed up."

"It's like every night he starts something, but he doesn't let either of us...finish. It's making me crazy."

"Okay, but you like what you and Roy are doing?"

I nodded. "A. Lot."

"Then just keep letting him do it."

"Until we die?!"

"Well, I don't think Roy is going to let it get that far. I'm pretty sure he's got a plan."

"You think?"

Mari's expression softened then. "Listen to me, Vanessa. From everything you've told me, Simon was a...D.I.C.K. If he wasn't making it good for you, that was more on him. Or maybe your body was trying to tell you something that your mind hadn't caught up with yet. `"

I sighed. That sort of made sense. Things had always been different with Roy. I liked him more. I trusted him more. He was a thousand percent more attractive to me.

"Some people have to feel an emotional connection with someone to enjoy having sex with them."

"That sounds... nice."

Mari laughed. "It sounds like you. You're not a casual person, Vanessa. I haven't known you that long, but I know that much."

"This isn't love though," I said.

"How do you know?"

Because love would be a disaster. Love would ruin me.

"I broke his heart two years ago. He's made it really clear he'll never forgive me and I think... I think you need forgiveness to feel love, don't you?"

"I don't know," Mari said quietly. "Love has always been too big a risk for me."

"Bah! Bah!" Nora held up her stuffed rabbit. We'd probably just hit her max distraction time.

I took the rabbit and held on to it until she wanted it back.

Then she started running around the small space like her pants were on fire.

"We should go," I said. "I need to take her to the park to run off some of this energy."

Mari walked us to the door.

"Hey, Vanessa, you made a mistake," Mari said. "You were young and you made a mistake. If Roy can't get over that, then he doesn't deserve you."

I laughed but it sounded hollow. "No, Roy definitely does *not* deserve me. He deserves someone he can love. But until then, he's stuck with me. Thank you, Mari. For listening."

"Anytime, my friend. Someday, I hope someone comes along to convince you, you're pretty special."

"I think he did," I said sadly. "And I let him go."

~

Same night
Roy

I WAS PRETTY sure I was going to die from blue balls. It was poker night and I was looking at my two holding cards, but all I could think about was my dick.

Three nights.

Three nights of foreplay, delicious fucking foreplay. Three nights of watching her whole body light up like a firefly at the slightest touch. Two nights of obsessing over what I was going to do to her at night once we got Nora in bed.

And Vanessa was loving it.

Ness wanted to touch and be touched. She wanted to please me and had no idea yet what I could do to please her. I mean... she had no idea.

What I didn't expect? How much I got off on it. This teasing shit? Jesus. It was like the strongest liquor and I was drunk on it.

"Roy," Bobby asked, leaning back in his chair. His hair that was usually so carefully swept back was falling into his face and he looked like a teenager again. "You in? Or are you folding?"

I had pocket eights. I totally should play this hand, but I was too pre-occupied with what was going to happen tonight.

Tonight, no more foreplay. No more stopping just before the orgasm. Tonight, we were going all in.

"Fold," I grunted and tossed my cards in the pile.

Before I'd sat down to play, I'd texted Vanessa her directions for tonight.

"You seem distracted Roy," Mal said with a raised eyebrow, as he tossed some chips into the pile of money. "Everything alright with your...what did you call it?"

"An arrangement," the rest of the table said in unison.

Fiona smiled. Matt grumbled about focusing on the cards and Bobby laughed outright.

I shifted in my seat still thinking about how unlike an arrangement we'd been the last few nights.

We shared the same bed. I'd stopped messing around with wearing briefs so she was used to me sleeping with her naked. My dick was perpetually hard, but I was okay with that if it meant that by the time I was ready to fuck her, she was going to love it. She was going to come so hard her whole body would feel it. I would feel it. The house might shake.

Three nights of teasing her. Watching her work so freaking hard to please me.

"Fuck," I grunted.

"What was that, Roy?" Fiona asked. "I know that's your preferred word of choice, but does that mean the arrangement is going well, or poorly?"

"Things are...good."

I thought of my text. Imagined her eyes getting wide when she read it.

Bobby shook his head. "I knew it. You're totally falling for her all over again."

"No," I said. "This isn't about feelings."

Mal's eyebrow lifted. "Be careful my friend. Take it from someone who knows a thing or two about inviting someone into their home to clean and cook for you. One minute they're your housekeeper, the next minute you're in love."

"Not going to happen," I insisted. Because I wouldn't let it.

"Yeah, but is she?" Mal said.

"Geesh, first it was baby shit, now it's love shit. Are we here to play poker or what?" Matt groused.

"We are here to play poker," Fiona said. "I raise. Five dollars."

The three guys left in the pot groaned. I was lucky to have ditched my eights.

"What do you mean, Mal?" I asked.

"I hurt Jolie pretty bad because she fell hard and I thought we weren't doing emotions. I was an asshole to her, and I'm just lucky she forgave me so I can spend the rest of my life making up for it."

Vanessa wasn't falling for me. I mean, we had ground rules. This wasn't about love.

Except Vanessa fucking stomped all over ground rules all the time. So did I, when I thought about it. Okay, tonight. We were going to fuck and then we were going to re-establish ground rules.

"I think I'm going to call it an early night," I said, and fake yawned.

Yeah, they saw right through that and gave me a chorus of "bullshit."

"Eager to get home to the missus?" Bobby asked. I smacked him on the back of the head.

"Hey! Did everyone see that?"

"No witnesses here," Matt said. "I fold."

Fiona quietly raked in her money.

I shrugged into my coat. I was eager. Flat out. In the past, having one night away from Nora was a major gift. Something to relish. I loved the kid, but everyone needed a break.

Now I was anxious to get home. It was too late to give Nora her bath and read her a bedtime story. She'd already be down for the night.

But I was going to go down on Vanessa until she came on my tongue and that was something to look forward to.

"Jolie will be home next time we get together," I said. "Do we need to move the game?"

Vanessa might like hosting poker night. She'd check out a poker night cookbook from the library.

"Jolie knows about poker night," Mal said, as he dealt cards around the table. "She wants to play with us."

"Still, if we ever wanted to shake it up...I could host."

Four heads turned in my direction.

"You never invite anyone over to your place," Bobby said.

Yeah, because the place usually was a chaotic mess. I

never had time to fix it up or make it nice, but Ness was into all that shit. On our last trip to Bullseye she'd bought *throw* pillows, whatever the hell that meant. I thought they were useless until I sat on the couch and propped one up behind my back.

"Well, I'm doing it now. But you might have to keep your voices down if Nora's sleeping."

Fiona smiled at me. "I think we can manage that."

I nodded once. This was good. These were my poker friends. It was no big deal to invite them over. Sure, Mal's place was bigger, but poker only needed a table. I could set something up in the living room. Vanessa and I could make it look nice.

"Night," I said. I made my way out of the house to the sprawling driveway that was bigger than my house. I got in the truck and looked down at my texts.

I got hard just thinking about what I'd sent her. Knowing that she'd read it. That she'd follow my orders to the letter.

Go to bed naked. Keep your thighs spread. Don't touch yourself.

It was going to be a good night.

15

Vanessa

This was agony. Lying here in bed, naked, which felt strange enough, but I'd done exactly what he'd said in the text and kept my thighs open.

He'd said not to touch myself, but the reality was, I'd never done that. Tried a few times when I was at boarding school because so many of the girls went on and on about it. Like getting themselves off was as routine as brushing their teeth. I could just never figure it out and there was something embarrassing about that.

Like one more thing to fail at as a woman. Like if I told my mother I had problems orgasming, she would roll her eyes and tell me I was eating too much.

Well, I was eating plenty these days, and I was closer to an orgasm than I had ever been.

Every night when we started, those *feelings* happened faster. Even now, just lying in bed waiting for him, I could feel the butterflies. Knew I was already slick down there.

Would he like that?

So far there was nothing he was turned off by. He seemed to enjoy every part of my body. He loved every sound I made. But he never touched me between my legs – where I was *dying* for him. Every time his fingers brushed between my legs, I tried to lift myself to meet him, but he pulled away with his husky, dark chuckle.

"No, no, Ness. I say when. Not you."

That was last night.

Tonight he wanted me already naked and my thighs spread. Surely that meant we were finally going to have sex.

The door opened and closed downstairs. His heavy boots were dropped by the door and the floor squeaked under his weight.

Ohmygodohmygodohmygod.

Finally, the bedroom door opened and in the hallway light I could make out his silhouette for a second. Then he reached out an arm and hit the hallway light, plunging everything into darkness.

Oh God, that was so fucking hot. The dark, the sound of his breath, the thump of his clothes hitting the floor. He said nothing. Just came over to my side of the bed and pulled on the duvet that I'd clutched to my naked breasts.

He tugged a little harder and I got the message and let it go. He flung it back, to the other side of the bed, and while it was too dark to see that I was naked, he ran his hand from my cheek, over my neck, over my shoulder, down the center between my breasts until his hand settled between my open thighs.

Oh. Oh. We're starting there tonight.

"That's my good girl," he muttered, his fingers sliding between my folds. "You're already wet for me. Were you thinking about me?"

"Yes," I whispered.

"Did you touch yourself?"

I shook my head. "I don't really know how."

He muttered something under his breath I couldn't exactly make out, but then he was reaching for my hand. I thought he was finally going to have me touch him. I mean, that's what this was all about, wasn't it? Allowing him to have a satisfying sex life while being stuck married to me.

But instead of pulling my hand toward his crotch, he pushed my hand between my legs.

"Feel how slippery you are? How warm and wet?"

I nodded, but in the dark he wouldn't be able to see.

"Now let's find your little clit. There, can you feel that?"

Yes, I did. It felt like a pearl, and when I circled it with my finger... "That's too much!"

"Okay," he said. "Then figure out what isn't." He kept his hand on mine, showing me all the ways I could touch myself. The degrees of pleasure I could feel. And I found a spot.

"You like that?" he asked, when I jerked under our combined touch.

"Yes, just... just like that."

"My girl likes it gentle, huh?" He pressed on the outside of my pussy, his heel putting pressure on my clit in a way that made my whole body feel electric.

"What about this?" he asked, taking my fingers and sliding them past my clit to the entrance of my body.

"Yes."

"Better?"

"Everything..."

He chuckled and I spread my legs wider, giving us room. I felt desperate and needy. There was something I wanted but it was just out of reach and I couldn't do it on my own.

"Please, Roy."

"Please what?"

"Please...can I... can you...help me get there."

"You mean you want to come?"

"Yes," I whispered. I'd never gotten this close. Never felt like I was working toward something.

Then I felt the bed dip, as it took on Roy's weight. Only he wasn't climbing on top of me, instead he was settling himself between my legs, lifting each of my legs over his big broad shoulders.

Oh my. I knew what this was. He was going to go down on me. Did I want that?

Did he?

"Ness, do you trust me?"

"Yes."

He wouldn't be doing it if he didn't like it.

Right. Because the sex wasn't for me. I didn't need to have sex to be happy in this marriage. Roy did. I was just letting him show me things he liked. So he must like this.

"Play with your tits," he said, even as he pressed kisses against my inner thigh.

"Huh?"

"Your hands on your tits," he said. Then he let out a hot breath right over my center and I could feel the warm heat all the way through me.

"Why?"

"You remember the rules, Ness?"

"Yes," I moaned.

"What are they?"

"I do what you say."

"Fucking right, Vanessa. Do what I say."

I brought my hands up to my breasts and he must have seen the shadow of movement. "That's my good girl. Now play with your nipples how you like and tell me when you're getting close."

"I'm already close, Roy. I'm so close."

He laughed against my skin and then sucked on my inner thigh. I jerked and moaned and wondered if I was going to die.

"You tell me when you're going to come."

"How will I know?"

"You'll know, baby. You'll know."

Then it was all happening at once. His tongue was gently nudging my folds apart and I was pulling on my own nipples which sent a buzz of something straight to my core. So I did it even harder.

I cried out. Because it was too much to keep inside my body. I was breathing heavy and Roy was relentless between my legs, his tongue now pushing into my body.

This is.. he's fucking me with his tongue. That was wild. And hot.

My legs tightened around his head and he pressed them back. He held them still in his firm grips, while he tongued me all the way from my center up to that pearl, and what was too much with my fingers was so fucking perfect with his tongue.

"It's happening I think. Roy, Roy, Roy...Can I?"

"That's it baby, okay. You can do it. Come on my tongue now."

At the same time he slipped his finger deep inside me and then flicked his tongue against my clit. He said I could, so I did.

I exploded with the most intense pleasure I'd ever felt. It was like being pulled apart by sunshine. It radiated from my pussy to my belly, out into my arms and legs until it felt like I was made of sunshine. I was nothing but energy.

I never wanted it to end.

"Fuck. Me." I whispered, shaking with the aftershocks of it all.

I heard him chuckle. "That's my line."

Roy carefully shifted my legs off his shoulders and then he reached for the lamp beside the bed. He turned it on, filling the room with a soft light.

"Noooo," I covered my eyes with my arm. I didn't want anything to mess with the current bliss I was feeling.

"Sorry, babe. Had to fucking see this." He ran his hands down my body. "Your nipples are hard little points, your chest is flushed red and you're wet down to your fucking knees. You're hot as fuck, Vanessa. That was your first one, yeah?"

I nodded, keeping that arm over my face.

"Look at me, Ness."

I shook my head.

"Ness," he said in that hard, do as I say voice I was becoming a sex slave to.

I dropped my arms and looked up at Roy, and he was... he was fucking gorgeous. Kneeling between my thighs, his muscles tight, his dick so hard.

"Roy," I whispered, my hips arching, like my body knew what it wanted. What it needed.

He took his dick in his hand, slowly pumping it.

"Should I..." I tried to sit up, but he used his other hand to press me back into the bed.

"Not this time. I want you to watch. I want you to see how much you turn me on. See how fucking hard I am for you right now."

His grip tightened and his strokes got shorter. Then he slid two fingers inside me and I cried out, and clamped my legs tight, trying to keep him. God, I felt so empty inside.

"So fucking needy," he said. "I knew you'd be like this. I knew it."

He slipped his fingers free of my body and they were wet in the lamplight, and he used those fingers against the head of his cock, making him wetter.

Cum leaked from the tip and a flush covered his chest. He grunted, fucking his hand harder.

This was what he wanted me to see. Roy, vulnerable and excited and covered in our come. This was what I must have looked like when I came too.

"Can I come on you?" he gritted out between his teeth, his hand moving even faster now. He closed his eyes like he was barely holding on.

Oh yes. I wanted that. I wanted to feel it and know I caused it. I wanted absolutely every drop of his passion and desire for me.

I didn't say anything. Just spread my legs wider and arched my back, my belly and breasts exposed to him, for him. I slipped my hands between my legs because he showed me what was possible, and when he opened his eyes, he saw the answer in my body. In my fingers on my clit. In my eyes.

"Fuck, yes," he groaned. "You're gonna come again." He stopped like he was going to wait for me and that wasn't what I wanted. Together – that's what I wanted.

"Come on me," I moaned. "Please Roy. Show me what I do to you."

"You fucking kill me is what you do," he groaned, and a spurt of hot cum hit my chest, and then my breasts, my belly. He was grunting and coming all over me and it felt so good. Then I was coming again. All the sunshine in the world was in this room. In our bodies.

"Fuuuuuuuck," he said, and then fell on top of me. His

forearms by my head, taking some of his weight. But his chest was pressed into my breasts, his stomach against mine.

"Good?" I whispered into his ear, even as I licked his neck. He tasted like sweat and soap.

He turned his head and kissed me the way I liked.

"So good," he grunted. "When I finally fuck you, you're probably going to kill me."

He leaned back, looking me in the eyes. I smiled at him like I was drunk.

"Did you like it?" he asked.

"Roy," I laughed. Like he didn't know? I thought my body made it pretty clear.

"I jacked off on your tits, Vanessa. Not every girl digs that kind of thing."

If he had asked me that question two weeks ago, if I would have liked a man kneeling between my legs while he jacked off on top of me.

Hard no.

Only now, with Roy, with our sweat and slickness all messed up together...

"I liked it," I whispered into his ear. "I liked watching you come on me. It made me feel..."

"What, baby?" he asked, gazing into my eyes.

"Like I was sexy."

He pressed his forehead to mine. "You're so goddamn sexy there are times I feel like I can't breathe when I'm around you. It's always been that way for me, Ness. Always."

I kissed what I could reach, which was his chin.

"Let's take a shower," he said.

"Together?"

"Don't tell me... never mind." He shook his head. "You're the most virginal non-virgin I've ever met, Vanessa."

"Does that bother you?" I remembered what he'd said,

months ago. "You didn't want to fix what you didn't break, you said that." I tried to wiggle out from under him. But he trapped me and kissed me until I melted against him.

"I was an ass," he said. "You're not broken. And this, what we just did, was the hottest thing that's ever happened to me."

Oh. Well. That was... that was really nice. I felt tears well up, but that was only because it had kind of been a big night for me. I didn't want to make this a bigger thing than it already was. I told Mari it wasn't love, but right now it only wasn't love because I wouldn't let it be. Like if I kept calling these feelings something else, then they couldn't be love.

He rolled off the bed, reached out his hand for mine and I took it. He led me to the bathroom, and when the water was warm enough he helped me into the tub like I was a piece of glass that might shatter.

Or, like I was precious.

The warm spray felt so good. Roy soaped up a washcloth and ran it down my shoulders, over my breasts, down my stomach. Between my legs.

I sighed with pleasure.

"Turn around," he said. It was a little tight in the tub with both of us, but I turned to face the wall and he washed my shoulders and back.

When he was done, he slapped my ass. I yelped and he wrapped his arms around my waist, hauling me tight against his body so I could feel his erection against my hip.

"When you don't do what I tell you, when you misbehave, I'm going to spank that ass," he grumbled in my ear. Which of course immediately made my stomach flip and my body grow heavy.

"Hmm," I said, as the water ran down our necks. "I guess I better not misbehave then."

Yeah, I was totally going to misbehave because I knew that's what he wanted. He wanted to put me over his lap and spank me. Knowing Roy, he'd probably wanted to do that for a long time.

He pushed the cloth in my hands. "Now me."

This was fun. The freedom to run my hands all over his body. His chest, around his nipples, down his abs which were stacked with muscle. That V that ran straight to his cock, which was now semi hard.

I hesitated for a second.

"Don't be afraid to touch my dick, Ness. Get used to it. It's going to be in your pussy, your mouth, your ass."

I let out a gasp.

He chuckled at my reaction. "We're going to be married a long time and there is a lot of stuff to show you."

This late at night his beard was coming in, darkening his face. His brown eyes were so dark and heavy, his square jaw and his mouth set in a perpetual frown, unless I got him to smile.

I was going to be married to this man for a long time and I couldn't be happier.

I ran the wash cloth over his dick until he was hard in my hand. I dropped the wash cloth then, just using my fingers, slick with soap to touch him. "Keep doing that and I'm going to come again," he said.

I looked at him through my lashes. A flirty look and he half groaned/half smiled.

"You want to make me come?" he asked.

"I want to do anything you ask me to," I told him.

He reached behind him, cranked the shower head so it wasn't spraying on me.

"You want to show me what a good girl you are?"

"Roy, I don't-"

"Just do what I say, Ness."

I let out a long trembling sigh and he told me how to jack him off in the shower. My hand was slippery and my grip was tight. He told me when he needed it faster and when I needed to slow down.

"Just the tip," he breathed.

"Like this?"

"So good. So fucking good."

I was. It was for him. His second orgasm of the night pumped out of him by me.

He said we were so good. So fucking good and I felt like we were.

16

The Next Day
Roy

I came down the stairs to find what was becoming a normal scene in my kitchen. Nora was in her high chair stuffing Cheerios in her mouth, while Ness was cutting up some vegetables on the counter which the kid wasn't going to like.

My coffee mug was filled and waiting for me. As was the new lunch cooler Ness had made me buy, because it was more environmentally friendly than using plastic bags like I had been using.

"Morning," she greeted me. A little flush on her cheeks, and I knew she was thinking about what we'd done to each other last night.

Fair enough since I was going to spend the day thinking about her.

Sex had always been pretty basic for me. I would have

said I was a meat and potatoes kind of guy. This dirty talk business? Spanking? Ness brought out something in me... but I didn't want to think about it too hard. I just wanted to enjoy it.

I cupped my hand behind her neck and lifted her up for a kiss. Deep and wet. She tasted like toothpaste and coffee and she practically melted against me.

"Morning," I said when I let her go.

I turned to Nora and she was staring up at me. With her big, wide, brown eyes. The kid wasn't used to us kissing yet. Or touching. Like she sensed there was a shift in our dynamic and she was trying to understand it.

She would need to get used to it, because I was going to kiss and touch Ness every fucking day I could.

"Can you say Roy?" I asked Nora.

"Bah!"

"Now I think you're just being stubborn," I said.

"I'm telling you, Dada would be a whole lot easier for the kid," Vanessa joked.

"Roy will be fine," I said, watching Nora stuff more Cheerios in her mouth. Why was I so resistant to dada?

"Going out well past the cove today, so I'll be late getting home," I said.

Ness dropped the piece of cucumber she'd cut up on Nora's tray. We watched as Nora lifted it to her mouth, pushed it in, then immediately spat it out.

"Cucumbers basically have no taste," Vanessa said.

"They taste green. That's all she cares about."

"I'm going to keep trying. You won't win, Nora," she said, wiping the little girl's hands with a wet towel. Ness removed her from the high chair before she could unleash her artistic efforts on what was left of her breakfast.

"We're heading into town to see Fiona today," she said.

"About a Christmas window display. I was thinking how cool it would be if she did dresses out of wrapping paper."

"That's really cool." I said. "How much are you charging her for that?"

"Roy," Ness said, like I was being ridiculous. Her hair was down today and kind of curly from going to bed with it wet. She was hiding behind it.

"Vanessa," I said back, sweeping her hair back so I could see her face. "You work for these people. They want your advice. They pay for it. Stop acting like they're doing you a favor."

"It just seems crazy to get paid for ideas."

I snorted. "I get to sit out on the water all day on my boat and catch lobster and fish. Seems crazy people pay me for that too, but they do. Understand your value, Ness. You can do this."

She sighed and nodded. "Okay. I guess the worst she can say is no."

"Exactly. No one is going to be insulted that you expect to get paid for your work."

Then she smiled. "Should I give her a poker friend discount?"

"Fiona? No. She already takes too damn much of my money. Oh, and speaking of that, I told the poker gang last night that we would host next month," I said grabbing my coffee and lunch bag.

I had a fucking lunch bag. What was happening to my life?

"Host?"

Ness had Nora in her arms and was following me out into the living room towards the front door.

"Yeah. We'll set up a table here. We just need some snacks and beer and shit."

"Okay. I like a party," Ness said.

"No, like poker."

"Food and drinks make it a party."

I stopped in front of the door. "Ness, it's not a big thing. A couple of bags of chips and we're good."

I opened the front door and lights flashed in our eyes.

"Vanessa Dumont, is it true you ran away from your wedding to Simon Turnberry to marry a lobsterman?" someone shouted.

At the bottom of the steps was a short bald guy who appeared to be talking into his phone. Next to him was a tall kid, no more than twenty or so, snapping pictures.

"Is that your child, Vanessa? Who is the father? Simon or the fisherman?" the bald guy asked.

"Get the fuck off my property," I growled.

"Is that viral video of you shopping at Bullseye real, or was that staged?" the guy persisted.

"Viral video?" Ness shook her head. "Yes. I was shopping at Bullseye. Just like millions of other Americans do. So what?"

"Who's the baby daddy Vanessa? Is that child the new heir to the Dumont wealth or has she too been cut off from the family money?"

Where do these guys get off asking such personal shit?

"I said it before," I came down from the porch, with all the fury of a storm. "You don't get off my property, I'm calling the sheriff."

"Hey, we're just trying to do our job," the bald guy said, even as he and the kid with the camera backed the fuck up. "Vanessa Dumont is celebrity news."

"Yeah, well, now she's my wife," I stated.

"So it is true!" The guy crowed like he got a scoop. "And is that your baby, Vanessa?"

"I'm the kid's guardian. That's all you need to know," I said.

"And your name for the record?" the bald guy asked.

"Fuck. You."

"Okay, I'm pretty sure that's *not* actually your name."

"Ness, get back inside and call the sheriff."

The guy with the mouth finally gave up. He put his phone away and held up his hands in surrender.

"Fine, fine. We're leaving. Grumpy much?"

I watched them get in the car and drive away. Then I waited another minute to make sure they weren't going to double back.

"Sorry about that," Ness said, Nora still in her arms. "I'm not celebrity famous but just being a Dumont comes with that kind of stuff sometimes. Me running away from the wedding probably made some news."

"Sucks," I grunted.

"Yeah. The perks of not having a smart phone, I don't even know what they're saying about me anymore. But no doubt my runaway bride deal had them going a little crazy."

"How would they know to even come here?" I wondered.

"Anyone in town could have told them. It's not like me being here is a secret anymore. It's over. Trust me Roy, I'm not interesting enough for them to want to follow up. My guess is, it was a light celebrity news day."

"Yeah," I grunted.

I didn't like it. Not the intrusion or the fact that people just got to get into your business because they felt like they could. Like you owed them something.

That was all part of Vanessa's old life.

Money, fame. Drama.

"Please don't," she said, and put her hand on my arm.

"Don't what?" I asked.

"Think too hard about it, Roy. It happened. It's over. Eventually, I'll fall off everyone's radar and then *Vanessa Dumont of the Dumonts* will no longer be click bait."

"And that's what you want? What you really want?"

She smiled and dropped a kiss on Nora's head. Then she leaned in and kissed me on the cheek. "This is everything I want. You go catch some lobster and I'm going to start planning for Poker Night."

"Ness. I'm serious. It's just a few bags of chips."

"You leave that to me," she said with a twinkle in her eye.

Vanessa

"HERE YOU GO," Fiona said, handing me a cup of tea. We were sitting in the back room of her boutique which she used as an office space. She sat behind a beautiful antique desk, cluttered with look books and paperwork. "Are you sure I can't get anything for the little one?"

"No, she's good with her sippy cup," I sat in the chair across from Fiona, with Nora on the floor by my feet. She had ahold of the two handles on either side of her cup and was chugging away on her water. It had been an arduous journey breaking her addiction to apple juice, but now her diaper rash was totally cleared up.

"So let's talk window displays," Fiona said, clapping her hands together. "Stephanie says you've got the magic touch."

"I don't know about that," I said, then remembered this was supposed to be a job interview and I should show a level of confidence. "But she did have some success with our last window concept."

"It was so colorful. It made her cupcakes look like art,"

Fiona said. "I always think I know what I'm putting in the window will work, but I would love a second opinion."

I shifted a little in the chair and took a sip of my tea.

Understand your value.

It's what Roy had said.

"Uh, here is the thing Fiona. I'm actually thinking about...well, it seems like maybe I could...I don't know..."

"Spit it out, Vanessa."

I let out a breath. "I'm thinking about starting a business. An interior design business. I don't have any formal training, however-"

"However, you've had plenty of on-the-job training," Fiona cut me off. "Vanessa, I wouldn't have asked you to come today, if I didn't believe in your work. Pappas' looks amazing, and I already told you what I think of Stephanie's window display. Everyone can't wait to see what you're going to do with the bar."

Right. Fiona asked me here for a reason.

There was a rumble of thunder outside that caught Nora's attention. I had this strange sense I should be afraid of it too, but I couldn't put my finger on why.

"It's just a little rain, Boop. We're okay," I said, running my fingers along her soft curling hair.

It was enough to settle her and she went back to her sippy cup.

"Anyway, the thing about helping you out, I would love to do it, but I'm going to have to...charge you," I said those last two words in a rush and watched Fiona smile and shake her head.

"Is that what you were afraid to tell me? That I was going to pay for your design advice?"

"Uh...yes."

"Of course, I'm going to pay you. I put together a

contract for the number of hours I think I'll need you for, I'm just waiting to fill in your rate."

"My rate?"

"Your hourly rate. What do you plan to charge? Unless you want to negotiate a flat fee?"

I twisted my fingers together and tried to come up with something, but I didn't know. What was my time worth? I looked down at Nora like she might have an answer.

"You don't have a number, do you?" Fiona asked.

"I'm sorry," I apologized, feeling stupid all over again. Who tells someone they are going to charge them, but doesn't know how much? I could hear my father's voice in my head.

You call yourself a business person?

"I should have been more prepared. It just never occurred to me that my advice had value."

"Well it does, and here's what we're going to do. I have a friend who does interior design work down in Boston. I'm going to give her your number and she's going to tell you all she knows about starting up a consulting business. Then, when you feel you have a sense of what you need to charge me, you'll come back and we'll finalize the contract."

My jaw nearly dropped. "Seriously? Just like that, your friend is going to help me?"

"Women who own their own businesses like to help other women in business. You and your brother, through CCIB, helped me grow my businesses significantly. Now it's time for me to repay the favor. You're one of us now, Vanessa. One of the businesswomen of Calico Cove."

God. That made me so happy.

Then a hard rumble of thunder shook the windows of Fiona's office and that low-level dread came back.

Roy said he was heading farther out today. That's why I was nervous.

Maybe he was already back. Maybe he saw the bad weather coming and turned the boat around.

I looked down at Nora who was now trying to take off her shoe. Grunting, her face turning red from the effort, until finally the Velcro came loose and she popped it off. The pride in her accomplishment was hilarious.

"Boop? Did you take your shoe off?"

"Bah!" she nodded, and handed me the shoe.

I plucked her up from the floor, put her on my lap and got her shoe back on.

There was a crack of lightening and we all jumped.

"That's quite a storm," Fiona said, looking out the window at the dark clouds. "Is Roy-"

"Out on the water? Yeah." I blew out a long shuddery breath.

"He's a professional," Fiona said. "I'm sure he's safe."

There was a monument in City Hall for all the fisherman who died in Calico Cove over the years. Roy's Dad was on that monument. All of them professionals. Storms didn't care how much experience you had. Or who you had waiting at home.

"You know, he told us this was an arrangement between you two," Fiona said. "Not a real marriage."

"He told you about us?" That was surprising, and not like Roy to share.

"Not a lot, you know how he is.

"Yeah, which makes it strange he told you anything." I felt a little bristly, not just from the storm.

"Well, it was Bobby, really. Roy might not have said a word if Bobby didn't bring up your past."

I tucked my hair behind my ear. "Is this the part where you tell me not to hurt him again?"

"Hmmm, it was going to be. But from the look on your face, I think you're in as deep as he is. It's good to see, Vanessa. Roy deserves some happiness. So do you, I think. I have a hunch things have not been as easy as it might have looked from the outside for you. Happiness and a fair hourly rate."

"Thanks for everything, Fiona," I said as I stood up with Nora in my arms, shoe now back in place.

"I'm happy to help. The woman who will be calling you is Sharon Wilstead."

"Sharon," I repeated. "Thanks again."

Outside, the sky was slate grey and pouring down buckets of rain. I didn't have an umbrella or a raincoat for Nora. So much for being the best mom a person could be.

"Boop, you ready to make a run for it?"

"Bah!" she exclaimed.

I ran, as carefully as I could with Nora in my arms, to the car and threw open the back door. Icy cold rain pelted me, sticking my hair to my head. I got Nora settled in her seat, but she was definitely soaked and not happy about it at all.

"I know, this isn't as fun as a bath," I said, as I got in the car and checked her again in the rear view. "Okay, kiddo. We'll get you home, get you a nice hot bath while we wait for daddy to come home. Sound good?"

This was what I'd always wanted. A family to love. Someone to shower with all my affection. To be myself, instead of this puppet version of what I thought they wanted me to be. It was here. It was happening. Someone who believed in me and had my back. Lifted me up instead of pushing me down.

Except this storm was freaking me out.

"Maybe he's already home," I said, hopefully, as we headed towards the house.

The thunder boomed overhead and Nora and I were both quiet for the rest of the drive home. Only the truck wasn't parked in front of the house.

It was almost three in the afternoon, the storm was raging.

And Roy still wasn't home.

17

———

5 Hours Later
Vanessa

"We need to call someone," I said over a crying Nora. I was bouncing her on my hip, but she wasn't having it. She was screaming at the top of her lungs. Her face was flushed, hot, from sweat or fever I didn't know.

It was my fault. It had to be. Because I let her get wet earlier because I hadn't thought to check the weather and bring an umbrella with us.

Did we even own an umbrella?

"Who are you going to call?" Mari asked, biting her lip.

"The police!" I cried. "Isn't that what they do? Find missing people?"

"Roy's not missing, he's just a little late," Mari said calmly.

I shot her a cut the shit look.

After ten texts had gone unanswered by Roy, I'd called Mari for moral support as my unease turned into worry. Which quickly exploded into outright panic.

Roy wasn't home. The storm wasn't easing up. Nora was screaming, with possibly a fever I was responsible for. Mari kept biting her lower lip, which only made me more nervous.

"Please, we have to call someone," I said. "If only to make me think I'm doing something."

Jackson and Lola were still off on their holiday. Too far away to do me any good in the here and now.

I could call my father.

He had money. He had resources. He could call the Coast Guard, maybe organize a search party.

But what would he want in return? Also, Roy would hate that I called him.

But if Roy didn't walk in that door in the next five minutes, I was going to lose my mind and just make the call.

"Look, I'll call Bobby. He'll know if there have been any maydays. He keeps on top of all that with the Coast Guard when there is a storm like this," Mari said.

"Yes!" Bobby Tanner was the local Sheriff. Roy played poker with him. Mari went to high school with him. He would help because that's what the police were supposed to do.

Mari was quietly talking into her cell phone, while I tried to rub Nora's back to get her to stop crying.

I'd tried the baby thermometer, but Nora wouldn't hold still long enough for me to put it in her ear for a proper reading. I tried holding her down while Mari held the thermometer in her ear, but she screamed so hard my heart broke.

This was my fault. Totally my fault. Why wasn't Roy home yet?

What if he was never coming home? What if he was lost at sea like his father?

I couldn't do this. I wasn't strong enough for this.

"I can't raise Nora on my own," I said.

"Hey, Vanessa?"

Mari's voice sounded like she was speaking to me through a long tunnel.

My breath was coming in pants. What if I fainted? What if I fainted holding Nora?

"Here, give me her," Mari said, reaching to take Nora out of my arms.

Don't let her go. She's mine.

"I got her Momma Bear," Mari whispered. "Now go sit on the couch and try and calm down."

Mari did a bouncy swaying dance move around the living room and Nora instantly calmed down.

"Your freak out was spreading to her," Mari said in a quiet voice.

"My freak out is deserved. Listen to it out there." As if to back me up a large clap of thunder shook the windows.

Mari kept swaying and rocking around the room, Nora's head on her shoulder.

I wasn't jealous that Mari could calm her down better than me. I was just upset that I was upsetting her. I couldn't do anything right.

"Vanessa, I get that you summered here a few times, but you must understand Calico Cove is a fishing town. These guys spend their life on the water. They can smell a storm from a mile away and navigate it appropriately. Roy might have had to go around it and that's what is taking him so long."

"Then why hasn't he texted back to tell me that?" I would text him again, I thought, thinking about where I'd left my phone. Maybe this one would do the trick. Except Mari was still trying to be rational with me.

"Reception in storms is tricky," Mari ticked off on her fingers. "Or, he's busy piloting the boat. Or, he's already in his truck and on his way home. Or he's helping someone else-"

"Okay," I said, falling back against the couch like all my bones had left my body. "So what do we do?"

"We wait, honey."

TWENTY MINUTES later and there was a knock on the door. Immediately I jumped to my feet. It wasn't Roy, he would have just come in. I threw open the door with my heart in my chest and froze when I saw a uniformed policeman on the other side of the door.

"No," I whimpered.

"Hey," the guy said, grabbing onto my elbows. "He's okay. Roy is okay."

It took me a minute to recognize Bobby. He'd hung out with me and Roy that summer we were together a few times. He'd been a cheerful contrast to Roy's grumpiness. They'd been their own little comedy routine.

"You promise?" I asked.

"I promise. Can I come in?"

I stepped back to let him step inside and his eyes immediately went to Mari, coming in from the kitchen, still holding the baby.

"Hi, Mari."

"Hey, Bobby," she replied.

"Oh, hey. Look at you with a baby. In your arms like that.

Sweet. I mean...uh...you look really good holding Nora," he said, turning red.

Mari wrinkled her nose. "Uh, thanks. I guess?"

"Why are we talking about Mari and not talking about Roy?" I asked.

"He's okay, Vanessa. Told me to come over so I could tell you in person not to panic."

"You talked to him?!"

"Not directly, no. When I checked in with the Coast Guard, they said they'd already reached out to him. Storm came in fast, and he had to go way out of his way to get around it. Apparently, he's been fighting all day just to bring her in."

"Can't they go get him?" I asked. "Isn't that what the Coast Guard is for? They have all those big rescue ships!"

"Roy said he was okay. If he said it, he meant it. Told the guys on the radio to let me know to tell you."

"What did he say? Exactly," I asked, as if the words mattered.

"Tell Bobby to tell Ness not to panic. I'm fine."

"Not to panic. What a stupid request. Of course I'm going to panic! This is what happened to his father! Are we all just supposed to forget that?"

"Yes," Bobby said, grabbing me by the shoulders to still me. Suddenly, his tone was very serious, his expression grave. "Yes, Vanessa, you are supposed to forget that. As a community of fisherman who live their lives on the water, we all forget it because it doesn't do us any good to dwell on it. What happened to Mr. Barnes was a tragedy, but this is Roy's life. And if you're going to be a part of that life, that means you need to adapt. Thunderstorms happen. Squalls come out of nowhere. Roy's a professional and he knows what he's doing. You have to trust that. Trust him."

"Bobby...she's new to this," Mari said.

He looked at Mari, with a silent command to stay out of it. "She is new. But if she's going to stick around she needs to learn. Roy's going to come through that door after a long hard physical battle against the ocean. He'll need a stiff drink, a hot meal, and maybe a blow job."

"Bobby!" Mari chastised. "Way TMI."

"Snuck that one in for a friend," the gravity in his voice was gone, replaced with his familiar humor. "I mean it, Vanessa. If you're serious about this, about being in his life, than you've got to man-up. Or woman-up. You're a fisherman's wife now and storms might worry you, but you've got to keep that shit inside. Can you do that?"

I nodded. A stiff drink, a hot meal and a blow job. I could do that. Right?

Mari had Nora all calmed down, so I took her. Her forehead was nice and cool now. She'd just been hot and sweaty from crying.

"I'm going to put her down," I said, as Nora curled into my chest. "She's tuckered out. Thanks for coming over, Mari. And thank you too, Bobby. For letting me know he's okay. This was just my first storm, but I'll get better."

"You okay?" Mari asked me, giving me a doubtful look.

She was right. I was lying through my teeth.

"What's the expression?" I said. "Fake it till you make it? Let's go with that."

She gave my arm a squeeze and I gave her a grateful smile.

"Let's go, Mari, we don't want to be here when the BJs start," Bobby said with a chuckle.

"Bobby! Will you stop talking about freaking BJs," Mari said, whacking him on the shoulder as she walked by him to the front door.

"What? I love talking about BJs with you."

"We have never once talked about BJs."

"It's a perfect time to start."

"You're such a dork," she muttered under her breath.

"That's why you secretly love me," he said, the door closing behind both of them.

∽

Roy

I PULLED the truck up into the driveway and sighed. Fuck me, it had been a long day.

Days like these were the worst, too. All physical effort with no reward. No lobsters because all my energy was spent just getting the boat back to the docks. I could have let the CG hall my sorry ass in, it would have been quicker, but there was nothing more embarrassing than not accurately predicting a storm like the one today and needing a tug.

I knew I wasn't in serious danger, and taking up resources like that meant that someone else who might actually need help wouldn't get it. I wasn't about to take that chance.

For a second, I sat in my truck looking at the house. Front porch light was on. Ness always left it on for me now that the sun was going down earlier. I was just sappy enough to acknowledge that I liked it. At least to myself, not to her. Didn't want her to think...

Fuck. I didn't want her to think I cared, but we seemed to be crossing all sorts of lines lately and it wasn't just sex. One of the things that irritated me the most when the Atlantic

Ocean was tossing me around, was I knew she would be worried about me. Scared for me.

She'd met me only months after losing my father at sea because of a storm.

Which meant I was going to go in there and she was going to be a wreck. Probably already freaking out about how she thought she was going to have to raise Nora on her own.

Or, what if she decided it was all too much for her? What if she had her bags packed ready to go back to her Daddy and the cold but comfortable life of being a Dumont?

If I was being honest, I wouldn't be surprised. Being a fisherman's wife was tougher than being a fisherman, and she was still pretty soft.

This, I thought with a sigh and a heavy heart, might just be the end of us.

I got out of the truck and headed up the steps of the front porch. I opened the door and the first thing that hit me was the smell of steak. We didn't eat a lot of steak, because it was expensive, but instantly my stomach rumbled. I hadn't had time for much more than sips of water from my thermos, while I tried to keep the boat steady.

"Ness?" I called out.

"Hey, back here," she said from the kitchen.

I walked through the living room, all Nora's toys were back in their cubbies and boxes, which meant the kid was down for the night. I'd check in on her later. I walked to the back of the house towards the kitchen, and when I turned the corner Ness was standing over a cast iron skillet cooking what looked to be a ribeye.

"Hey," I said.

She turned and smiled. "Hey, babe. Figured you would be hungry after a rough day."

Okay. No freak outs. No crying. No hand wringing. No bags packed that I could see.

Hmmm. "I am."

"Sit down at the table. I found your bottle of bourbon in the cabinet over the fridge. I'm thinking tonight you could use a stiff drink."

She already had the bottle on the countertop and my bourbon drinking glass next to it. She left the steak and put some ice in the glass and filled it with two fingers of bourbon.

"You want to go take this, get a quick hot shower and when you're done the steak should be ready."

Okay, this wasn't the socialite debutant version of Vanessa. This wasn't the *save me* version of her either. This was a version of Vanessa Dumont I'd never seen before.

Still a people pleaser, sure, but that was always going to be her thing. As long as she was pleasing me, I didn't see a problem with it.

But this version of Vanessa Dumont also seemed completely in control of her shit.

"Or..." she said, her voice trailing off.

I stood in the kitchen with the bourbon over ice in my hand, the smell of steak in my nose, and feeling like I'd walked into an alternate universe.

"Or maybe you would like me to give you some...release first," she said in a soft voice, getting up in my space, pushing her hair back behind her ear.

"Release?"

"You know..." she ran a finger down my chest, towards my waist and stopped just at the snap on my jeans. "I could...bl...blow on you. Blow you. You know, down there. A...blow job, for the release."

A steak. A bourbon. And a blow job.

That's when it all clicked.

"You were freaking the fuck out weren't you?"

"Of course I was!" she shouted, although she did it in that whispering shouting way so as not to wake the kid.

She turned back to the stove and turned the heat off the steak.

"I'm not burning the good meat, but let me just tell you today was awful. I was so worried and Bobby was like *you have to be a good fisherman wife* and I'm like fuck that! But I'll try because you're tired and had a hard day too. So I got the good meat out of the freezer and I've been on the computer looking up blowjobs. And I swear to God, I know exactly how big you are and how much I can reasonably fit in my mouth and that doesn't even seem remotely possible. But Bobby was all like *a hot meal and blow job is a wifely requirement in Calico Cove.* So fine! Let's just do it. Before or after the steak?"

She was flushed and out of breath from her rant. I thought she was the fucking cutest thing I'd ever seen. That's when it started to sink in. *This* was Vanessa. Caring. Thoughtful. A little high strung. Always trying and sometimes failing. But sometimes getting it just right even when she didn't realize it.

I cupped my hand that wasn't holding my drink around her neck and brought her close. I bent down and touched my forehead to hers and for a few breaths we shared the same oxygen.

"Sorry you were worried," I said.

"Sorry you had such a rough day," she whispered.

"I know what I'm doing out there and I know when I'm

over my head. My dad was a stubborn fuck about that shit. He never would have called for help, and it cost him his life. Me, I got too much shit to live for now."

She let out a breath and looked up at me. "Am I one of those things?"

"Yeah," I admitted. "Yeah, you are."

Her smile was nearly blinding.

"Did you really look up blow jobs on the computer?"

She nodded, then winced. "There was a lot of gagging. Do guys actually like that sound? Because all I think about when I hear someone gagging is how it makes me want to gag too."

I laughed. "I wish I had the strength in me to show you how much you're going to like it. But I'm dead on my feet, babe. I'm going to take that shower. Eat some good fucking meat and then I'm going to crash. But I want to do that with you in my bed. Yeah?"

"Yes, Roy."

18

The Next Morning
Roy

The crack of thunder pulled me out of a bad dream. I was on the water. The waves were breaking over the bow of the *Surly Bird* and I knew I was taking on too much water. The radio was dead. It was up to me to get the boat to safety. That's when I turned around and saw Ness on the deck holding Nora. The boat was rocking, but somehow she maintained her footing in a fancy dress and high heeled shoes. Her fancy hair untouched by the crashing waves.

It was what she'd been wearing the night of her engagement to fuckface.

"It's okay," I shouted to her above the noise of the storm and the ocean. *"I'm going to save you!"*

"Do you want me to save you too?" she called back.

I blinked a few times, looking up at the dark ceiling, and

ran a hand over my face. That wasn't how this worked. I saved her. Not the other way around.

I turned my head to the alarm clock on the bed stand. It was just after five in the morning. Another clap of thunder boomed and I knew I wasn't heading out to sea today. No point. Typically, on bad weather days I had a massive to do list. Shopping, repairs on the boat, repairs on the house. None of it was ever easy to do while watching Nora, but now things were different.

A tiny foot kicked my kidney.

That's right. Nora was in bed with us.

Nora hadn't loved the storm and woke up in the middle of the night crying. Ness just brought her back into the bed with us and she settled down immediately. Content to sleep between the two adults responsible for caring for her.

I rolled over and lifted the blanket. Nora had one tiny naked foot pressed up against Ness's nose, and the other one dug into my armpit. This kid was in constant motion during the night.

If someone told me a year ago this was going to be my life, I would have laughed in their faces. If someone told me how much I was going to fucking like it, I would have called them a liar.

But here I was. Loving my life. Foot in armpit and everything.

Carefully, I peeled back the covers and slipped out of bed. Then I slid Nora along the sheets until I could lift her in my arms. While she liked to move around a lot, she was still a sound sleeper. When she was out, nothing was going to wake her.

The book I was reading had two whole chapters on letting kids sleep in the bed, but the bottom line was it was important for them to be able to settle in their own space. I carried her back to her room, settled her in the crib, and waited to see if she stirred.

Nope.

I'd been trying to tell myself she was mine. I was the only thing she had left in this world, and I would give my life for her. However, and maybe I could just see this now, I knew I hadn't been emotionally all in with the kid. I'd been keeping part of myself distant.

Protected.

I was just so afraid they would take her. Tell me I wasn't up for the job, find her a better home. If I let myself love her...then I'd be losing my dad all over again.

Except, that's just not how love worked. You could try to fight it and sometimes it just wormed it's way inside you and took hold. I'd stayed away from the word *dad*. I stayed hard away from the word *daughter*.

But that's what I was. That's what she was to me.

Maybe it was time to let go of the fear.

"When you wake up, I'm going to teach you how to say dada," I whispered to her. "'Cause Ness says it's easier than Roy."

Quietly, I made my way back to my bedroom. Ness was awake, her eyes squinting against the light in the hallway, so I turned it out.

"What time is it?" she asked.

It was time to make love to my wife.

"Take your pajamas off," I said quietly. Instantly, my dick was hard as stone.

But she went still, and I wondered if maybe I'd taken our game a little too far. Maybe it was too early, she was too tired, hell, I didn't even know when her period was due.

I was about to tell her it was okay. We didn't have to have

sex. When she sat up and lifted the tank top she was wearing over her head.

My eyes went to her pretty little tits, which had gotten fuller in the past few weeks. My girl was eating actual food. Filling herself up with food I'd provided for her.

It was satisfying as fuck.

I pushed down my boxer briefs and freed my cock, while Ness scrambled under the covers to shimmy out of her sleep shorts. Fuck those covers. Fuck anything in between us. I climbed up on the bed, using my thighs to spread her legs out wide.

The smell of her - the lavender of her skin, the sweet musk between her legs – was delicious. Slow, I reminded myself. We're doing this slow.

"You've had sex before?" I asked, hating the idea that I was bringing fuckface into this bed with us, but I needed to know.

"Yes," she whispered.

"Does it hurt?"

"It did. With... him."

Yeah, we're not in the business of saying fuckface's name.

"You on the pill?"

"No, I ... ah, have an IUD."

Oh thank fuck. "That means I'm coming in you. You okay with that?"

Her body arched against me. Yeah. I'd say she was okay with that.

"But here's the thing, Vanessa. You gotta tell me if it hurts."

"I will. I promise."

"Don't do that shit where you lie because you think I need you to."

"I won't."

"Oh God, Vanessa," I put my head in her neck, breathing in the sweet sleepy smell of her. "I'm barely hanging on here. You gotta-"

"What... what do you need me to do?" So eager to please, this girl. The things I could do to her, the things I could make her feel.

"Just be honest."

She pulled on my hair, lifting my head so I met her eyes in the dark. "I will, Roy. I promise. But what if..."

"Spit it out."

"What if it never feels good?" she asked quietly.

Fuck me. That fucking *fuckface*. Not only didn't he take the time to get her off, to make her feel good, he'd also hurt her. No wonder she'd always pulled away from sex.

I was going to make up for everything that asshole did. I was going to give her so much pleasure, she wasn't going to remember her own name.

I shifted down the bed, spreading her legs wide until she got the hint and slid them up over my shoulders. I was never going to get tired of that smooth skin against mine.

I slipped my hands under her perfect little ass and pulled her pussy closer to me. She wiggled trying to help me.

"Yeah," I breathed against her pussy. "Look at you. So hot and wet for me. But I need you dripping, baby. I need you soaking wet."

I tongued her hot wet slit and let the rush of heat just wash over me.

"So good. Like fucking honey," I muttered. "Tell me, what do I like, baby?"

"Me," she said, like that was some kind of miracle. This woman, fuck, she wanted to be loved so much.

"That's right, but when I'm sucking on your little clit, what do I like?"

"For me to touch myself," she said. Her fingers already twisting her nipples, finding the pressure she liked. One day I was going to stand by the side of the bed and watch her pleasure herself from beginning to end. Maybe introduce a toy...

Shit! My hips jerked against the mattress, my dick needing some kind of relief. I used my tongue to lap against her clit. I found that she was so sensitive, just gentle circles worked instead of full on sucking her clit into my mouth.

I fucked one finger deep inside and she sighed with the pleasure, pushing down on me. I added another and then scissored the two fingers to stretch her out a bit. She whimpered.

"Good or bad?" I asked.

"Unh."

"That's not an answer, baby." I sent my two fingers deep again and she spread wider for me.

"Good," she whispered.

I rewarded her with my tongue on her clit, as I finger fucked her as deep as I could.

"Roy! Roy! Yes, yes, yes."

I could feel the walls of her vagina squeezing against my fingers, another tongue flick over her clit and her whole body arched into an orgasmic stretch.

I slipped my fingers from her, dropped her legs back to the bed and watched my wife come.

"That's my good girl," I told her. "Look at how fucking beautiful you are when you come like that. Did that feel good?"

I took myself in hand and started pumping into my fist.

"Yes, soooo good," she said. Her head back against the pillow, her eyes closed.

I leaned over her and took her tit in my hand and sucked on her hard little cherry nipple. She jerked against me.

"Good or bad?"

"Good. Always, Roy."

"Fuck, you're so damn hot. I can't wait." I planted my palms on either side of her head. "Ness, look at me."

Her blissed out eyes slowly opened.

"I need you to keep looking at me, yeah?" I reached down with my one hand and notched my cock against her pussy. Slowly. I needed to be so careful not to hurt her.

I pushed inside, the head of my cock stretching her sensitive skin.

She gasped.

"Good or bad?"

"Good. Good."

"Take a little more," I said, easing in another inch, holding it there.

"Hmm," she whimpered, and started to close her eyes.

"No, eyes on me, remember?"

"Yes, Roy," she breathed.

"Such a good girl. Such a good fucking girl. Take more. You can take it."

Her eyes got wider and her knees came up around my hips. I slipped a little further in. And then after one slow, last push I bottomed out. My cock was buried in her slick tight pussy and I could die from it. Actually die.

"Roy?"

"Baby?"

"You're all the way in?"

"All the way." It took everything in me not to pull back and thrust. "How do you feel?"

She wiggled her whole body like she was adjusting herself around me. Her hands slid around my waist and gripped my backside. Then she tilted her hips up and rocked against me.

"Holy fuck," I groaned, and dropped another kiss on her tit. "You fucking yourself on my cock, baby?"

She stopped then and bit her bottom lip.

"No, no. None of that shit. You take what you want. You want my cock deep inside you?"

"Yes," she said.

"It feels good deep inside you?"

"Yes."

I pulled out nearly to the tip and she whimpered. Fuck me, I loved that sound. Like she was a little desperate for it.

"Roy," she said, gripping my ass even harder.

This time I thrust in hard. Hard enough to make her tits bounce.

"Talk to me, Ness."

"More, like that," she groaned.

I flexed my hips and gave her another hard thrust. The sound that came out of her mouth that time was nothing but pleasure.

"That's my good girl. See, you like fucking just fine." I watched the bliss just roll over her in waves. "Oh, I'm going to fuck you nice and hard and then I'm going to spill my load deep inside your wet cunt. And you're going to come again for me, because that's what I like."

"Roy," she gasped, like she was already there.

I got up on my knees and looked down at where I was deep inside her. I wanted to watch this. I pulled her leg up and dropped her ankle over my shoulder, and then I fucked her so hard the bed shook. Her tits kept bouncing. I could feel my balls tightening.

"Get there, Ness!" I dropped my hand and rubbed her clit with my hard calloused thumb.

"Roy!"

She clamped down hard on my cock and I let go. Pump after pump, my cum shooting so deep inside her. Barely breathing, my heart pounding in my eyes. I lowered her leg to the bed again, my cock still semi-hard, still deep inside her. I was shaking. Trembling really. My arms, my legs, even as I braced my weight over her, giving her some of me but not all.

It was by far the hottest fuck of my life. As soon as I could breathe, I would tell her that and it would make her so fucking happy.

Ness's hand rubbed against my cheek. "Roy?"

"Yes, baby?" I panted, pushing her sweaty, damp hair off her face

"I want to do that again. Please and thank you."

My fucking wife was going to kill me in bed.

It was going to be a helluva way to die.

19

Vanessa

"So we're going to install these light fixtures on either side of the bar." I showed Stu the models from the website I'd pulled up on his iPad. "I'm going for an overall American Craftsman meets Modern Industrial feel."

Stu blinked. "Am I supposed to know what that means?"

I laughed and handed him back his iPad. "No, you just have to trust me."

Stu looked around the space and I tried to see it through his eyes, a professional contractor, assessing all my choices. The white oak beams on the ceiling that ran the length of the barn, the stain on the hardwood floors, and the wainscotting throughout the room that I believed made the space feel more intimate.

"It's good," he grunted. "I'd come to a place like this."

Ever since Roy's visit, Stu had been perfectly agreeable

with me. Even helpful. He gave me estimated dates of completion when I asked for them and so far his team was hitting all of them. The bar was scheduled to be open in time for Thanksgiving weekend.

Now it was time to focus on the design details, which was my absolute favorite part.

Fiona's friend Sharon had called me and given me tons of good advice. I now had an hourly rate, which was a little below average for most interior designers, but I thought it was fair since I didn't have a formal degree.

However, Sharon had explained the biggest parts of the job were developing relationships with contractors, wholesalers and suppliers. Most clients didn't just want advice, they wanted someone to manage the job. From ideas to budget to timelines.

Once the bar was done, I was going to ask Jackson to help me set up an LLC, which was fancy talk for a legal business name, and then I was actually going to do it. I was officially going to have my own business. I was still considering school, which seemed a little crazy, but these days I felt like I could do anything.

If I could bring in some money, real money, that would take so much pressure off Roy. We'd started a savings account for the Family Lawyer and I could help fill it up faster. Plus, Nora was getting bigger every day. Her need for clothes and toys never ended.

Roy worked with her every morning to say dada now.

Freakin' adoresvillee, by the way.

However, the minute after he gave me my goodbye kiss, which always made my toes curl, and took his coffee and lunch cooler to leave for the boat, I tried to get Nora to say momma.

I was afraid I might be confusing her, but I couldn't help it.

I was someone's momma.

Nora's momma.

Roy was my husband and we were a family.

Oh, and did I mention the sex?

I felt like a race car. I'd gone from zero to eighty in less than ten seconds flat.

I actually felt bad about it. Roy was on the water all day long hauling in lobster traps, and then at night I made him have sex with me at least twice a night. Some nights three times.

I was insatiable!

I'd been living in this sexual coma for years, and now I knew how good it could feel – I wanted to try all of it..

And when he got bossy with me, when he told me what a good girl I was...I tried to summon up some feminine outrage, and failed.

All it did was make me wet.

"Hey, Vanessa, you there?"

Stu was snapping his fingers in front of my face. I immediately blushed. "Oh sorry, I was thinking about...table tops."

"Yeah. My crew and I are done here today. We've got another job outside of town so we won't be back until Friday."

I nodded. "Yep. All good. Jackson will be back next week so you won't have to put up with me much longer."

Stu shrugged. "You're alright. I'm usually an asshole with most project managers because people who stand around and watch, instead of do, piss me off. That's just how I roll. But you're not afraid to get your hands dirty."

I held up said dirty hands because I'd been busy today doing some touch-up painting.

"Thanks, Stu. That means a lot coming from you."

"We'll be in touch?" he asked.

I nodded. "I need to get a client first, but absolutely I'll keep you in mind for my first actual job."

I waited until the crew was gone, before locking up the bar behind me. Nora was with Mari today, because I knew I was going to have to do some hands on work on the place and didn't want her distracting me.

Since Mari was one of Nora's favorite people, and she knew spending time with her also meant a trip to the bakery downstairs, I didn't get any tears when I dropped her off.

I made my way toward the town square. I'd parked by Mari's place since it was an easy walk to the bar, and thought about everything I needed to do to get ready for tonight.

Roy's poker friends were coming over tonight and I wanted to make sure it was perfect. He said to keep it simple. Chips, dip and some beer. But I could do better than that. Maybe some homemade guacamole. A veggie tray. Everyone loved a veggie tray.

"Vanessa?" I was just about to cross the street to go to the bakery on the other side of the town square, when I heard my name.

The hair on the back of my neck prickled. It wasn't some random paparazzi person.

It was my mother.

Slowly I turned, trying to keep my face blank. Our relationship had been strained since I was a little girl, but she hadn't reached out at all since the wedding. Not once to see how I was. I expected that from my dad, but it hurt a little from my mom.

Even though in hindsight, I could see how manipulative she was.

She was still my mom.

"Oh my word, Vanessa. What are you wearing?"

I sucked in a breath. "Jeans and a hoodie. I'm very comfortable, thank you."

She huffed. Her cheek bones were sharper than I'd remembered, and all the under eye concealer in the world couldn't hide her dark circles.

Beyond that she looked perfectly fit in a Burberry rain coat and kitten heeled pumps I knew were worth more than my entire wardrobe. Her hair was the same ash blonde bob it had been for decades. She wore her diamond studs and the classic Tiffany gold necklace.

Meanwhile, my hair was pulled back in a ponytail. Not styled or curled. My hoodie was yellow and my jeans were a size bigger than the last designer pair she'd seen me in.

I could see her doing the calculations in her head. My mother could nail the dress size of a woman from fifty yards away.

"Well, I see this husband of yours has been feeding you."

"He has," I said. "What can I do for you, Mom?"

"I brought you things from the house," she said, and I realized she had a wheely suitcase with her. "Just some basics. Your wool coat and the Hunter boots. Though, I don't know if they'll fit."

I wished I could be tougher. I wished I could turn my nose up at a suitcase of expensive designer clothes, but I was not that strong.

"Thank you," I said, taking the suitcase. That I didn't do a happy dance was the real win. The wool coat was super warm and it would mean I didn't have to shell out any extra cash for a coat this year. "Was there anything else?"

"Yes. I want you to end this nonsense and come home."

"Home? That's funny coming from you."

"What is that supposed to mean?"

"I haven't heard from you at all, Mom. Not one word in almost two months. So the concern you're pretending to feel seems a little disingenuous."

"When your father told me what you'd done, married that...fisherman, I had to take to my bed for days."

Well, that rang true. In times of stress, we Dumont women liked to pull the covers over our heads.

"But I've had a chance to think things over, to try and see things from your perspective. So I've come back to Calico Cove to tell you this."

She fidgeted with the strap of her purse, which was practically a sign of the apocalypse. Wow, I thought, this is going to be good.

She took a deep breath and said, "You don't have to marry Simon Turnberry if you don't want to."

"Mom," I laughed. "You say that like it's still a possibility. Of course I'm not going to marry Simon. I ran out on our wedding. I know I let you down, but nothing is going to change what happened."

"Fine. We can move on from that disaster of a wedding and start over. But you have to come home to Boston. This is a summer destination for people like us, not a place to live."

"Mom, did Dad tell you everything?"

"I assume you're talking about that fisherman," she said. "You'll divorce quietly and we'll never speak of it again. Our social set doesn't ever have to know anything about it."

I shook my head. "That's not going to happen, Mom."

She stepped closer to me, her hands now clenched into tight fists. I wasn't worried about her getting physical like Dad. Mom didn't scream or shout or use violence. Her weapon was words and a complete understanding of her opponent's weak spots.

I braced myself for something awful. Something devastating.

"Vanessa Dumont, I did not raise you for this life. You have responsibilities to this family. To our brand. To our name."

"My name is Barnes now."

I hadn't legally changed it. It hadn't really occurred to me until now, but I liked the way that sounded.

Vanessa Barnes. Mrs. Vanessa Barnes.

"And you think you're prepared for the life that this fisherman can provide you?" She could barely say the word fisherman without curling her lip in distaste.

"Lobsterman," I said with a chin lift. "And yes. We've been doing okay so far."

"So far," my mother said with all kinds of meaning. "Here is the thing, my darling. While you might think you're doing fine...while you pretend to play house and be a good little wife...ultimately you will fail him. "

I sucked in a breath.

"You see that, don't you?" She asked, her forehead creased like she cared. "I raised you to host parties. To sit on boards. To shop. To gossip. To smile pleasantly when someone is slashing you to pieces with soft words. To understand the politics of money and high-power marriages. You were born to look pretty on someone's arm and to fit into the society of rich trophy wives. That is who Vanessa Dumont of the Dumonts was meant to be. You don't have the first clue how to be a *lobsterman's* wife. He needs a partner. Someone who can contribute to his household. Someone who can keep a budget, cook and clean. Pop out dozens of lobsterman children and then keep them in line." She shook her head, her lips twisted in a cruel smile. "Does that sound like you?"

"It might surprise you, but it does. Yes. A little bit actually."

It kind of surprised me too. I'd done all right on the budget and with the cooking. Nora and I...well, we were a team now. Could I handle more kids? I wasn't sure, but I thought so.

"Oh, you never were very good at understanding what people thought of you."

"What does that mean?"

"A man like that needs more than you, Vanessa. The passion will fade and you'll see it's not about *love* for him. A man like that is far too practical for such sentimentality. You'll only become another burden for him."

I wanted to be stronger. I wanted to channel my inner Roy and tell her to go fuck herself. That I had to return to my family and my home. But her words found their way in.

Those stupid boards on the porch I got wrong. Plus, I'd stopped doing the other repairs on the list because I was working on Jackson's bar and Roy was just handling all that now.

I always cooked expensive steak too long. He liked medium rare, not well done. I just could never figure out when to stop. Why was meat so freaking hard?

The other night we'd both thrown out the stew I made, because it was way too salty. We'd made sandwiches instead. I apologized and he said it didn't matter, but it did.

Of course it did.

I already knew he didn't love me. He'd made that clear. It was in the ground rules.

How long could the passion last without love?

"Tell him you're the problem," my mother said, with

something like a sympathetic expression on her face. "Make the right decision for him so he can find the partner he was meant to be with. A true helpmate, someone he could actually fall in love with if he allowed himself to."

I stepped away, instantly rejecting the idea of Roy with some other woman.

I found him. He was mine.

"I have to go," I said. "We're having people over tonight and I have to shop."

Again my mother sniffed, looking at me as if she pitied me. "Do you have any idea what you're shopping for? How to plan an event like this when you've only ever known how to oversee a catering staff? This is what I'm talking about, Vanessa. You will only mess this up because you don't understand his life."

It was just poker!

The words screamed against my skull. How hard could it be to make it a fun poker night?

I was going to find out. I was going to make sure it was the best damn poker night Calico Cove had ever seen.

"Good bye, Mom," I said desperate to get away from her.

"Let's just say, goodbye for now. I'll be staying at the estate for the next few weeks, or until you come to your senses."

No, I thought. I could do this. I was determined to do this.

I took my wheely bag and left.

∿

Later That Night
  Roy

. . .

I PULLED the truck up to my house and cursed. I was late because of an engine problem on the boat I had to address. Then Madame Za caught me on the docks and talked my ear off. Apparently, Vanessa's mom was back at the Dumont Estate and Madame Za had seen the two of them talking near the square.

That was no big deal, I told myself. It wasn't like I wanted to keep Vanessa from her family completely, just specifically her father who was obviously dangerous to her. Still, something about the two of them talking made me nervous.

Mrs. Dumont would no doubt remind her daughter about everything she was giving up to be with me. It would be great to have a minute alone with Vanessa to ask about the conversation with her and her mother, but I could already see there were a bunch of cars parked out in front of the house.

Like a bunch more than just Mal, Fiona, Bobby and Levi.

I opened the front door of my home and stopped in my tracks.

It was wall to wall people. There was a poker table in the center of what had been my living room. Like a professional poker table. With a felt top and leather trim.

This table was nicer than Mal's.

This table was nicer than anything in Las Vegas.

And there was a guy wearing a black shirt and tie, dealing out cards to the crowd of people around the table.

Jackson was back from his trip, sitting on one of the stools, which meant Lola was probably here, too. Jolie had returned from her chef internship, and was sitting on Mal's good leg even as she chatted with Mari. Bobby was trying to show Mari his cards, but she was waving him off.

Ness came out of the kitchen with a plate...holy shit, was that shrimp cocktail?

She was wearing a fancy dress I had never seen before. It was deep green, long and flowy, with a belt around her thin waist. Her hair was that long shiny curtain I hadn't seen since her engagement party.

It was like looking at the Ness from before. Before she was mine.

She spotted me standing by the door and handed the plate of shrimp to Lola, who was coming out of the kitchen behind her with a drink.

"Oh good! You're here," Ness said with some excited claps, making her way through the crowd to me.

"Ness," I said. "What the fuck is all this?"

Matt came up behind me and slapped me on the back.

"Your first time hosting poker and you go all out. Nice, Barnes. Way to show off."

"Hi Matthew and welcome," Ness said, put on her brightest smile. "There are some extra stools near the staircase. In the kitchen, I have a bar set up where you can find our signature cocktail for the night a 'HoldemTini.'"

Signature cocktail. What. The. Fuck.

"Cool," Matt said. "Sign me up."

When he walked past us, I caught Ness's wrist and tugged her outside onto the porch.

"Ness, what the hell?"

Her face fell. "What? It's not enough? You think we need another cocktail? I can probably pull something together quick."

I shook my head. "It was supposed to be a couple people over for poker. I said chips and dips. Not shrimp cocktail."

She blinked a few times and I could see she was rattled. "Yes, but this was your first time hosting poker so I wanted it to be super amazing. Then Jackson texted that he and Lola were back from their trip, so I thought it would be fun to turn it into a little party."

"Where's Nora?"

"She's with Mari's mom. I didn't want to be distracted, there was so much more to do last minute, so Stephanie said she would have her over for a sleepover. I...I mean... that's okay, right? Stephanie said she's done it before."

"Yeah, when I had some serious shit to do, Ness," I bit out. "I don't like leaning on people for help. And I only ever ask for it, if it's serious. Not for you to throw some damn party."

Ness swallowed. "I wanted to make it nice. You don't think it's nice?"

"How much did all of this cost?" I asked, raising my voice more than I liked, but this was so typical of her. To take something that should have been basic, and turn it into a fucking event.

"No, it's okay. I paid for all of it," she said quickly.

"With what money?"

"Mine."

I remembered what Madame Za said about Vanessa and her mother. "Did you see your mother today?"

She blinked. "Yeah, what does that-"

"Did you take money from her?"

"No!"

"Are you lying?"

Vanessa's face went hard and sharp.

"Fiona's been paying me for some consulting work, and Stephanie contracted me to do her window displays every month and paid for some of that work upfront. I didn't take any extra money out of the budget and I didn't take anything from my mother."

She broke eye contact with me and bit her lip.

"Vanessa!"

"These clothes, okay? She gave me some clothes. But they're my old things," she gestured at her dress, the high-heeled booties she was wearing. She looked like a million bucks, because it probably cost a million bucks.

"You're mad?" she asked. "That I'm throwing a party with my own money."

"It's just...too much. A poker table and a dealer? Signature cocktails. We have more important shit to spend our money on."

Her eyes went wide and I saw the guilt punch her hard. We lived on a tight budget because all my pennies went to the lawyer now. But that was my money, not hers.

"I'm sorry," I said, trying to reign myself in. "It's your money, you can do what you want with it. I just don't need this fancy shit."

"My mom told me I'd mess this up," Ness muttered, crossing her arms over her stomach. And just like that, I could see her start to spiral in that way she did.

"Hey." I wrapped my hand around the back of her neck and squeezed just enough so that her eyes met mine.

"I'm sorry," she whispered, and I could hear the tears in her voice. "My mom just...got in my head."

"What did she say?"

"That I wasn't the right partner for you. That you need someone better than me and that I should just go home."

"Is that what you want?" I asked, forcing the words out. "To leave? Find someone better suited to your life?" I jerked my thumb back at the party. "Someone who doesn't live on a budget and likes expensive parties and-"

"No," Ness said, looking me in the eye. I could see the

truth. I felt it in the tension in her body. "No, I want what we have. I want this life."

"You're an amazing partner, Vanessa. I don't need professional card dealers and shrimp cocktail. I don't care about fancy. So you got to get it out of your head that you need to worry about impressing me. *You* impress me. You take care of our shit, you take care of our kid, you take care of me. Your parents are fucking toxic. I know it's easier said than done, but you can't let them get inside your head."

She nodded slowly, then bit her lip. "You're a good partner too, Roy."

I wasn't so sure about that. The word *love* hung in the air between us. The one thing I knew she really wanted to give or get. Or both, I wasn't really sure.

Maybe I was an asshole for making it part of the rules, but I wasn't prepared to change them. Still, there was one thing we could share.

"You just like the way I fuck you," I said, pulling her towards me and kissing her lips, softly.

"I do...I do like that," she said softly. "But I like the way you believe in me too. You make me believe in myself."

Well. That was pretty fucking...awesome.

"Can you kick all these people out so I can take you to bed?" I asked her.

"Roy, no. It's a party." The sound of laughter was pouring out of the house. "People seem to be having a good time."

"Yeah, because we're fucking feeding them shrimp," I told her. "Who doesn't have a good time when shrimp is being served? You got any more surprises I should know about? Strippers popping out of cakes? Pony rides in the back?"

"No," she said. "No more surprises. But..." she gave me

full flirty eyes. "After everyone leaves, we do have the house to ourselves tonight. All night."

I pulled her in for another kiss.

"You good?" I asked against her lips.

"So good."

"Let's get back in there before everyone eats all your shrimp."

"It's okay," she said as we walked back inside. "When you texted that you were going to be late, I made sure to put a separate dish aside just for you. I didn't want you to miss out."

Of course she did that for me. I shook my head. There was only one thing to do in repayment.

Give her a shit ton of orgasms.

20

Vanessa

The last guest left and Roy locked the door and turned off the porch light.

"You know," he said. "I hate to admit it-"

"But it was fun!" I said.

I knew it. I knew he had a good time. We played a bunch of cards games and everyone was laughing and eating the good food. It had been a stupid and over the top expense, but it had been *fun*. Roy had sat on one of the stools most of the night. He had a few beers and a few of the sliders I'd made.

Towards the end of the night though, he pulled me onto his lap, his arm around my waist, and held me there. We just talked to our friends and laughed. Never in my life had I ever belonged in a place, like I belonged in Roy Barnes' lap.

"It was," he agreed. His lips curled in a small smile, his eyes getting hot as they looked me up and down.

"Uh oh, I know that look-"

"Take off that dress."

"Here?" We were in the middle of the living room.

"You do what I want, yeah? And I want you naked. Here. Now."

I took off the belt and set it on the arm of the couch. He picked it up.

"Might come in handy," he said. Maybe I should have been nervous, but this was Roy, and everything Roy did felt good.

"I need you..." I said, as I turned my back to him so he could get the zipper that ran from the neck of the dress all the way to the top of my ass.

I smiled, thinking about what he could see.

"What the fuck is this?" he asked, his voice rough. He pushed the dress off my shoulders and then ran his finger along the black thong I was wearing. Mom had packed a bunch of my underwear too. Once upon a time, all I wore were thongs.

"La Perla," I said, looking at him over my shoulder. He was fixated on my ass.

"You were wearing this under that dress. All night?"

"Like a secret," I said.

His eyes flashed to mine. He palmed my ass and slid a hand around my throat, pulling me back against his chest so he could kiss me. It was a good kiss. An *I mean business* kiss. A *brace yourself, things are going to get dirty,* kiss.

I loved it. I loved him.

I did. It was another secret I was keeping.

I had to swallow the words a million times tonight. I told myself that I just needed to be patient, that Roy would get there. He had to. We'd come so far for him not to love me.

Unless he couldn't.

Unless I'm not the kind of woman he could love.

I wasted that money on the party. I let my mom get in my head. I...

I pushed the thoughts away, staying in the here and now with his hand shoving aside the lace of my bra, his other hand slipping down between my legs.

"You're already so wet for me," he breathed in my ear.

Always, I wanted to say. For him I was always wet.

I reached behind me and put my hand over the hard length of his erection and he pushed into my palm. "I want you on your knees," he breathed in my ear. "I want you to suck my cock tonight. Just like I taught you."

"Yes, Roy."

He groaned in his throat, turning me around. He grabbed one of my throw pillows off the couch and put it on the ground at his feet.

Wearing nothing more than black lace and my Gucci heeled booties, I got down on the pillow. He tore off his shirt and went to work on his belt buckle, the zipper of his pants. His cock sprang free and I sucked in a breath.

I fucking loved his cock.

"Open," he said, holding his dick so he could slip it into my mouth. "Wider," he whispered, and I looked up at him as my lips stretched around him.

"Suck, just the tip. Close your...yes. Fuck, just like that." I sucked the tip of his cock, licking the slit like he'd taught me. I didn't need him to tell me what to do anymore though, it was easy to see what he liked. The way he hissed and swore when I tongued him. When I used my hand to stroke the hard length of him.

"Just like that. You're so good at this. So fucking good." He curled his hand into my hair, pulling it until I gasped.

Until I moaned around his cock and the vibrations made him swear.

His thigh muscles bulged as he braced his legs out wide. He was slick with my spit and I put my hand against his stomach because I liked to feel his muscles tremble when I took him deep and held him there.

"Ness, you make me feel so fucking good. Keep it slow though, I don't want to come in your mouth."

I let his hard heavy girth slip from my mouth and looked up at him.

"I want you to."

He grunted. "No, I want to come inside you. I like it better when you come on my cock that way. For now just suck me deep and I'll tell you when to stop."

Heat pooled between my legs. I held on to his hips, pressed my hard nipples against his thigh so he knew I was turned on too, then sucked his heavy length deep into my mouth. As deep as I could. Giving him all of that wet warmth.

"Fuck, what did I do to deserve you?" he groaned.

My heart pounded. That sounded like love. Felt like love. I wanted it to be love so bad it hurt. I pulled away from his dick, stroking him with my hand, but my face turned away. I just needed a second. A second to get myself together. To not need so much from him.

Roy stepped back.

"Are you okay?" he asked. "Did I... was it too much? You need to tell me when it's not working for you. I told you that."

"No, no," I said, even though I knew my eyes looked wet. "It was good. I loved it."

He looked down at me, not angry, but with his brows furrowed.

"What's going on in that head of yours, Ness?"

Should I tell him? Could I be that honest?

Love me. Please, just love me.

"I'm sorry. I'll try-"

"Get up," he said, cutting me off. He was still stroking himself, which I thought was always kind of hot, watching him do that. Once I was on my feet he pulled me up against him, his erection squished against my belly, wet from my mouth.

"You're thinking too much," he said. "When we're doing this, you're with me. Not off in your head. With me."

I nodded, because he was right. I was thinking too much.

I was thinking about how much I wished he loved me and it was ruining our sex. And sex was one of the things he wanted from me. Sex and dinner and caring for Nora. He didn't want love. He'd been clear.

This is what I'm screwing up. Not the party. This.

He walked us back toward the couch and made me bend over one of the arms. Oooh, I thought. This again. I loved it when he did it to me from behind. He got so deep. I wiggled my butt in the air and put my weight on my forearms on the couch cushions. I waited for him to yank my thong out of the way, but-

Swap!

I jumped as his palm landed on my ass, and it took a second for my brain to register what I was feeling. A slight sting of...

Swap!

Roy slapped my other butt cheek. Not so hard. Just enough...

Swap, swap, swap.

"Talk to me, Ness," he growled. "How are you feeling?"

Like I wanted to bury my face in a pillow and scream.

Only I didn't have to because there was no one in the house besides Roy. I couldn't form a coherent thought in my head if I tried.

"More," I said and lifted myself on my toes. Offering myself up completely.

"Yeah, this will get you out of your head."

Swap. Swap.

He slipped his hand beneath me and cupped my breast and teased my nipple. Tugging it hard, then gently circling it with this thumb.

He spanked me and then rubbed away the sting. Pain and comfort. Over and over again.

I was nothing but shaking, incoherent need when he slipped his finger deep inside my pussy.

"Yes, Roy," I groaned, and tried to fuck myself back on him.

He used his other hand to twist up my hair and tugged just enough to lift my face off the couch.

"What do you want?"

"Roy, more, please more."

"You ready for my cock?"

"Yes, please."

"You like it when I fuck you?"

"Yes, please," I whispered. "I like it so much."

My hair in his fist, his other hand on my hip, he pressed me into the arm of the couch and thrust deep.

I screamed. I was so full of him, stretched and feeling every inch. My husband was a big man in that department and I loved it.

"Gonna fuck you so hard, Ness. Not holding anything back. Couldn't if I wanted to."

Please no, don't hold anything back. But I was too far gone to say the words. I felt his thighs spreading me wider.

There was no finesse. No careful love making. No technique Roy was using to prolong it, or to get me off. He was just fucking me as hard as he could and it felt insanely good. I never wanted him to stop.

"Ahhhh fuck!" I shouted, and that felt good too. "Harder, more. All of it. I want all of it!"

When he hit that spot deep inside, I knew to just let go and let that wave of feeling sweep me up. Take me over.

"Gonna come hard, Ness. You want that inside you?"

"Yes! Yes!"

I came so hard I thought I might faint. My leg got a cramp. My ears were ringing and still he kept plowing into me, holding my arms back for leverage.

"Fucking love this hot wet pussy, so fucking much. Mine. Mine."

Then his legs were shaking and he was bent over me. I could feel him coming inside of me and I clamped down my internal muscles to hold him as tight as I could, and he groaned so loud above me I felt like a freaking hero.

He owned me, but I owned him too.

He collapsed against my back, his dick still semi-hard inside me.

"I love fucking you, Ness," he muttered.

For a moment my heart stopped and joy choked me, but as fast as it came, it left. He didn't say I fucking love you. He said I love fucking you.

Those two things were worlds apart.

21

We'd finally done it. Roy and I had finally broken through. Nora's official first word, well, first words, were...*uh oh*.

They had come about totally by accident, with no coaching at all. I'd put her in her highchair, and we were doing our normal dinner routine, when she slapped her sippy cup off the tray and I said *uh oh*. Like it was nothing, she said *uh oh* back.

"It's not dadda," Roy said. "But I'll take it."

Roy and I high fived, then we taught Nora how to high five, and now she was doing it constantly.

Today was Sunday and I had convinced Roy to, wait for it...take the day off. An unheard-of event.

I had two new clients besides Fiona, Stephanie, and technically Jackson, who I was working for at the bar. I'd given him my hourly rate, told him what he was going to pay me, and he'd smiled at me like he was proud of me.

It was heady stuff.

So I had some money coming in, which meant Roy didn't have to work seven days a week. He balked at first about using the money I earned for us, but I reminded him that we had decided to commit ourselves to this marriage. For Nora's sake. Which meant his money was my money and my money was his money.

The account for the lawyer was growing. We all had good winter clothes.

So, we sat down, crunched some numbers, and decided after over twelve years of fishing seven days a week, weather permitting, he was due to have one day off a week.

"What the fuck am I going to do with a day off?" he'd asked when I first suggested it.

Today it was time to show him what he was missing.

"Are you ready for the Barnes' Family Day of Fun?!" I asked everyone.

Roy was sitting at the kitchen table, drinking his coffee and shaking his head at me. But Nora had her arms in the air, sensing my excitement.

"First, we're going to Pappas' for breakfast so we can show off Nora's new language skills."

"It's *uh oh*, not Shakespeare," Roy muttered. But when Nora held out her hand for a high five, he gave her one.

"Then we're going to the...park!"

"Bah!" The park was her favorite place.

"Then I thought we would take a drive out to the Peterson farm," I said, oh so casually.

"The Peterson farm? Out in Chester? Why would we go out there?" Roy asked.

"Well, I have it on good authority from Stephanie that they recently had a litter of puppies, and I was thinking..."

"No," Roy said.

"No?" I asked. "But I would be home to take care of it, and what little girl doesn't want a puppy?"

"Nora, do you want a puppy?" Roy asked her.

"Bah!"

"That means no," Roy said.

I walked over and plopped into Roy's lap. He grunted, but put his arm around my waist, holding me close.

"Give me one good reason why we can't get a puppy?"

He held up his hand and started counting. "They're a ton of work, it costs money to feed them, we don't know if the kid is allergic, you have to walk it when it rains and snows, they fart all the time, and they get old and die and you never get over it."

"Awww," I said, kissing his face. Pressing my breasts against his chest because that always cheered him up. "What was his name?"

"Buddy," he admitted. "I had him from six to nineteen and he broke my fucking heart."

"But you loved him. That's the part you have to remember." I placed a hand over his heart.

He arched his eyebrow at me. "Did you have a pet growing up?"

"Are you kidding me? Let an animal into any one of the Dumont properties? That was a hard no."

"Then how do you know all that shit about the love staying with you?"

I shrugged. "I love sad animal movies and that's what they always say."

He grunted.

"Let's do this, we'll think about it over breakfast and

then there will obviously be some dogs at the park. Nora loves to pet them and I haven't seen any type of an allergic reaction. Then, once you've seen her play with one, we can decide."

He squeezed my hip. "Why do I get the sense this is a trap?"

It was totally a trap.

~

I LOVED WALKING INTO PAPPAS', because the second I stepped through the door, people said hello. Like we were in a TV show. Madame Za sat at the counter chatting away with Georgie, who was sporting fabulous pink eye shadow today. They both lifted their hands and waved. Annie Piedmont from the book store was also at the counter reading something on her Kindle. She said hello.

Levi and Matthew, who I had gotten to know better the night of the poker party, were sitting in a booth together shoveling down pancakes. Roy lifted a chin in their direction and Levi lifted a hand in acknowledgement.

It was a typical Sunday morning at the diner with all the locals, and it just felt like home.

"Vanessa!" Lola called out, as she took plates of omelets from the kitchen to a booth in the corner. "Take the first open booth you see and I'll bring out coffee. Then I need to find something we can drop on the floor so we can hear Nora say *uh oh*!"

Madame Za turned around on the swivel seat. "Oh my. Did I hear that right? The child can now speak. How exciting. Our little lost girl is growing up."

"She says *uh oh*," Roy grunted. "That's it."

"Well, it's a start. How are you doing, Vanessa? Fiona

tells me your business is already growing. I do my readings primarily under a tent in the town square so I won't be needing your services, but my sister is thinking about moving here permanently and opening a crystal shop. What do you think of that idea?"

"Ooh, I love crystals. They're so pretty."

"And have so many different properties that can impact our auroras. Healing, love, energy."

"Geezus," Roy said into my ear. I elbowed him in the stomach.

"Absolutely," I said. "Next time I come to town, I'll bring some business cards I had printed and drop one off for you. Then if your sister wants some help or ideas, she can give me a call. The first two hours of any consultation are free."

"Excellent. Look at you, Roy. Don't you just have the sweetest little family? I told you one day you would open up to what the Universe could provide."

"And today we're going to get a puppy," I added gleefully.

"No, we are not. I said I would *think* about it," Roy said.

Madame Za clapped her hands together. "A puppy!"

"I know, right?"

Roy grabbed a booster from the stack in the corner and took it over to an empty booth. Nora and I followed.

It was late October now, so the weather was getting decidedly chilly. I pulled off Nora's coat and opened my carry bag which had all the Nora necessities. I started with a wooden spoon and a bath toy she stole on a recent trip to Bullseye.

"You're a real buzz kill on my puppy news," I told him.

"Because we're not getting a puppy," he said. "My cold hard heart cannot be turned by cuteness."

"Your cold heart is constantly turned by cuteness," I said, as I batted my eyelashes at him.

He laughed and The Barnes' Family Day of Fun was off to a fantastic start.

"Hey guys," Lola said, appearing by our table with a coffee pot in her hand. Her hair was up in a ponytail, she wore jeans and a long-sleeved Pappas' t-shirt. I was wearing basically the same thing without the Pappas' logo.

"Hey. I didn't really have a chance to catch up with you at the party," I said. "But how was your trip? That was the longest you were ever away from Calico Cove."

"By like a mile," she agreed as she filled our coffee mugs. "It was great. Jackson wanted to show me absolutely everything in Boston, all his favorite places. Then we visited a bunch of Shells restaurants, and that was exciting too. Then we went down the coast for a little bit, but after a few weeks, I have to say, I just wanted to come home, to my place, my people. You know?"

I did. I knew exactly what she meant. I looked at Roy out of the corner of my eyes to see if he was nodding along, but he was looking at the menu.

Since the night of the party, I'd pushed those words... the words I couldn't say, and probably shouldn't even think, as far away as I could. I focused on the day to day life we were building, and I tried very hard not to want anything more from Roy than what he was already giving me.

"You know what you want?"

"Pancakes!" I said. A little too loudly. I really loved pancakes. No wonder my mom wouldn't let me have them growing up, I would have wanted them at every meal.

"Bah!" Nora screamed, repeating my excitement.

"Okay, that's pancakes for the both of you. I got some fresh blueberries in just yesterday. Do you want to make those blueberry pancakes?"

Nora had never had blueberries in pancakes and I didn't want her to spit them out at the diner if she didn't like them.

"Do two blueberry, two plain just in case she freaks."

"Got it. And Roy? Your usual?"

"Yeah, thanks, Lola."

Lola left us and we sugared our coffees and pushed the forks and knives out of Nora's reach.

Roy wasn't big with small talk, and I never felt like the silence between us was ever awkward. It had always been that way, even that summer we first met, after his dad had passed. Roy had needed a lot of silence back then, and someone who was willing to sit with him in it.

"I was thinking about something," Roy said.

"What to name our puppy?" I teased.

"I swear to God, Ness..."

"Okay, fine. I'll back off. For now."

"We're married and we've agreed we're going to stay that way for the foreseeable future."

I wasn't crazy about the word *foreseeable*. It sounded too much like he was still-keeping his options open regarding me.

"That's my plan," I said cautiously.

My plan. Our plan. To stay together. For Nora.

"What do you think about changing your name?"

I blinked. Of all the things I expected him to say, that was definitely not one of them.

"You don't like my name?"

He gave me his *don't be ridiculous* look. "To my last name. Vanessa Barnes. I'm thinking you can put the socialite, Vanessa Dumont, to rest."

Vanessa Barnes. Mrs. Vanessa Barnes. I'd only thought about it a hundred million times since that day I told my mother I was a Barnes.

"I like that idea," I said, smiling at him. "I like that idea a lot."

"Good," he grunted, like it didn't mean much to him either way, but I understood Roy speak. He didn't say or do much that wasn't meaningful. Because if he didn't care about it, it wasn't worth any of his energy. For him to want this for me, it meant something to him.

"You're going to need to get your birth certificate," he said. "From your parents."

"It's here at the Dumont Estate," I said. "I was going to need it for..."

"Fuckface?"

I nodded.

"I'll go with you," he said. "To pick it up."

"Okay, but not today. I don't want to ruin Barnes' Family Day of Fun."

Lola served us our breakfast orders, and both Roy and I watched as Nora ate bite after bite of pancakes filled with blueberries. Not once spitting it out.

"Do you think they make vegetable pancakes?" I asked Roy.

"I can't think of anything more disgusting."

After we finished, Roy paid the bill and I gathered Nora's stolen toys and kitchen utensils. Together, we were headed out the door when it opened and a stranger stepped inside.

Nobody in the diner looked up and said hello to him. He was young, maybe twenty something. Dark hair that was shaved on either side of his head, but long over his forehead. Both arms covered in tattoo sleeves. Revealed by a distressed short sleeved t-shirt.

His gaze darted around the diner like he was looking for something. Or maybe he was just a little twitchy. I shouldn't be one to judge so quickly, but when his gaze landed on me, I had this tingly feeling in the back of my neck like something was wrong. Then his gaze switched to Nora, and my instinct was to protect her face as we walked past him.

That feeling didn't go away once we were outside the diner. I looked back through the window and saw that he was still looking at us.

"What?" Roy asked, when he saw I was stopped and looking back at the diner.

"Nothing," I said. The young man had looked away and I was seeing danger when there probably was none. "On to the park!"

∼

Roy

I WAS A SUCKER. All my tough guy talk, and all it took was watching Nora chase around a dog at the park for me to cave like a house of cards.

Now I was standing next to a pen of Golden Retriever puppies, smiling like I might never have smiled before, as Nora laughed and played with the puppies. She would stand up, only for three of them to pounce on her and knock her over, which she thought was the most hilarious thing ever.

I lifted her out of the pen before they smothered her with puppy love.

"Can you say dog?" Ness asked her, pulling on her foot to get her attention. "Doggy, dog."

"Dog!" Nora declared and pointed. "Dog, dog, dog!"

Well, holy shit. Vanessa and I looked at each other with wide eyes.

"That's my girl," I said, bursting with pride. Nora put her hand against my cheek and said: "Dog!"

"No, I'm dadda." I pointed to my chest. "Dadda."

"Dog!"

Vanessa thought this was hilarious. "She'll get there, I promise," she said. "Now what are we going to do with this adorable girl who clearly *needs* a dog."

"Mr. Peterson," I called out to the farmer who had given us space to play with the puppies. Peterson wasn't a dog breeder. His goal was just to breed his two goldens together, for more farm dogs, but he was willing to part with two from the littler.

"When will these puppies be ready for adoption?"

"They get weaned at eight weeks," he said, pushing a faded John Deere ball cap up on his head. "So they're about a week away."

"We'll be back," I told him.

"Good to know they're going to a nice family," Peterson said.

I nodded, even as my chest tightened with that feeling again.

Family.

My family. That now included a kid, a wife and soon to be, a dog.

Immediately I was flooded by all the ways that could change. The ways they could be taken away from me. Things that didn't make sense. Accidents. Vanessa could decide she wanted to go back to her family. She could get so successful as a designer, my life as a fisherman wasn't good enough anymore. Someone could come and claim Nora. CPS could decide the life I was giving her was garbage.

"Roy?" Vanessa put her hand on my back and I sucked in a breath. "Are you okay?"

"Fine," I said, and leaned in to kiss her. Needing her. She hummed against my lips.

Barnes' Family Day of Fun. Family.

It didn't need to be a bad word. It didn't need to be scary.

"Dog." Nora patted my cheek.

"Hi Nora."

"Dog, dog, dog," she chatted.

"Dadda. Dad. Daddy," I tried.

"Dog, dog, dog."

I shook my head and that irrational fear crept over me, whispering garbage thoughts in my ear.

Roy, you're too fucking happy. That's usually when everything gets taken away.

Not this time, I decided. Not this time.

I don't have to be afraid of this. I can have this.

IT WAS late afternoon when we finally got back to the house. "For a day off, I'm freaking tired."

"I never said Family Fun Day wouldn't be work. Nora and I take our playing very seriously. Don't we, baby?"

She was babbling in the back seat not paying attention to us at all. I think her head was still back there with the puppies.

I pulled into the driveway and stopped. There was a car already parked. A car I knew.

"Why would Mrs. Hughes be here?" Ness asked me. "On a Sunday? Is this one of those surprise visits?"

A cold chill dropped down into the center of my gut.

"Let's go see what she wants."

I got out of the car and let Vanessa handle Nora. Just as I approached the car, Mrs. Hughes got out.

I knew immediately from the expression on her face there was trouble. Of course there was. Hadn't I just been thinking about how damn happy I was?

"Mrs. Hughes," I greeted her.

"Roy," she said with a brief smile. "I've got some news."

"Figured. Let's go inside."

We all went inside the house. Vanessa asked Mrs. Hughes if she wanted some tea, which seemed ridiculous. Except Mrs. Hughes said yes, and now I was putting the kettle on the stove as Ness got Nora out of her coat and set her down on the floor to play. Once the kid was distracted and Mrs. Hughes had her tea, Ness and I sat on the couch together to hear the news.

I had this thought that I should take Vanessa's hand. Hold it. Instead, I crossed both arms across my chest.

"I'll get right to it. Nora's father has come forward."

I'm her father.

"What does that mean?" Ness asked. "If there is a father in the picture, where has he been?"

"He claims he didn't know about Nora's mother's passing. As soon as he found out, he contacted social services and now... here we are."

"There was no father listed on the birth certificate," I said calmly. "I checked."

"Any claim Mr. Anderson has on Nora will only be validated after a paternity test has been conducted."

"So let me get this straight, a man-" Vanessa began.

"Gil Anderson," Mrs. Hughes supplied.

"This guy, Anderson, says he's the father, even though he wasn't listed on the birth certificate, wasn't part of Diane's life. But now what? He wants Nora back?" Vanessa put her hand on my leg and I flinched away. I was so angry I couldn't be touched. I wanted to stand up. I wanted to grab Nora and get her the fuck out of here.

"He hasn't brought up the matter of custody," Mrs. Hughes said. "He's just concerned with his daughter's welfare and wants to make sure she's being well taken care of."

"Well, she is," Ness snapped. "She's been very well taken care of. Roy, tell her. We're saving money for a family lawyer so we can make it official. We're a family."

My brain told me to stretch my hand out and put it on her knee. To comfort her because she needed comfort. But if I unlocked my arms, I thought my guts might just spill out onto the floor. My arms were the only thing keeping me together.

"What are the next steps?" I asked her.

"He wants to meet you. Both. And Nora, of course."

"No, he doesn't sniff Nora until I see the results of a paternity test," I said.

"That's fair. But if you decline his offer to meet, things go immediately to court. If you meet...perhaps there's a way to stop that from happening. "

I could feel Vanessa staring at me. I could feel her expectation. I was going to make this all right. It was what the hero did. I needed to rescue us from this shit situation.

Only I didn't know how.

"We'll meet him," Vanessa said.

Mrs. Hughes nodded, but her expression was grim. "Roy, Vanessa, I just need you to be prepared. The rules are pretty clear about this. If Mr. Anderson is Nora's biological father, and he chooses to make a claim for custody, in the state of Maine I can tell you, judges are more likely to lean in favor of the biological parent. You understand?"

"Oh my god," Vanessa whispered, "We could lose her?"

"I understand," I said, cutting them both off. "Are we done here? Nora needs her dinner. It's been a busy day for us."

"Yes, that's all I have. I'll set up a meeting for this week?"

"Fine," I said.

Mrs. Hughes stood and pulled her coat on.

"I'm sorry about this Roy," she said as she stepped out onto the porch. "You've done very well by that little girl so far. Don't think it's gone unnoticed."

As soon as Mrs. Hughes left, Vanessa collapsed into my arms and I held onto her like she was going to be taken away, too. Like everything was going to be taken away.

22

Vanessa

I woke up to Roy's hand slipping under my shorts, pushing them over my ass, down my legs. His fingers sure and knowing. His breath hot on my neck.

"Roy?" I whispered.

"I need you, Ness."

"Yes," I said. I needed him too. I wanted him to fuck me until I didn't feel afraid. Until I stopped running the worst-case scenarios through my head.

"Shh...."

We were on our sides, his chest to my back. He pushed my leg up over his and slid into me from behind. I moaned, back against him. I wrapped my fingers around his wrist, his palm flat between my breasts, and held on. I waited for his voice in my ear, telling me I felt so good. That I made him feel good.

But he was silent.

"Roy?" I whispered, shifting so I could look at him. He turned his face away, like he couldn't meet my eyes.

It was him, so it was good and delicious and I could feel my climax building.

But I wanted the words. I wanted the connection. I needed the connection.

"Roy, kiss me."

I reached back, trying to pull him down towards me.

He resisted. Just a tug of his neck, but I knew with that small gesture that he was rejecting me at some level.

"Stop," I said.

Maybe I should have just let him finish. Maybe I should have just enjoyed the orgasm he seemed so determined to give me, but that's not what I wanted. That's not what we'd promised to each other.

"Stop," I said again, a little louder.

Roy held himself still inside me. Hard and throbbing and that alone felt so good, but it wasn't enough.

"What's wrong?" he panted.

"You're not with me," I said, turning so he slipped out of me. "You're off in your head and you're not with me. You don't like it when I do that during sex. I don't like it either."

Roy rolled onto his back, his arm across his eyes.

"Sorry. I just..."

I curled up against him. "I know. You're scared for tomorrow."

Mrs. Hughes had set up the meeting. We were meeting Gil Anderson at Pappas' tomorrow morning at eleven am, after the morning rush of customers so we would hopefully have some privacy.

"I'm scared, Ness. I'm really scared."

God, if I could take this on for him, I would.

He turned to me. "Did I hurt you?"

"Of course not."

"Come up here and sit on my face, I'll make you come."

No, I wasn't going to do that. Roy was stressed and worried, and had been for days, with good reason.

Nora had been part of my life for two months, and the idea of losing her was soul crushing. He'd been raising her on his own for over a year. There could be no words for the fear he was experiencing.

"I just can't sleep," he said, staring up at the ceiling. "Every time I close my eyes..." he couldn't even finish the sentence. He ran his hands over his face. I'd never seen him like this. My hero, Roy Barnes, was scared. And he was at a loss.

I curled my hand down around his cock, still half hard, and at my touch he only got harder. "Let me help you."

"Ness, you don't have to."

"This is for you. Let me make you feel good."

I slid under the covers, curling my hand around his cock, still slick from being inside of me. When I put him in my mouth, I was going to taste him and me.

Us.

I didn't hesitate. I sucked him in my mouth and listened as he groaned. I felt him push down the covers so he could watch me. I worked him with my tongue and my lips and then gently rolled his balls with my fingers.

He groaned and thrust his hips, fucking himself deep into my mouth to the back of my throat.. I gagged, but tried to hide it.

"Fuck, don't do that," he said, tugging on my hair until I was forced to release him.

"It's okay," I said, wiping spit from my mouth.

"It's not okay," he snapped. "You don't let me choke you like that when you don't like it."

I stroked his shaft, played with the head of his dick with my tongue. "Oh I like it. I like it when you get out of control," I told him. "Like you can't help yourself."

"You're killing me, Ness," he said hoarsely.

I sank my mouth down over him again.

"Ah fuck, baby that feels so good. You do me so good."

There was that connection. The words of praise I needed.

I knew at least in that moment he was back with me. That we were in this together.

THAT MORNING NORA woke with a stuffy nose. No fever that I could tell, just a runny nose and a lot of sneezing.

"Oh no, baby. You might have a cold," I said, as I lifted her out of her crib.

"Oh no," she repeated, rubbing her stuffed nose.

My baby.

I swallowed the fear and went about our normal routine. I wasn't surprised to see Roy sitting at the breakfast table already. Despite coming hard in my mouth, then taking time to get me off with his fingers, I knew he'd slept restlessly.

It was nearly nine in the morning, so he'd probably already been out to the docks and back.

"Nora has a cold," I said, setting her down in her chair.

"Fever?" he asked me.

"No. Just some gross snot."

He grunted.

"Maybe we should cancel the meeting," I said. I got Nora some yogurt and Roy poured me a coffee. "I don't want to leave Nora if she's sick."

"We're getting this done, Ness. Putting it off doesn't keep her with us."

"Fine," I huffed.

"I'll go alone, if you don't want to deal with it."

It was on the tip of my tongue to tell him yes, that's exactly what I wanted.

Only that was the cowardly way out, and if I was going to be Nora's mother going forward, then she deserved more than a coward. She deserved a lioness.

And Roy deserved someone who would do the hard things right beside him.

"No, I'm going with you. We're Nora's parents."

He cupped his hand around my neck and kissed my forehead. "Yeah, we are."

WE SAT side by side in the booth at Pappas'. We told Lola we were meeting someone from CPS, so she just kept filling our coffee cups and shooting us worried glances without asking too many questions.

It wasn't quite eleven when the door opened.

Instantly, I recognized him. The stranger from Sunday who had watched me and Nora so intently.

He wasn't dressed any better today. Distressed jeans, a worn faded t-shirt. It was fifty degrees outside but he wasn't wearing a coat. It wasn't because he wasn't cold either. His thin frame seemed to shiver the second he entered the warm diner.

He slid into the other side of the booth. He smelled like cold air and cigarettes.

"Hey, I'm Gil Anderson," he stretched out his hand toward Roy, but Roy didn't take it.

"Mrs. Hughes will be here in," Roy looked down at his watch. "ten minutes. We should wait to say anything until she's here."

"Nah, man. That's why I came early." He checked out the area around us, and then leaned forward and dropped his voice. "So look, we can make this go away. If I take a paternity test, it's going to show I'm the kid's dad. Diane and I had been together...what...like six months when she got pregnant. She was all about keeping it. I wanted nothing to do with it. Not really parent material, if you get my drift."

"Yeah. I get it," Roy said. "Then why are we here?"

Gil jerked his chin in my direction. "The story I told the old lady was true. I only just heard about Diane offing herself, so I checked in with CPS to see what happened with the kid. Curious, I guess. They said she'd left you custody. I remembered she'd mentioned a cousin who was a fisherman or some such shit. Figured okay, cool, kid's fine. Then a couple of months later, and I see you both on the news. Roy Barnes, Diane's cousin, and Vanessa Dumont, holding my kid. I think wow, looks like the kid is going to come into money someday. Dumont heiress money, right? Figured I should get paid a little something for my part."

A wave of shame washed over me as I realized what this was. Why this person was here, now, after seventeen months.

The viral video of me shopping at Bullseye. The reporters on our doorstep.

I clapped my hand over my mouth feeling like I was going to vomit.

This was my fault. This scum of the earth, sitting in front of me, didn't want Nora. Or anything to do with her. All he wanted was money.

Money I didn't have. Because I wasn't a Dumont heiress anymore.

I did this. This was my fault. I put Nora in jeopardy because I made Roy save me. I couldn't breathe. I wanted to scream.

"How much?" Roy asked.

"Fifty K. That's worth my time as a sperm donor, isn't it?"

"What guarantee do we have, that if we pay you now, you won't be back for more?" Roy asked him. How could he be so calm? How was he not strangling this asshole with his bare hands? How was he not looking at me with scorn and hatred?

"I'll sign whatever waiver you need me to."

"A waiver?" I choked out. "She's a little girl."

Anderson shrugged. "Not my problem. I'm just looking for what's fair."

Fair? None of this was fair!

The door to the diner opened and Mrs. Hughes stepped inside, looking around until she spotted us.

"We cool, right?" Gil asked Roy.

"Yeah," Roy said, like he'd done this a million times. "We're cool."

"Well, I see you're all here," Mrs. Hughes said, as she approached us. "Great, we can have a nice chat and just get to know each other for this first meeting."

"Sounds great. I'm really impressed with Roy and Vanessa already," Gil said. "They seem like they really care about my daughter."

I reached for the silverware that was on the table and dropped it into my lap. Under the table, I quickly unwrapped it and found the fork. Then, as hard as I could, I pressed the fork into my thigh. Through my jeans, I felt tines press into my skin, the pain radiating out through me.

Because it was the only way I was going to be able to sit through the rest of this meeting without screaming and crying.

I sat there wearing my polite smile. The smile I'd learned to get me through pain. Through pinches and hard twists of skin. Through cruel comments and a childhood without love. Nora was never ever going to know a childhood like that.

It didn't matter what I had to do, I wasn't letting Gil Anderson get his hands on her.

~

THE MEETING LASTED NO MORE than fifteen minutes. I could tell Mrs. Hughes wasn't happy with Roy's silence. Mine too for that matter, but Gil was a skilled conman.

He talked about Diane, Roy's cousin. Their relationship and how it ended before the baby was born. He'd said she was desperate to be a mother, but she struggled with depression even when they were together.

It was impossible to know what was real and what wasn't. How Roy held his temper, I had no idea. Not with a fork to the thigh, I was sure.

"I need to get back to work," Roy finally said, cutting off Gil when he'd started in on another story about Diane.

"Oh, of course," Mrs. Hughes said. She shuffled out of the booth and stood up. "Should we talk about next steps?"

"I think I would like some time to think about things," Gil said with a smarmy smile. "This meeting was really important, but I need to consider what's best for my daughter. If I could have your contact information?"

"Ness," Roy said. "Give him your number."

I rattled it off.

Then Roy walked away without so much as a goodbye to anyone.

"You have to understand," Mrs. Hughes said to Gil. "He's raised her for the past year. That bond is obviously very strong."

"Sure, yeah, I get that. I don't want to do anything to hurt this whole family thing you've got going, Vanessa. I just want to make sure I make the right decision."

I swallowed hard to stop myself from screaming. Instead, I nodded, smiled, and followed Roy out the diner door.

I could hear Lola calling out to me, probably saying goodbye, but I couldn't turn around. I couldn't let her see the devastation on my face.

I needed to fix this. I needed to fix this for Roy.

It was the only thing I could do.

23

Roy

Once we were in the car she turned to me, but I already knew what she was going to say.

"Don't."

"Roy..." her whisper was ravaged. Her pain was all over her face and I couldn't look at her.

"I don't want to hear it, Vanessa. I really don't."

I needed to check my rage. I needed to check every emotion I had right now, because it wasn't going to do anyone any good. Not me, not Ness and certainly not Nora.

"You have to let me say this is *my* fault. I did this to you. I have to fix it." Her eyes were filling with tears.

I reached over and cupped my hand behind her neck, tugging her toward me.

"You didn't do shit. That fucking blackmailing asshole did this, Ness. Not. You. You didn't ask to be Vanessa Dumont, you didn't ask to have some teenagers take a video of you while you were shopping, and you sure as shit didn't know that asshole was going to put two and two together."

"We have to pay him," she whispered. "We'll just pay him and he'll go away. Before he even takes the paternity test."

I turned on the car and pulled away from the curb. Deep breath in. Deep breath out. I shoved all my fear, all my fury, into something manageable. Something I could live with.

"We're not paying him anything. We're going to get Nora and then we're going home. Tomorrow I'll come back into town and talk to Bobby about our options. Pretty certain blackmailing someone over custody is illegal."

Ness was shaking her head. "He'll just deny it. There's no proof. All this can be solved with money."

"Spoken like a true Dumont."

She sucked in a wounded breath and I knew I'd gone too far, but I was in it now.

"There's no money," I said. "You know that. The account for the lawyer barely has five grand in it."

She folded her arms over her chest and closed her mouth. I could tell just looking at her profile, she was wrecked, but she was also thinking.

"Don't you do it, Ness. Don't you even suggest it."

"I haven't said anything," she snapped at me. "But you know that's the easiest answer here. My mother is still at the estate. I'll ask her to give me the money. I won't even talk to my dad."

"And she'll give it to you without strings, will she? Just open up the old purse and count out fifty grand?" I demanded. I stopped at a stop sign and turned to her. "Or will she demand that you divorce me and go back to Boston? Maybe she'll ask you to apologize to your father – who, if you don't remember, smacked the shit-"

"Stop it!" she snapped.

"That money will come with strings and you know it!"

"That money will keep our baby girl safe!" Ness folded over in her seat. Her head in her hands. "I can't stand this. I can't stand that anything bad would ever happen to her. We have to fight!"

"We're going to fight," I pushed back. "With the law. No one is taking Nora anywhere. But I'm not sacrificing you to save Nora."

"Why not?" she said, gesturing with her hands like I was insane not to take the path of least resistance.

"Because you're my fucking *wife!*"

At least she didn't argue with that. We pulled up in front of the bakery and I turned off the car.

"No one can see this on us, Ness. We have to be chill."

She nodded and wiped her hers. Tucked her hair back. Got herself together. "I'll go in and get her. Wait here."

It made sense. If we both went inside, there would be chatter and bullshitting. If Ness told them I was waiting for them in the car and we had to get home, she would make it quick.

When the car door closed behind her I wanted to shout. I wanted to scream louder than any man ever has. I was so close to having it all and it was all slipping through my hands.

I didn't want to resent her fucking Dumont name. I didn't. But my life would have been so much freaking simpler if she'd just been born Vanessa Smith. Of the nobody Smiths.

Except she wasn't, and I had to remind myself again that it wasn't her fault.

I would find the answer to this problem and I would protect my family. There was no other choice.

∽

The Next Day
Vanessa

I SAT on the couch watching Nora play with her stuffed bunny. The bunny was threadbare and ragged and I washed it every few days. Sooner or later it was going to fall to pieces.

Just like everything else.

Roy had left for his meeting with Bobby, and even though he'd only just left, it still felt like time had come to a screeching halt.

"Dog?" Nora said, holding up the bunny to me.

I shook my head. "No, baby girl. That's a bunny. Can you say bunny?"

"Dog."

It was silly, but she was so freaking cute I almost started to cry. I came into her life, and because I did, people thought she was some kind of commodity. Something to be traded for cash. Nora was the most precious, most priceless thing in the universe. The idea that Gil only asked for fifty thousand was laughable. When I would have paid all the money my family has made over a life time.

I stood up and started pacing again, feeling like I was going to crawl out of my skin.

Roy felt confident Bobby could help us. But I knew there was nothing the sheriff would be able to do without proof. We should have seen this coming and recorded the conversation we had with Gil, but he'd blindsided us.

I'd gotten used to good people doing good things in this life I'd made with Roy, I'd forgotten all the old lessons from my years as a Dumont.

Money is King. Greed brings out the worst in people, and everyone deep down is greedy.

The knock on the front door startled me.

"Dog?" Nora asked.

"No, it's not a dog," I said. I was cautious as I approached the door. What if Gil had decided to get more aggressive and was here to physically take Nora away?

Over my dead body, I decided.

"Who is it?" I called through the door.

"Vanessa, it's me. Lola said something weird happened at the diner yesterday. She wanted me to check up on you."

Jackson.

He'd made a new life without a penny of our family money. He'd turned his back on the name and created something new and successful. He had love. He had happiness. My brother could help me figure this out.

Jackson took one look at me and pulled me into his arms. He wore a wool coat and smelled like the ocean, Fall, and a little bit like pancake syrup and french fries. Lola had rubbed off on him.

"Are you okay?" he asked.

"I just really need a big brother right now." I said into his chest as he squeezed me tight.

"Lola said you and Roy had some meeting, and when you left you looked crushed. What's going on?"

"Oh, Jackson," I sobbed. "It's all my fault."

AFTER I'D MANAGED to calm down, give Nora a snack, and fill Jackson in on everything that happened with Gil, I was able to think clearly again.

"Roy thinks we should be above board with this and

handle it legally, but money is the easiest answer," I said. "Anderson just wants to get paid."

Jackson sighed. "Ness, I agree but... Roy's right. Asking that much money from Mom or Dad is going to come with strings. The first of which will be you moving back home to Boston. Is that what you want?"

No. It was the last thing I wanted. I was Roy's wife. The way he'd shouted it in the car – it gave me a little faith that he believed that too. I was his and he was mine.

But it wasn't love, was it?

For Roy, every single part of our relationship was for Nora. He saved me so I could take care of her. He married me to help with CPS. He even fucked me so the marriage would be more real in order to get custody.

But the only thing that would really make it real was love. Until then we were just playing house.

It was an arrangement. A marriage of convenience.

"I was so freaking happy here, Jackson. Like really happy... for the first time in my life. So no, I don't want to go away. But Roy can't lose Nora. She's his family and he's already lost his family once. He can't go through that again. I won't let him."

Jackson nodded and smiled a little sadly. "You love him."

"With everything I am."

"Well, then it's lucky for you I have some news," Jackson said with a little gleam in his eye. "I know a thing or two about outsmarting bad people. And you, my sister, have options you're not even aware of."

"Jackson, I am stressed out to the max right now, so if this is bad news..."

"Oh, quite the opposite, Sis. It's about the CCIB."

Roy

"You didn't record the conversation?" Bobby asked me.

We were in his office in the municipal building where the Sheriff's offices were, on the second floor. People were in and out, but Bobby's office was private. He hadn't been on the job that long, so he still had a stack of boxes in the corner. But there was a wall of pictures behind his desk. A couple with his two dads. His sister and his nieces. There was an old high school yearbook picture of him and Mari – they'd been voted Most Goody-Two-Shoes their senior year. Not sure why he'd wanted that framed.

"No, I told you. It didn't even occur to me."

Which in hindsight was stupid. I should have known someone coming out of the woodwork after all this time would be suspicious – it was my exact fear. No one decides eighteen months later, after walking away from a kid, that he suddenly wants her back. Every gut instinct I had told me this claim wasn't legit, but I was too worried to think clearly and take precautions.

"Okay, well, he's made his intentions clear. We know this is a shakedown. What we need is proof. Maybe another call to work out the logistics of the payoff. We can record that."

I frowned. "You think he'd be that stupid? Now that I know what he really wants?"

Bobby lifted his hands as if to suggest it was better than nothing. My phone buzzed. It was Vanessa. She'd buzzed me about two hours earlier, but I'd let it go. I needed to be focused on this.

I sent her a quick text telling her I'd call her back in a minute.

"Fine. I can try," I said. "But can't we do a background check on him? The guy has to have something in his past that would make him unfit to be a parent."

"Yeah, I could run a check on him, but as long as he's actually the biological parent, it won't matter. You know how many people out there are unfit to be parents, but still they're raising kids?"

"I don't like this," I said. "I don't like that a sting operation is my only out here."

"You could take him to court," Bobby said. "I'm no legal expert in this area, but there are grounds for terminating a biological parent's legal rights. This guy has been out of Nora's life for eighteen months. You could possibly make a case for abandonment."

Although Gil could argue that he hadn't known about the child until recently. Would a judge see through all that? I didn't know, but it seemed as uncertain as setting up a sting operation and recording it.

There could be no uncertainty when it came to Nora.

"I'll think about it. I need to talk it over with Ness. We should make this decision together."

"Yeah, I'm pretty sure that's what being married and being parents is all about. At least that's how it works with my parents."

I didn't have the kind of role model Bobby had growing up. His dads had been supportive and always present. Bobby used to joke about how much they talked. When his sister recently got a divorce, they'd tried to get the entire family into counseling.

My dad made his own decisions every time, never told anyone about them. Certainly didn't worry about what I thought about them. Or how I'd be impacted. And maybe it was too easy for me to revert to those same habits. I'd told

Vanessa how it was going to be without really hearing her out.

Last night we'd gone to bed without a word between us. It hadn't felt right.

It hadn't felt right leaving her with Nora this morning either. We should all be here together. Fighting this together.

The fault was mine. I was the one putting up the walls around myself, especially when it came to Ness. She'd left me to go back to her family once, and the harsh reality was I was scared she would do it again.

She would tell herself it was for the right reasons. She would tell herself she was doing this for Nora. For me.

I'd shouted at her and then shut her down. I needed to apologize to her and convince her of how much I needed her. Then I had to sort out my legal rights when it came to Nora.

Which meant I needed help.

"You said you're not a legal expert," I told Bobby. "Then find me someone who is. I need the best damn family lawyer in the state."

"That I can do."

I had five grand in that account. That had to buy us a few hours of legal advice.

I stood up and shook his hand. Getting a lawyer felt like a more solid plan. I had no idea how I was going to pay for it, but I would worry about that shit later. Right now all I wanted was to go home and be with my family.

My family, who I wasn't going to let anyone, certainly not someone as depraved as Gil Anderson, destroy.

I was just coming out of the building heading toward my truck when my phone rang again. I assumed it was Ness checking in to see what was happening, but saw Mrs. Hughes name on the screen.

"Mrs. Hughes," I answered, putting the phone to my ear.

"Hello, Roy. I'm calling to ask how this all happened."

I stopped walking. "How what all happened?"

"The termination agreement," she said, as if I should understand what that meant.

"I'm sorry, Mrs. Hughes. I have no idea what you mean."

"Oh. I assumed...Judge Webb called our office to let me know. Gil Anderson filed for a termination of his parental rights. He's agreed to allow you to retain legal guardianship of Nora. Which I have to say pleases me very much. You and Vanessa seem very committed to each other and that little girl. I thought maybe you had another conversation with Mr. Anderson that I wasn't aware of, but I suppose he did this of his own free will. Congratulations, Roy."

"Yeah. Thanks," I muttered, then ended the call.

How the fuck...?

There was only one answer. She did it.

Vanessa Dumont did what Vanessa Dumont does, she went back to her family for the money.

24

Vanessa

I heard the truck pull up into the driveway and I couldn't wait. Nora was upstairs napping, so I opened the front door and ran out to greet Roy with my news. The envelope Jackson had just dropped off was clutched in my hand.

"Roy! You're never going to believe this-" I said as he got out of his truck.

"I'm surprised you're still here," he said sharply. His brows were drawn together, his face more severe than I'd seen in years.

He was worried, I told myself, but he didn't have to be anymore. Nora was ours and we could make everything official now.

"Why wouldn't I be here?"

"I thought your parents would have locked you away by now. Put you in front of the nearest judge to divorce me."

"What are you talking about?"

"I know what he did," Roy snapped. "Mrs. Hughes called

to tell me the good news. Gil Anderson relinquished custody. She thinks it's because we showed him what amazing parents we are, but you and I know different, don't we?"

Oh my god. He wasn't even interested in listening to what I had to say. He had this all decided in his head. It was two years ago all over again.

I fought my panic, and tried to stay calm. This wasn't two years ago. I was a different person now.

"What do you think you know, Roy?"

"You paid him off," he snapped. "I told you, I was handling this. I told you we were going to do this the right way. And instead of listening to me, you did the thing you always do, which is run back to daddy and his money!" He grabbed the envelope in my hand and tore it open. "I'm glad once again that I'm so disposable to you. I wouldn't have thought you could walk away from Nora too, but you, Dumonts, man. You've got ice for blood. Are these the divorce papers? Your dad sure works-"

He looked down and saw it wasn't divorce paperwork. It was my birth certificate. He looked up at me confused, but I was shaking with fury and hurt.

"You didn't answer my calls," I said, my voice so calm I could hardly believe it was mine. "I wanted to just get it all done, so I did what I thought was best and I paid him off-"

"With your daddy's-"

"With my money!" I shouted. "Mine. My money from investing with Jackson."

"Vanessa-" he reached for me and I flinched away.

"You immediately believed the worst about me."

"I'm sorry."

I shook my head, the urge in me to tell him it was okay was so hard to resist. I could tell him that I understood. That he was scared and angry and he was lashing out at me. He didn't mean it.

Only it wasn't okay. Months of living with him, of devoting myself to him and Nora. It still wasn't enough for him to see me as anything more than that scared, weak girl I'd been. The girl who had run home to daddy.

I deserved better than that. I deserved the kind of love I gave to him. Unconditional. Strong. Forgiving and fierce.

"Do you love me?" I asked.

"What?"

"Do you love me?" I shouted. "Because I love you. I have loved you for years. I never stopped. I have been holding the words inside, waiting for you to say them, because surely you can't live like we live and not love each other? Right?"

He was silent and it felt like I was being pulled apart by the seams.

My hands shook. My breath shook.

"It's pretty simple," I said. "Yes, Vanessa, I love you. Or no, Vanessa, I don't."

"Why..." he rubbed a hand over his mouth. "Why do you need that?"

Tears I'd been holding back fell over my eyelashes.

"Because I do," I whispered.

"And what if I can't do that?" he asked me.

I put a hand over my mouth to cover my sob. "You *can't* love me?"

Oh, this was worse than I thought. This was the end then. We were over. If he couldn't love me...because I was me...Messy Nessy and I couldn't be loved...then we had nothing.

"What if I can't love anyone?" he asked.

I rejected that. "You love Nora."

He looked at me and I could see everything he was feeling. The locked box that was Roy Barnes was flung wide open. He was nothing but pride and fear and a little boy whose mother had died. A grown man whose father had died so suddenly.

"What are you scared of?" I asked him.

"Everyone leaves," he said, his jaw clenching.

"Not if you love them."

"Especially when you love them."

I looked up at the house where Nora was sleeping soundly in her crib. I wanted to kiss her one last time, but I knew that wasn't going to be possible. I wasn't going to be able to do that without breaking down. Without crumbling to shattered pieces on her bedroom floor.

I had to do this now, while I could still walk. While I could still manage to put one foot in front of the other, even though my knees were shaking.

"I'm the best thing that ever happened to you," I said, shaking back my hair. "And I never would have pegged you for a coward, Roy Barnes."

I walked away then. From the house. From Nora. From him.

From my birth certificate my brother had dropped off, so I could officially change my name to Barnes.

I wouldn't be needing it after all.

❧

Three Days Later
Roy

"IT'S GOING TO BE OKAY," I said for what felt like the thousandth time, as I held Nora in my arms and tried to bounce her on my hip.

Nora wasn't buying it. Her cold had turned into a full blown thing, with green snot all over her face. Neither one of us had slept. Nora walked around the house all day and night crying, looking for Vanessa.

Nora wanted her back.

It was after seven in the morning. I needed to get out on the water. Three days of no income was not sustainable, but what the hell was I supposed to do? The kid, my daughter, was sick and miserable.

And sad. Just so sad.

"We're going to be okay, Nora. I promise."

"Oh no, oh no, oh no," she said through the sobbing.

Yeah, I didn't believe me either.

"What the fuck are we going to do, Nora?"

"Dog!" she screamed back at me, and I knew that was her word for Ness. Her word for love really.

"You're breaking my heart, kid."

I didn't know where Vanessa was.

When she'd walked away from me I'd tried to offer her a ride, but she'd ignored me. Just kept walking. Back straight. Eyes forward.

Vanessa Dumont had spent her whole life wanting to be loved and she finally put her foot down. All she was asking for was what she so easily gave.

I never pegged you for a coward.

Fuck. The look on her face, defiant and crying. She was miraculous.

I'd taken her birth certificate back inside the house. She must have gone back to her parent's house at some point. I imagined how much courage that must have taken. I imagined her mother putting all kinds of strings on it and Vanessa slicing through every one of them.

A knock on the front door startled both of us, and for a second Nora stopped crying.

"Dog!" Nora screamed.

"I don't think it's dog, kid. I'm too good at building walls and putting people on the other side of them."

I opened the door and was surprised to see Mari.

She looked me up and down with no small amount of scorn, and then held her arms out for Nora.

Nora, who'd been done with me for days, cheerfully went to Mari. Immediately, the kid stopped crying and put her head down on Mari's shoulder.

"Let me get a tissue," I said wearily, stepping back to let her inside. "She'll get snot all over your sweater."

"I can handle a little snot," Mari said, following me inside the house.

I can only imagine how it looked to her. Shit was everywhere. Glasses, bottles, toys, blankets, pillows. On the floor, on the couch. Nora and I slept in fits, and it happened on the couch or upstairs in my room. The few times I could get Nora in her crib, she screamed if I tried to leave the room. So I slept in my childhood bed that smelled like Vanessa.

Torture in a thousand different ways.

I hadn't cleaned a dish, or made anything to eat other than what Nora could stomach, which was mostly crackers.

Shit. What if the kid was hungry?

The box of tissues had been knocked to the floor at some point. I picked it up and pulled out a tissue. I tried to get it under Nora's nose even as she twisted her head on Mari's shoulder in an attempt to avoid me.

"She doesn't like me much these days," I told Mari.

"Can't imagine why." Mari's tone told me she wasn't a fan either.

"What are you doing here?"

"Came to check up on you. Wanted to see if you were as miserable as Vanessa, and I'm delighted to see that you clearly are."

It took a second for that to penetrate the fog in my brain. "Wait. You've seen Vanessa?"

"Seen her? Uh...yeah. She's living with me." Mari sat on the couch. Nora content and drowsy in her arms.

Sleep. The kid needed to sleep and I'd been too wound up to settle her down.

"Thank you," I said, jerking my chin in Nora's direction.

"What the hell did you do to her, Roy?"

"Well, she got sick and then I got sick and she's overtired and-"

"To Vanessa. What did you do to Vanessa?"

I fell into the chair across from the couch. The one Vanessa sat in when she first started living here.

I rubbed my forehead like I could get to the headache behind my eyes. Once we'd decided to "make it real" Vanessa sat with me on the couch. Her legs over my lap, while I read my stupid parenting book that didn't teach me fuck all about what being a real parent meant.

Because the first and most important thing about being a parent was loving your kid. It didn't say that in the book, because it was fucking obvious.

I hadn't let myself do that with Nora for the longest time.

Because I was scared I might lose her.

Except while I was trying to hold off that emotion with both hands, it was sneaking up behind me. Of course I loved her. She was my kid. I was her father and one day she was going to say it. Out loud.

Dad. Daddy. Dadda. However it came out.

Thinking I could build walls and stay safe from that kind of love was messed up. Thinking I could be safe from loving Ness, when I'd never really stopped...

Equally messed up.

Marriage of convenience. What a crock of shit.

"I tried to put her in a box," I said. "I tried to keep myself safe by putting all these walls up, by having all these ground rules." Oh god, my stupid ground rules. No wonder she laughed at me.

"Safe from what?"

I shrugged, too exhausted to care how much I was revealing to a woman who walked in here to rub salt in my wounds. "From Vanessa. From getting hurt."

"That woman would walk through fire for you."

"I know."

"That's only half of what she'd do for this baby."

I hung my head even lower.

She asked me if I loved her and I didn't answer her because... fuck, love felt small compared to what I felt. Love felt like an empty word when I was full of emotions.

Emotions so big I couldn't function without her. I was a boat without an engine. I didn't work.

Was that love?

It was need. It was want... it was so much want, I ached to touch her.

"She's living with you?" I asked.

"For now."

"I thought she might have gone back to her parents."

"No, Roy," she said, like I was an idiot.

I was an idiot. I knew better. The girl she'd been, was not the woman who'd walked away from me this time. That woman wasn't settling for anything. Least of all a house without love or fuckface for a fiancé.

"She's with me until she finds a place of her own. The condos where Jackson lives are almost done. She's probably going to buy one of those."

Another record screech in my head. "She's going to stay in Calico Cove?"

"Her business is here, Roy. Her friends. This little girl... this is her home."

Home. Geezus. That was what I felt. Vanessa was my fucking home.

"Mari," I said wearily, running my hands over my face. "I think I screwed up."

"You *think*?" she laughed. "This is what's going to happen. I'm going to take this beautiful girl back to my place where Ness and I are going to spoil her rotten. You are going to sleep, shower and eat, in whatever order needs it first. Then I think you should talk to Vanessa."

"She won't answer my calls." I'd tried. Of course I'd tried. Every night. Like a tongue poking at a toothache.

"I'm going to put in a good word for you."

I looked over at Mari, my guardian angel in a vintage Friend's t-shirt with green snot on the shoulder.

"Can I fix this?"

Her face was sad and it felt like a knife to my chest. "I don't know, Roy. Vanessa was...destroyed when she finally got to me. I don't know if you can come back from that kind of pain."

25

Vanessa

Mari walked into the apartment with Nora in her arms, and it was as if all the breath was knocked out of my chest in one solid punch.

I hopped off the couch, where I'd been trying desperately not to text Mari for updates.

She'd told me she was going to check on Roy when she left. Apparently, there had been no Roy or Nora sighting in town for days, not even down at the docks where the *Surly Bird* had sat idle.

His texts and calls to me had stopped in the last 24 hours. It made Mari nervous enough that she wanted to check on them.

I'd played it off, like it didn't matter to me one way or the other, but I knew Mari could see right through me. I needed to know they were okay. I needed it, like I needed air.

The second Nora saw my face, she started crying.

"Oh my precious, baby girl. Look at that red nose. Was daddy not using the super soft lotion tissues on you?"

She sneezed and I hugged her into my chest.

"Oh no, oh no, oh no, dog!" She said making her frustration with my absence perfectly clear.

"I know sweety, I'm sorry I've been away."

How the hell was I going to do this? How was I going to live in this town and not be part of Nora's life? When I couldn't be part of Roy's? We'd have to get some kind of custody agreement. Maybe I could still babysit during the day?

Nora settled against me, panting a little now that she'd cried it out. I rubbed her back and kissed the soft curls on her head over and over again.

My poor baby. She'd had a cold, her nose was full of boogers and I wasn't there to cuddle her, or make sure she had her favorite bunny or anything.

The thought of it all was gut wrenching.

Mari was shaking her head at me. "You're pathetic."

"I know," I sniffed. "What am I going to do? I love her so much."

"Well, if it makes you feel any better, Roy is in worse shape than you are."

"Good," I mumbled.

I was still so mad at him. For not listening to me, for jumping to conclusions that weren't true. For not loving me the way I deserved.

"He admitted he screwed up," Mari said.

"He did?" I asked, hating the sound of hope in my voice. Then some reality settled around me. Roy had been three days with a sick toddler. Which meant no sleep, no one to help out. He wasn't fishing, which meant he was probably anxious about money.

Exactly what had he screwed up? His treatment of me, or the cushy set up he had with me as his wife/not wife.

"He's going to call you," Mari said. "And I told him I'd put in a good word for him."

"Are you kidding?" Mari had been firmly on Team Vanessa when I showed up here three days ago. We'd gotten drunk and proclaimed Roy an ass of the highest order. She'd been nothing but on my side. "One visit and you're on team Roy?"

"I'm on Team Roy and Vanessa," Mari said. "I haven't had a whole lot of reasons to believe in love," she said. "But that guy today. He was heartbroken."

"He doesn't love me," I insisted. Or he would have just said so.

"I think he's going to surprise you."

~

Roy

I'D DONE EXACTLY what Mari instructed me to do. I'd taken a hot shower, fallen into bed for a few hours of sleep, and tried not to sniff Vanessa's side of the bed that still smelled like her shampoo. I slept for a few hours and woke up to my phone ringing.

"Vanessa?" I said, before I even read the name on the caller ID.

"Close. It's Jackson."

"Sorry, I-"

"Come meet me at Pappas'," Jackson said.

"I'm actually going to go see Vanessa-"

"No. I'm pulling the big brother card and you're going to come see me first."

Jackson hung up and it felt like I'd been summoned by the Godfather of Calico Cove.

When I walked into Pappas' no one gave me the happy greeting they used to give me when I came in with Vanessa. Word of our break up must have gotten around. From across the diner, Madame Za gave me the evil eye.

My only comfort was knowing Nora was with Vanessa. My baby girl might still have a cold, and might still be sneezing her head off and smearing snot all over her face, but I had no doubt she was doing all of that perfectly content in her mother's arms.

Her mother. Fuck me.

It's what Vanessa had been since the moment she came searching for us down at the docks in that ridiculous beaded wedding gown, my Wife Wanted ad clutched in her hand. She'd taken to the role like a duck to water, and I'd tried to give her ground rules when I should have gotten on my knees.

Jackson was sitting in his preferred booth, a laptop open in front of him while he typed furiously.

"Hey," I said, coming up beside his booth.

He stopped typing and looked up at me, his face grim. "Dude, you are not my favorite person right now."

I sat down across from him. "Yeah, well I'm not my favorite person right now either."

"Heard from Matthew you haven't been out on the water for a few days. That's not like you."

"Nora has a cold, and well...we're pretty much a wreck without Ness." There was no point in not admitting it. I didn't have much pride left.

"Hmm," Jackson said, closing his laptop. "Maybe you

should have thought of that before you jumped to all the wrong conclusions and treated her like trash."

"Is she okay?" I asked.

"No."

"Does she need...money or anything? Her winter coat? Her favorite hoodie? I mean, she left with nothing."

Jackson leaned back and laughed. He laughed so hard everyone looked over at us. Swear to god Madame Za cursed me.

"No," Jackson said. "Vanessa doesn't need money. You really didn't listen to her, did you?"

"She said the investments came in, but I don't know? How much can that be?"

"Oh, man," Jackson wiped his eyes. "Joke's on you two ways. Turns out my father is in a bit of a financial pickle. One I've put him in over the years by buying up properties he's needed to grow the business. That's why he was so desperate for Vanessa to marry Simon. The Turnberry family was willing to make a sizeable investment in Dumont Hotels, but only if that came with the Dumont name. Classist bullshit if you ask me. No, Vanessa didn't take our parents money, not because they didn't have it, which they don't, but because she came into a chunk of money on her own. We've been investing in the businesses of this town for a couple years now. Vanessa calls a lot of those shots, and when she suggested the Dumont Hotel become a wedding destination, then invested in all the businesses that supported weddings...well, it paid off. Big.

"That day, after your meeting with Anderson, I'd just transferred over two hundred thousand dollars we'd made back on our investments into her account. She called you and while you weren't calling her back, we found a family lawyer. Got her to write up the termination of rights agreement for us. Then took that, with twenty-five thousand in cash, and found Anderson staying at a motel just outside of town. He saw the cash, was willing to take what was offered, and didn't blink before he'd signed away his legal rights to Nora."

I closed my eyes. She'd done it. All on her own. After all of her hard work, and solid business instincts that she didn't even give herself credit for, she'd made it.

"You should have seen her," Jackson said. "She was so freaking proud of herself. She thought she'd saved you and Nora. All of it was possible through the work she'd done. Not from any handout she'd taken. She sent me to our mother's house to pick up her birth certificate, because she'd been so desperate to change her name to Barnes. She thought you were going to be proud of her. Instead, you kicked her to the curb."

There was no way to sink lower into the booth. No way to hide from my shame.

"Well, if it isn't the love of my life and the biggest asshole on the planet." Lola came up to our table, a half-filled coffee carafe in her hand. She slapped me upside the back of my head and I frowned at her, but I didn't object. I couldn't.

"What do I do now?" My voice was rough, maybe a little desperate.

Jackson shook his head, even as Lola scooted into the booth next to him.

"I don't know, man. Vanessa has spent her entire life being told she wasn't good enough. She said she was happy with you, for the first time in her life. I understand that big time, because I have Lola in my life now." Jackson turned to Lola then. "But if Lola could forgive me for the shit I pulled, I'm guessing Vanessa might be able to forgive you. What do you think, babe?"

Lola pinched Jackson's chin between her fingers. "I think she's a fool if she doesn't kick him in the nuts at least twice."

I winced. It was going to hurt like a mother fucker, but that seemed fair.

"I was scared to be happy," I admitted. Because that's what I did now. I admitted shit. "Scared that it would go down like last time, where she took all the happiness away."

"Don't tell me that," Jackson said. "Tell her."

~

I HAD to run home before heading back to Mari's. Before I knocked on the apartment door, I could hear the laughter on the other side. It was Nora and she was giggling. For the first time in three days. Her cold obviously forgotten. I had to make this work. I had to fix this.

I needed my family back.

One sharp knock and the laughter stopped.

Ness opened the door, her expression shut down, like she was purposefully trying not to show me anything, but her red-rimmed eyes and the dark circles underneath them told me everything I needed to know.

"I'll get Nora," she said.

"No. Wait. Can you come out here and talk to me for a second?"

I could feel her hesitation.

"Please, Ness," I rasped, my throat suddenly dry. "Just hear me out. Then you can kick me in the balls or do whatever it is you think I deserve."

She stepped outside and shut the door behind her.

"Jackson told me what happened," I began.

"So you believe him? Not me."

"I'm sorry. I'm so sorry. That whole day I was a fucking mess. I was scared and I was angry-"

"So was I. It doesn't make what you did right. Every time you get scared or angry, is that how you're going to act?" She stared at me, her breath coming in plumes in the cold air. "Roy, it's freezing out here, can we-"

I pulled out that green sweater of hers. The one I kept from that summer. The one I'd buried in the back of my drawer the second she walked back into my life, because I didn't want her to know.

How I'd never forgotten.

"What..." her eyes widened when she realized what it was. "What are you doing with this?"

"You left it in my truck that summer."

She took it and slipped it on, the green brought out the blue in her eyes. The pink in her cheeks.

"I loved you that summer," I said. "You made me happy in a way I'd never been happy before. In a way I never thought I could be happy after my Dad died. When you left, the way you left, it just kind of... cemented this idea in my head that if anything was too good it would be taken away."

"Roy," she said. "I'm sorry."

"I know, but it's not about that anymore. It's not about what you did at all. I got this fucking thrill telling you I would never forgive you, but I did. Right away, I did. You asked me if I loved you and it was like I didn't understand the word. What I feel for you is so much bigger than love. It's need and want and comfort and pride. It's home, Vanessa. You are my home. You and Nora. You are all I could ever imagine wanting in this world, and not having you with us the last three days has been hell."

She stepped back, eyes narrowed.

"Tell me the truth, Roy. Is this really about me, or how smoothly your life runs when I'm a part of it?"

That was fair. I'm not sure I would have believed me either after the things I'd said.

So how did I tell her? What one thing could I say that would convince her it was all about her and how I felt about her? I wasn't great with words.

I was better at actions.

"I want to knock you up," I said.

"Excuse me?" she asked, clearly shocked.

"I want to make a baby with you. I want another little girl who looks like you and has your sweetness. I want a boy who will look after his older sisters. I don't want one more sibling for Nora, I want like five."

"Five!" she cried.

I felt myself warming to the idea. "I want a whole gaggle of kids with you because you have more capacity for love and caring than I could ever imagine. And I know that, because all the love and caring you give me, you give Nora, it's all instinctual. Because no one ever showed you how to be that way. So the last thing I want is a smooth, orderly life. I want all the kids and all the chaos and so much love. All the love. But I only want that with you, Ness."

She lifted her hand to her heart and there were tears in her eyes.

"Marry me, Ness."

"I already did," she said.

"This time because you want to. Not because you need to. Because in case there was any doubt in your mind, I didn't save you that day. You saved me."

She reached out and took my hand, and suddenly it felt like I could breathe again. She entwined our fingers and then looked up at me.

"Please take your family home now, Roy. I need to get our daughter some children's cold medicine on the way. Oh, and I'm going to need you to make things up to me through multiple orgasms tonight. Please and thank you."

"Yes, wife," I agreed instantly. Looked like my nuts weren't going to get kicked after all. "Let's take our family home."

EPILOGUE

Thanksgiving
Roy

"Let's go over the plan, Ness."

It was eight am in the morning. Nora was already fed and in the living room playing with her new puppy, Tillie. Yes, I'd clearly lost on the dog front, but it was one of many concessions I was willing to cede, to make my wife happy.

Letting her host Thanksgiving for friends and family was yet another one.

"I've got it, Roy," she insisted as she pushed up her sleeves, getting ready to stuff the turkey that was butt up in the sink.

"Do you? Because things are starting to look over the top in here."

"You're only saying that because of the decorative gourds, but I saw them at the grocery store and thought they would look awesome on the tables. They were really cheap and I'm still within the budget we set."

I eyed her suspiciously. In the last few weeks, Vanessa had re-invested a lot of her earnings back into the CCIB, so we were back on a budget.

A budget supplemented by her interior design work. Which gave us enough room that I was only out on the water five days a week now. Day six was a half day for boat repairs and paperwork. Day seven was family day.

The same held true for Vanessa. She never booked appointments with clients on my day off, so that day was always ours.

"So the menu is still the same?" I questioned.

When we decided to host, I agreed only on the promise she wouldn't go overboard like she had last time she got a bug in her head about having people over. Turkey, stuffing, and potatoes, and that was it. Jackson and Lola were bringing a vegetable dish. Stephanie and Mari were bringing a cake for desert. I told Matthew and Levi just to bring booze, whatever they wanted to drink. Both of them were bachelors with limited cooking skills, so no pressure there.

However, it felt like there was way more going on in this kitchen. There was a pot on every burner of the stove. The new crock pot had something in it too.

"Basically," she said, with a slight shoulder shrug even as she rubbed butter inside the skin of the turkey.

"Do you know what you're doing with that? Because it looks gross."

"It's so totally gross, but YouTube says this is the only way to have a moist turkey."

"What's in that?" I pointed to one of the pots.

"That's for gravy."

"What about this one?" I pointed to another pot.

"Going to be cranberry sauce," she said, as she turned the water on with her elbow so she could wash her hands in the other side of the sink.

"Nobody actually likes that."

"Nora does."

"You're lying."

"I'm manifesting."

Oh my god, this girl. She'd checked an *abundance mindset* book out of the library, and it was all she could talk about.

"What about this pot?" I asked, pointing to the third burner.

"That's going to be glazed carrots," she huffed.

"Jackson and Lola were bringing the vegetables," I argued.

"They're bringing a green vegetable dish. I needed something with more color."

"This is hinging on out of control."

"This is perfectly within my control. For now. I'm doing this, Roy. My first real family Thanksgiving not put together by chefs and servants. It's going to be messy and fun and I can't wait."

"You're still excited by the whole thing?" I asked. That's all I wanted, for this to be something she still wanted. Still loved. If she got stressed out about it, I'd shut it down in a heartbeat.

She beamed at me and it did something to my insides. "Yes. It's everything I want for us and Nora. Family, friends, a mishmash of tables and chairs, wine spills and burning the crescent rolls. The whole experience."

"Okay, but don't burn all the rolls. I like those things."

She gave me a little salute. "Now, for your list of chores. I need you to run to the grocery store."

"Are you mad, Woman? Look at all this food!"

She sighed. "I know, but I just realized I forgot the crescent rolls and you just said you like them."

Tillie barked and bounded into the kitchen, which was tight with me, Ness and the seven hundred pound turkey.

"Tillie! Tillie! Tillie!" Nora shouted, running in behind her.

She was heading in the direction of the oven, so I scooped her up before she got close.

"No running in the kitchen. Not safe."

She slapped her palm against my cheek. "Dadda, Tillie go, go, go."

"Yes, Tillie is on the go, but you can't always chase after her."

"Momma, Tillie go, go, go."

Vanessa leaned in and kissed Nora. "Why don't you go with daddy to the store to get rolls?"

"Dadda rolls!"

"Oh, and if you could take the dog too so I can try to get this stuff sorted out without interruption?"

Tillie barked and I relented. "Okay troops, you're coming with me so Mom can lose her shit cooking all this stuff."

"Don't say shit in front of Nora. She's learning words every day," Ness groaned.

"Well, then she's going to learn to say shit, because I don't know what else to call this mess."

Ness put Nora in her winter coat. I got Tillie's leash.

"You probably should also get ice cream," Vanessa said, following us to the door. "It will go well with the cake."

"Crescent rolls and ice cream," I repeated. "Got it."

"And I hate to ask," Ness said, biting down on her lip

"But another thing of butter. I just don't think I have enough for the carrots."

"Crescent rolls, ice cream and butter."

"Oh, one last thing," Ness called just as I opened the front door.

"Geezus," I growled. "What else?"

She smiled sweetly. "A pregnancy test?"

I blinked. Then blinked again. "Already? We just had the whatsitcalled removed last month."

She shrugged. "What can I say? I'm late and maybe you're just that good."

I set Nora down on her feet and walked over to my wife. Then I bent her over my arm, in the fine tradition of Rhett Butler, and planted a wet hot kiss on her.

"I fucking love you," I said against her mouth.

"Don't say fuck in front of Nora," she said, even as she smiled at me. "And I love you too."

"Fuck!" shouted Nora.

～

Not done yet, right? Of course not... sign up for the bonus epilogue of Roy and Vanessa here: Download Now!

And turn the page for a sneak peek at Bobby and Mari's Christmas Novella: Buy now!

HER FAKE DATE FOR CHRISTMAS

Senior Year of High School
Bobby

The door to the wrestling room burst open and Marianne Smith came stomping in like a painting brought to life.

Her overalls, hands and a part of her neck covered in splashes of green, yellow and blue paint. Her dark hair curled its way out of the extremely insufficient scarf trying to keep it under control.

"Have you seen it?" she asked, holding up an early copy of the year book.

I had just worked out had and was actively dripping sweat onto the gym mat. I really didn't want to have a conversation with her in the wrestling room that smelled like feet.

Which made me think I probably smelled like feet.

"Seen what?" I asked, using the bottom of my shirt to wipe all the sweat off my face I could reach with it.

"Bobby," she sighed and I bit back my smile.

This Mari *mood* would not appreciate me smiling right now. She had a few moods that resisted any signs of joy. Irate Mari was one of them.

"The Senior page." She came to stand close to me, close enough that I could smell the oil paint and bitter linseed scent of her. Eau de Mari. Sometimes she smelled like heavy duty soap. Sometimes she smelled like freshly sharpened pencils.

I tried to take a step back, so she couldn't get a whiff of me and she must have noticed, her eyes darting sideways to me and then away. I felt my face get hot with a kind of embarrassment. An awareness I never knew what to do with. She made me feel my own skin and it was amazing and awful at the same time.

"What are you still doing here?" I asked and it sounded like an accusation I didn't at all mean. The windows outside the wrestling room were dark. It had to be close to ten at night.

"Ms. Weidmann gave me keys so I could work on my senior thesis after school." She looked out the window too as if the dark night surprised her. "How are you still here?"

"Coach Papini gave me keys so I could work out and clean the mats after I was done." I walked over to where coach had left the bucket with the mop shoved inside. I pull the mop out and started swishing it over the sweat covered mats to give me some sort of distraction from everything that was Mari.

"See!" Mari said, her eyes wide. "This is the problem."

"That we have keys?" Seemed kind of amazing to me,

but Mari was all worked up about something. Her hair was practically vibrating.

"Look." Mari flung open the yearbook to the senior section. Specifically, to the Most Likely page. The senior class voted on people they thought most likely to become president (Amber Martinez) or an Olympic athlete (Matthew Sullivan) or get arrested (Declan Armitage).

"The Declan one is a little mean-spirited," I said. "Is that what's got you mad?"

"The bottom," she said and pointed at the Best/Biggest section. Biggest flirt. Best smile...etc. Standard high school stuff.

"I don't..." I trailed off when I saw my name. Not under the category of Most Likely to become town Sheriff. Which was my plan. "Biggest Goody Two Shoes."

"Yeah. They voted us Biggest Goody Two Shoes," she said, like it was a shock.

I blinked at Mari. Mari blinked at me.

"Well, I am going to the police academy," I said. "And you-"

"And I what?" she asked. Crossing her arms over her overalls. She wore a tank top under them and I absolutely did not look at where her arms had fallen. Or her boobs. Her body at all. She was a floating head.

A beautiful irate floating head.

"You're always in the art room?"

"That makes me a goody-two shoes?"

"It makes you too busy to get in trouble." It also made her too fascinating, too cool, too everything in my opinion. "You're off to New York, Mari. Who cares what the Calico Cove Senior Class thinks?'

"I don't care what everyone thinks. I'm upset because... it's true. It is true, Bobby. For me at least. I've been so

focused on what I want to do with my life that I haven't...
done anything."

That rang a strange bell in my head. I'd wanted to be a
police officer, much to my parent's chagrin, since I was in
the fifth grade and Sheriff Pollier spoke at a school assem-
bly. He'd said his job wasn't to punish people but to protect
them.

It was his job was to take care of this town.

Ever since then – I'd been thinking about the academy
and taking care of Calico Cove.

Every move I made served that purpose.

"At least you went to prom," Mari said.

"You didn't want to go," I said. Maybe too fast.

I hadn't asked her myself only because I'd watched her
tell Luka Daniels in the hallway between classrooms, she
didn't want to go. At least a dozen people had seen that
particular slasher film. "You said you wouldn't be caught
dead at that stupid waste of time."

"I said that?"

"Exact words."

Poor Luka had been so embarrassed he'd called her a
bitch before he's stormed off. So of course, I had to have a
few words with him about his manners around women.

Not that Mari knew about that. She'd hate it if she did.

"Well, maybe I was wrong. Maybe...maybe I should have
gone."

"You didn't miss much," I said. "You know what
happened to me at prom?"

"You got drunk and had sex with Caroline in a hotel
room?"

"Is that what you heard?" I asked, shocked and outraged
on Caroline's behalf.

"No. But, that's what they do in the movies," she said, lifting a shoulder. "I guess I just assumed."

"I drove people home. I drove drunk Luka, drunk Dec and the entire drunk wrestling team, home. Caroline passed out in the back seat of the car and I drove her home too. I basically spent the night as the designated driver for our entire senior class."

She looked like she wanted to laugh. And fine. She could laugh. It was funny. If you weren't the one doing the driving and not being with the girl you really wanted to be with.

"You really are a nice guy, Bobby."

"You say that like it's a bad thing. You're pretty nice, too."

"Ha!" she snorted.

Okay, she wasn't. Not really. Not to everyone. To everyone else she was sharp and hyper focused on her goals.

Only I knew that deep down she was really sweet. But you had to work hard to get to that layer. It was like she only showed the soft parts of herself to people who earned it.

I loved that about her.

"Don't you want to see what it's like though?" she asked. "I mean, before you go away to the academy. Don't you want a glimpse of what's so fun about being bad?"

No. I did not. But I could see where she was going with this.

"You want a walk on the wild side before settle down in art school," I assumed.

"Yeah, I mean. Artists are supposed to live, you know. Experience things so we can use it all as part of our craft. We need to squeeze every bit of juice out of life so we can serve the art. What have I done? What juice have I got? None. I have no juice. I am juiceless."

She looked at me like I should have an answer.

"Uh...You got in trouble in third grade for stealing-"

"Art supplies. That doesn't count. I thought art supplies were like library books and everyone could just take them when they needed something."

"You broke into the boy's locker-room this year."

I wasn't sure why I said it. That memory had never been spoken of between us. Mostly, I tried not to even think about it. It happened at the beginning of the year. She'd been on a rampage about the wrestling team using her oil paints to decorate their faces before a wrestling match.

She'd stormed into the locker room, but instead of catching the team in war paint, it had just been me there. Naked. Like all the way naked. Like my dick was in the breeze.

She'd looked at my face – paint free of course – I would never steal her supplies.

Then at my dick.

Then she'd run out of there.

Mari has seen my dick.

Every time I thought about it my dick wanted another moment in the spotlight.

"That was... hardly..." she coughed, looked away. "I mean...I didn't *do* anything. I never *do* anything."

You could have. If you wanted to. I would have let you do anything.

"What about sex?" she asked suddenly. Her face was bright red but she was looking me square in the eyes.

"What about it?" I had to press the mop handle against my dick so I wouldn't get a boner in my sweatpants.

"Have you done it?"

My whole body was going to burst into flames. "No."

She rolled her eyes dramatically and threw her hands in the air. "Oh my god, they should have just called us Most

Likely to Stay Virgins our Whole Life. Are you like waiting for marriage or something?"

I'm waiting for you.

"No," I said. "I'm just..."

"I'm doing it," she said, cutting me off. I was grateful because I had no idea how I was going to finish that particular thought without revealing more of myself to Mari than I wanted to.

"Doing what?"

"All the things I'm not supposed to. I'm going to get drunk and smoke cigarettes and weed. Maybe more. Maybe all of it."

"All of it? What does that mean?"

"I don't know what that means! That's the point. You in, Mr. Goody-Two Shoes?"

Well, I couldn't let her do this stuff alone. Or with some other guy who might take advantage of her. This was Mari. It was a no-brainer.

"Okay. I'm in."

Buy Now!

ALSO BY HAILEY SHORE

Happily Ever Maybe?

Not My Prince Charming

Printed in Great Britain
by Amazon